MW01706027

Through the Psyche of Ambrosia

◊

Part I

Byron Fortin

Through the Psyche of Ambrosia - Part I:
A Nexus of Numen
Book 1 in the Worlds Beyond Scripture series
By Byron Fortin

www.byronfortin.com

1st print edition
ISBN: 978-0-9881178-0-8

Cover art: Sarah Keith Smith ©

Published in Canada

Table of Contents

Prologue
◊
Through the Psyche of Ambrosia

There in the north, atop a mountain ridge, a once-great king of the horn overlooks the bloodshed below five peaks—bloodshed for which he is responsible.

Down in the valley turned desert, far below the elevation, a colossal army marches in from the west. The army of earth and air forces having broken through several barriers to the region now stand at their adversary's gates.

These wretched-minded soldiers are bent on conquest; they and their enslaved accomplices will not stop until the land is taken, to be claimed in His name. They work together to mirror the enemy and drive them back further towards annihilation.

They, the lionhearted brave, defend their kingdom's keep with tooth and claw, holding back the horde even as creatures of unfathomable origin gather to surmount the opposition. Their kingdom smoulders in the ash of an ongoing assault as the fury of hellfire rains down upon them. The fourth wall is about to be breached, as from the east a great horde readies, those the dead and glorious gone await to be led out across the river Styx, flooded well beyond its borders to touch much of the land and reach the guardian. Even as the gold-plated knights fight to hold the line, a true last line of defense can be seen in the distance as a beast from the sea lies in ruin, its insides spilling over. Surrounded on all sides, her fallen army can now only hope for its queen general to lead them to their inevitable end.

Above the cries of war, a serpent's shriek spreads fear, signalling the approach of doom.

On the cliffside, she approaches: the Lady adorned in red. She holds open her cloak as she puts a stinger in the air and steps up beside the horned figure dressed for battle. As they gaze upon the wreckage, his eyes do not falter from his achievements.

"The stage is set then?" says the battle-sung warrior son.

"As are its figures…they conspire against you," the Lady answers.

"To make a last stand. They will try to bend the rules to their will, and She will allow it," he says. "Al Sharatain must not be allowed back into the fold; he must not find her. Neschamali must not be allowed to reawaken."

"Do not worry, she will not…and he will never again realize her. I will not allow it to come to pass. They are, for now, forever lost, as they forever shall be. You will see, where they allow for a bend to be made, I shall put a full break to the levee. For I am able."

"Remember that what you do still has consequence—the dark hole becomes ever larger. You cannot allow for this anti-matter to spread any further."

"I shall go only so far," she says, clenching her fists.

The king gives an incredulous snort. "And what then of the forsaken? Will he be an ally to the cause?"

"If ever he wants to see she who holds his love again, he will."

"Then he is a fool…and so a fool who will have his own special part to play in delivering the prophecy. You are prepared to do whatever it takes to secure our measures, I am confident."

"Of that I can assure you," she says. "I've waited too long for this. The child will come to me, I am certain. She must—my future relies on this."

"Everyone's future relies on this. But will she be able to lead them?"

"Yes, I am confident…and we will control her."

"Good. Then go, and let *no one* stand in your way."

"I would die before I'd again see that come to pass."

"But my dear," he says, "you are already dead—and a dead heart beats for no longer."

PART I:
A NEXUS OF NUMEN

CHAPTER 3
◊
LOST THOUGHTS CAUGHT IN EMOTION

Fall 2012

Who knows how long I was out? When I finally came around, I found myself in a whole world of curious circumstances.

I awoke in an unfamiliar place, my body twisted in a compromising position. Quickly I scanned my surroundings; it seemed I was in an enclosed compartment of some kind. I could see daylight coming in from above my head, which rested on the floor of the compartment. I stared up at the ceiling of my encasing.

Now, I trust that for most who find themselves in such a state, their first instinct may very well be fear or panic. These would be sensible feelings to have. But I never had much tact for sensibility.

Yes, for certain I was more curious than anxious with my latest conundrum, not to mention too subdued to fashion any alarm. My actions of the previous night had only just begun to catch up with me. My mother always said you can't love the lady without respecting her—she'll burn you. *Strange, I've drunk more and always been fine the next day…*

Returning back to that first moment in my tight-knit box, indeed it looked as though I had gone head over feet. Somehow, there in the midst of sleep, I must have turned myself completely upside down. With my neck cricked to one side, the weight of my body rested heavy on it. My long hair behind me was pulled and matted, and my kimono stretched uncomfortably across my chest, bunching up in the back. The rest of me was in no better a condition; my back arched out high and my buttocks curled in low, my knees knobbed with ankles crossed. Oh, and it appeared I was missing the geta on my left foot.

That's when I sensed it, an immediate and most overwhelming suspicion that, though I remained at a physical standstill, the space in which I presided over was in motion. I wasn't at all partial for this mood set before me, so naturally this feeling took precedence over all temperaments. Suddenly a fast rush of heat flushed over my system, causing me to break into a cold sweat. Then I noticed a powerful humming noise coming from the floor—it stabbed at my skull, the shock growing with intensity with the speed of each breaking second. The more I tried to ignore it, the stronger it pushed against me, so that soon the sound shredded through my eardrums. It was then I felt a piercing and most sickening pain echoing through the sphere of my mind's eye.

I made an effort to move away from my malice, but like a shroud of smoke that engulfs the eye I was blinded by a sting in my mind's marrow. I closed off my gaze, took in a deep breath, and tried to collect myself as best I could. Then, with a dizzy concentration, I carefully dragged myself up from the floor and sunk down along the second plateau of the space. *Soft.*

At least I wasn't on my head anymore, not that this made me feel any better. Now, on to discovering where I was and why.

Looking around, I suddenly realized it. Burgundy upholstery, seated plateau, humming motion, glass on either side and just slightly above where my head rested. Clearly I was laid up in the back seat of the automobile I admired the past eve. *It actually works, and with me in it. Astonishing.*

How had I ended up in the back of Mona's car, I wondered, as I pulled myself up into an upright position so that I was able to look at the windshield in front of me. Suddenly I felt my temperature rise and stomach turn. The thought of moving was still too much, and to have to see it...

I felt sick, and a little scared. To put it in more poetic terms, these were the moments of urges, urges to bring forth from my body my lower intestinal tract and then strangle myself with it. This, followed by a great flush of dizziness.

I knew two things: I was no longer home, and I was very much not alone. *Has to be someone behind the wheel...*

The scene was more frightening than I had imagined it. There were cars all around me, zinging past and travelling at incredible speeds. We were moving at quite a pace ourselves, beaming down a stretch of concrete roadway, seemingly endless. Had to be the highway (not that I had ever seen it up close before).

I then heard a sound I'd become accustomed to the night before—the noise of a flicking lighter, coming from somewhere in front of me. What followed was the sound of a familiar voice.

"Finally awake, are we? I was beginning to think I would be alone with my thoughts for the rest of the ride," said the charismatic voice. Smoke followed in a stream from whence it came.

Mona. Of course it was. I was at once relieved at the sound of her voice.

I ever so slowly made my way to the middle seat, and immediately was thrust into a looming cloud of smoke. I was taken aback by the strong stench in the air. My nostrils burned with its toxicity as I mistakenly inhaled the foulness of its fumes, suddenly feeling as though my lungs might collapse in on themselves. I was nauseated and began to cough violently. Cigarettes...not at all as clean as what I was used to smoking.

I moved downwind of the smoke, and a knife-like pain shot through my temples. It pounded like a kettledrum, echoing unwelcome crescendos and deafening me. My head felt like it had been set on fire by a force of terrible anger. I exhaled a great moan.

"Too much to drink last night, I would say," Mona chuckled to herself. Her laughter, which on any other day might fill me with a sense of joyous serenity, carried with it a dry sickness that pierced my ears.

Huddled over my knees, I stared at the ground and held my head between my hands for support. Best to take it easy, I thought, lest I wreak any more havoc on myself. "Ugh … I'll never drink again," I muttered.

I looked up and met Mona's gaze for a moment. She looked just as radiant as she did the night before. Clothed in the same smart brown blouse, with the same piercing green eyes, same strawberry locks flowing down upon her shoulders. She was a picture. Her full lips now took the form of a genteel smile. Her right hand moved slightly towards a tray filled with cigarette butts. Between her index and middle fingers was the carcinogenic stick, fast becoming her trademark. I watched her hand, studying the slightness of each finger as she flicked the ash in one smooth, fluid motion. *Magnificent.*

"You've been out an awfully long time, Ambrosia," she said.

"Have I now…?" I didn't doubt it, and so the question could no longer be ignored. "So would you mind telling me where in the Sheol we are then?" Blunt and direct, a good route to follow.

Mona kept up a smile. "Tell me, son, what do you remember?"

I rubbed at my swollen temples. "Not much… The last thing I remember, we were at the gazebo…and now I'm here in the car, wherever here is. I can't believe it's actually running."

"I told you it would."

"Yes, you did. But what you haven't told me is what I'm doing here now." I was through with the unknown. "For the love of Dao, Mona, will you please just tell me?" My head pounded.

Mona took another drag off her cigarette before answering.

"Well, my friend," she said, as calm as an untouched pool of water, "you were, for lack of a better word, a bit *faened* when the events of this past evening did expire. Too much wine, I'm afraid. I presume you do remember our little conversation earlier, where I stressed the absolute importance of making for an early start."

I knew where this was headed. "Yeah, I remember." It was the only response I'd dignify her with.

Mona continued, "You, my friend, should respect the fact that you are with me at all. It is after all a rather significant favour on my part, is it not?" Without time for retort, she began in on me again. "We really did all that was in our power to bring you around, you know, but it was of no use. You were three sheets to the wind."

"I'm sure you could have—"

"No, Ambrosia, I don't think you're seeing the gravity of the situation. You were out, and nothing was bringing you back." She paused for a haul off her cigarette.

I don't know if it was the smoke combined with the headache, but I began to see red. I leapt forward towards her so I could see her face, yet another bad idea to add to my ever-increasing list of bad ideas, as it made my brain feel like a pea in a rattle. No matter—it would only help urge on the fire.

"So what are you saying, then?" I demanded. "You mean we've left, we're gone for good? Mona, what have you done?!"

"What I had to do, son."

"You…you dreadful wretch! You just took me away from them like that, ripped me away from the only home I've ever known! I didn't even get a chance to say goodbye! I mean, what if…? I may never see them again!"

"Dreadful wretch, am I?" Mona's lips curled slightly, mocking my verbal assault. "My, my, your Mothers did tell me you were a tad outspoken at times, hmm." Mona paused to butt out her cigarette. "If you must know specifics, my young friend, then specifics you will have. Your Mothers and I spent the better part of a half hour attempting to wake you, even with a cold splash of water and repeated slaps across the face. I must admit, that part I did enjoy. Yes, you were passed out cold, and really who can blame you—I saw how much you put back. We had no other choice then but to pile you in the car. It was either that or miss the flight, 'less you would rather I left you there?"

I put a hand up to speak in my defense, but again I was cut short.

"Am I wrong here, or was it you who said to me only yesterday that your only wish was for escape? Because you felt trapped. Under lock and key, as it were, ferried away from an entire world of possibilities, all existing outside your humble abode. Condemned to a life less lived. Were those not your words? Maybe I'm remembering someone else…."

She had me and she knew it. For as long as I could remember, I had longed for this chance. As the years went by, the passion to discover something more past the borders of my forest haven had only grown. A caged thing, my destiny would not allow for this exploration, so I knew I would have to leave my life behind me, lest it consume and destroy me within its solitude.

So came along Mona, lifelong friend of my lovely Mothers four, who had never spoken of her before. She had been the first person I'd met outside the sanctuary of our home—a woman of great wealth who offered me escape, who had on her person an extra plane ticket and a car to shuttle me out. I'd never been so close to achieving my dream of leaving, of making my own way in the world. But then, I'd never been so close to an actual car before either.

So she had me, yes. I was beat, but not beaten. I had to make her see things from my perspective. She needed to know the sincere discord I felt towards her for not allowing me to give my loving family a true and proper farewell. Even if it was, in a way, my fault.

"Yes, Mona, you are right. I did wish to go with you. But you are not understanding the gravity of the matter, and worse you are openly mocking me. The fact is that the only family I have in this world are who knows how far away from me now, and you don't seem to care in the slightest!"

I took a deep breath in as I sat there, rigid with silence. My muscles were sore from tensing, and I was ferociously grinding my teeth. My head was still pounding, and my stomach shared its hunger for discomfort as I felt a stabbing sensation down through to my bowels. Mona's calm disposition didn't help. I couldn't understand why she wasn't frazzled or discontented in the least.

Not saying a word, she peered out at the road with the same smile of contention etched upon her face. And while she sat there, poised as she was, her left hand remained on the wheel as her right motioned towards the cigarette pack resting on the dash. Was she going for another already? She pressed the filter to her mouth and set the paper ablaze with the lighter, a smoke line burning down into the crevice of her lips. For a moment, I forgot our argument and stared at the smoking blunt as if in a trance. Mona pulled the cigarette away as she gently exhaled, another breath of smoke exiting her passage, encircling her face for a moment before drifting away. Why did this pacify me so?

I cut through her silence. "You do realize they were my whole life up until now?"

"Yes, so you have told me."

"Just saying, you could have tried harder is all… before taking me into that dark night!" I always had a flare for the dramatic.

Mona took an easy glance into the mirror, raising an eyebrow before turning back to the open road.

Too much, I wondered, or perhaps not enough?

"Try more like hitting it out of the park," Mona said.

What? Did she just reply to what I was thinking? No, but one could read it well enough on my face.

"Listen, my handsomely frank young sir, whether you care to realize it or not, we are on a schedule, and it is a schedule I intend to keep." She spoke sternly while maintaining a soft, classic beauty. "You had your chance to say your goodbyes last night, and so you did."

And so I did. She was right, and there was no point in arguing further. What would it change, really? She wasn't about to turn us around. *Best not to think about it, what's done is done.*

I sighed and looked away from Mona, focusing on the outside to take my mind off things. There was so much to see, so much to take in all around me, and yet I still felt a strange disconnection from it all. A feeling too often felt…

I watched the many vehicles move around me, so many shapes and sizes, colours and sounds. As they sped past us, I watched them go. Some I'd seen the likes of depicted in books and magazines, but there were others altogether new to the eyes. I'd not ever had the chance to be this close to the genuine articles before. That in itself was enough to make me question my own reality, more than once. Pinched so hard I nearly broke the skin.

It was all so much to take in. The simple and beautiful life I had known would never feel the same way again. For how could something so delicate and natural not be crushed under the weight of such an assiduous circumstance as this? Everything moved so quickly in the outside world.

At least something here reminds me of home, I thought as I saw, beyond the fast cars and concrete roadways, a vast reach of forested heights that flourished all around us with a touch of colour spreading its mark along the tree-lined atmosphere. In the fall of nature's brush, a palatine rose blossomed and brought to life a deep colour-stream visage. The main base of green that lingered intermingled with hues of red, orange, and yellow. Like a used palette, the colours ran together in a blended wash of splendour that was truly all their own. The skyline draped behind the oaks, curtaining them in an azure luster. As a midday sun touched down on the foliage below, its shimmer captured the trees as a spectrum of dazzling radiance. I wished I had my oils at hand to capture if only a piece of the diorama.

Turning away from the scene and resting my head on the back of the seat, I took a deep breath to gather myself. At last the throbbing in my temples was beginning to dissipate. Staring up at the car's ceiling, I began to think about those I'd left behind. *How could I have not awoken to say goodbye?*

"It happens," Mona said.

I immediately looked forward, her eyes meeting mine in the mirror. They were such a beautiful shade of green, a heavy gloss of thick luster.

"What happens?" I asked.

"You're still wondering about last night, aren't you? I can see it in your eyes, dear boy. I'm just telling you that it happens. Best not to trouble yourself over such things. What's done is done."

I broke eye contact with her as I looked out the window again. "Well, now I know and I'll never do it again…"

"Then you did learn something."

I let out a small sigh to acknowledge my defeat at the hands of the liquor. "Just, you know, I wish I had maybe done things differently."

"Don't beat yourself up, my dear. You all had a wonderful last night together, and I'm sure it won't be too long before you are all together again. It's not like it's goodbye forever."

"Yeah, 'cept I have no idea how to make it back there again."

"When you are ready, my boy, I have no doubt that you will find your way home. It's as easy as drawing you a map."

"I suppose it would be."

I watched from behind as Mona took in a final puff and then extinguished the rest of her cigarette.

"In this world of possibilities, Ambrosia, there are roads leading everywhere. It's all up to you which direction you take. But choose your path wisely and remember your family will always be there to take care of you whenever you reach out for them. Your hopes and aspirations are out there, just waiting for you to reach out and grab hold of them. Take hold your dreams and trust in your heart, and you will find what you're looking for. Know I believe in you."

"Uh…okay? Thanks." *What in the House of Dao was that all about?* I wondered, for rather long winded had she been in her words of wisdom. Just a pep talk to ready me for the world outside, maybe? Some heartfelt advice from someone who had managed to find her own dreams and make them happen? Or perhaps it was to combat homesickness by offering up a reminder that I would always have people who cared about me and wished only for my success. They were the brightest stars in my sky, I would not forget.

Mona then reached a hand over to the passenger seat and threw a felted bag in my lap. As I looked inside I found a number of folded up articles within.

"What the faen is this?" I replied as I held up the garments to examine them.

"Why, they're your new clothes, my boy." Mona spoke as if this should be an accepted fact. "I took the liberty of planning a whole new wardrobe for you. After all, I can't have you moving through this new world of yours with only your silken robe, tantalizing to the eyes as it may be."

I looked down at myself, at the brilliance of my gold sash accented with ruby red. "Robes—not the attire of choice, is it?"

"No. Your studies, they included cultures and civilizations of the modern era, did they not?"

"It was touched upon."

"And fashions of the time…"

So far, even I knew the names for each of the garments: boxers, blue jeans, vermillion button-up short sleeve shirt, maroon zip-up hoodie.

"Oh, and let's not forget your jacket," she said, throwing another article my way from the passenger seat. "It is fall, and you'll soon find out that not all places are as climate pleasant as the mountains you're used to, with their seemingly permanent Chinook winds."

The coat fell into my lap, and I quickly examined it—a deep textured rosewood and a classic design with double zip pockets, button sleeve tabs, and multi-stitched inset back belt. I, in truth, had studied the fashion thoroughly as I had in secret always longed for one to call my own—even if only to wear over my robes. It reminded me of the pelts I would wear while hunting, only with more class.

"Leather, is it?" I asked.

"Oh, by the Goddess no. It's synthetic."

"Plastic leather? So…pleather, then?" I wasn't exactly pleased with the knock off.

"Just as good as the real thing, and no animals were harmed in the making of it."

"I guess…still…"

"Still nothing, boy. I know you would argue that every part of a hunted animal should be used, and I would agree with you. But you must understand that, in this modern era of the outside world, our animal friends are overhunted, put on the verge of extinction for such senseless possessions…"

"I understand." *Geesh.*

"I hope you do."

No point in arguing that a synthetic lookalike could be just as damaging as the real thing—when viewed through the eyes of another, it all sends the same message if someone cannot tell the difference. I couldn't tell the difference, not that I had any more basis to go on than an onscreen image of what leather should appear to be.

"Trust me, son, they'd know. That right there in your hands, it sends the appropriate message. As for the rest of the uniform, well…so sorry, my boy, but believe me, wearing your present attire will do you no favours. Why, you look like you're preparing for some kind of samurai showdown."

"Well, I should only hope. And it's not a 'robe'. The correct term is 'kimono'. The uniform also requires a juban, obi belt, odori tabi boots, geta sandals, and hakama pants—all missing thanks to our hasty departure, by the way." I didn't have to look to know she was rolling her eyes. No matter—I could abide the jeers, let her take her swings.

"And what of the bloodstone around your neck?" she asked. "Is that part of the attire as well?"

"I'm sorry, what?" I immediately looked down at my chest and noticed the beaded strand hanging from my neckline. I picked it up to examine it. "I've…never seen this before."

"No? Your Mothers put it on you before our departure. A gift, they told me, a piece of home to take with you."

And so it was. The bloodstone that made up the neckpiece was the very same stone that covered my home garden path. "It's quite…beautiful, really."

"So it is…and so it is that you may keep that, but the rest must be coming off." Mona spoke with her right hand pointing backward, waving it around to indicate I should get on with it. "Now, Ambrosia."

I looked over the clothing, gave a sigh, and in humouring her, began to strip off.

"No need to be bashful," she said. "The underwear goes on first." She winked in the rearview mirror.

I smiled back her way. "I know, Mona, I know."

When finally dressed in what can only be explained as the most uncomfortable of circumstances (let no free fly enter here), I expressed another soft sigh of defeat and crumpled into the back seat once again. I held the kimono as I stared idly down to the floor where each of my geta sandals did lie.

Mona looked in the mirror to catch a glance of the finished product. "Marvelous, my boy! You certainly look very suave. The ladies will just eat you up."

"That's a comforting thought," I replied. It wasn't, nor was any part of the situation she had put me in. The undergarment piece was especially unpleasant, having ridden its way up certain unmentionable crevices. My feet felt cramped as they were boxed in now by a pair of black sneakers, stuck in socks that itched, unable to breathe. As I tugged and pulled at them, I wondered how anyone could endure such constriction every day. It didn't matter, however; I could manage if I had to. *Just don't ask me to be happy about it.*

Mona only smiled and shook her head. She removed yet another cigarette and her lighter from the front right pocket of her blouse. She daintily placed the cigarette between the softness of her lips and the lighter to the smoke's head. As she ignited the spark, a glimmer befell her face like a spectral glow shower. "You do look good, Ambrosia, very modern. Now if we could just do something about the hair."

"We're not touching the hair." I was stern in my rebuttal. My blonde, voluminous hair stuck six inches out from my head in all directions. It was sublime.

"It's chaos. But very well, we'll keep it...for now." I was fast learning that Mona had a certain way of doing things. But could I get her to falter?

"Sit back and enjoy the ride, my friend. It's not yet noon and we've still an hour before reaching the airport."

And so I did. Still it all looked surreal to me—the people, their vehicles, this seemingly neverending stretch of highway. But that was okay. I was enthralled by it all. Too bad my body chose to make others plans, as though I hadn't slept enough already. I felt exhausted, my muscles ached, and my head had not yet snuffed out the fire in full. It was not long before my eyes grew heavy, and no matter how I fought it, the lids began to fall. Tranquil slumber soon took me, and my first experience with the outside world ended much the same way it began, as held in the arms of sleep.

*****

I was awoken for the second time that same day by a violent shaking; it didn't take long before I was able to focus my gaze on the cause of my slumber's upheaval. There was Mona, half bent over me, hands on my shoulders, jolting me from sleep with great vigor. I guess she had had some practice already.

Beside me the right side door stood ajar, and Mona was standing half outside the car. My head still held on to the idle impulses of a hard headache.

"Damn it, faen off with it!" I said. "I'm awake!"

Mona merely gave me a look and then backed away from the car.

"Sorry about that," I said. "There was no call for it, just I get a bit testy when awoken. It's nothing you did."

Mona did not look like she cared either way. "Let's get to it, then. Up with you and out."

I sat up and emerged from the car. It was now well past midday, I thought, judging from the sun's placement in the clear sky.

The air, it slapped me, much more brisk than I was used to. I was immediately thankful for the hoodie and jacket Mona had supplied me. The jacket looked good on me too, I thought as I took a second to check myself out in the car window's reflection. I then looked out over my surroundings, and it was apparent to me that I wasn't in the woods anymore.

"May I introduce you to the airport terminal," Mona said, pointing out the rather hard to miss building structure that stood before us.

Having not ever seen a building of such magnitude up close, the reality of it left me dumbfounded. So much glass, so much steel, and the people, they were everywhere around it, walking in and out through the building doors. And what doors they were, long glass panels as tall as two grown men, moving on a revolving axis. It was stunning to watch. Row upon row of vehicles were parked there too, cars to the either side of us stretching out beyond where we could see. Others still moved between rows, looking for empty spaces or simply leaving them behind.

For the first time I felt like a tiny, less significant part of a greater whole—and I knew I was only scratching the surface. There was so much happening in the region, so much I'd never been exposed to before. A buzzing society had grown up all around us. I had never interacted with, much less seen another person aside from those who raised me, and then Mona. This, my first real societal interaction—it was overwhelming. It was one thing to see the world rushing by through the window of a moving car, and an entirely different thing to take part in the commotion. I loved the magnitude of it.

That's when I heard the sound, a great roar that resonated throughout the atmosphere, shaking the ground in its thunder. As the sound started to climb, I gazed above me. What I saw next made my body shiver as every hair stood straight up on end. A jet airliner emerged from the clear skies, ripping its way through the airspace, its sonic vibrations splitting the stratosphere. It was unlike anything I could have imagined. I stood in awe.

Turning to catch Mona's reaction, I was a little disappointed to find that she was paying no heed to the sight before us. Instead she motioned towards the rear of the car and opened the trunk.

I went back to people watching, gazing at them with wonder as they went about their business. Many carried with them parcels while wheeling heavy suitcases behind them. There were a multitude of shapes and sizes, ages and races. I could see families, parents and children, and couples hand in hand. Others walked alone, and some in groups, friends immersed in conversation. Some smoked cigarettes like Mona, and others talked on their mobile devices. People stood hailing the many yellow vehicles along the strip with the word "taxi" atop them.

As I took the time to observe each person's chosen apparel, I noticed the many differences between individuals. A signature of that person's individuality, perhaps? There was quite a large assortment of colours and ensembles, leather jackets (real leather) and cowboy hats, high-heeled shoes and long-sleeved shirts, streaming dresses and jean jackets. Sunglasses also seemed to be a popular choice.

Oh, and let's not forget the other hairstyles out there (as I noticed people were noticing me and the way that I looked). Long, short, frizzed, spiked, curled, even shaved; it seemed there was no lack of originality to be had there. Yes, it was all quite the visual treat.

Then there were those people that just looked like duplicates of one another; stuffy three-piece suit phone talkers, black shoe-polished speed walkers. Heads slick with the grease…

Actually, the more I looked around me, the more I began to notice something else also, something almost disturbing. It was the way they walked—the sway of their body language, different from anything I had seen before—a portrayal of disdain, almost? A troubled and almost defensive demeanor? Words like "anger", "confusion", and "fear" came to mind as I took in the scene. Fear: it spoke volumes to me.

"That's just frustration you're seeing, Ambrosia," Mona said as she walked up beside me. She now had on a pleather jacket of her own. Brown was her colour.

"Huh?" I asked, unsure of what she was saying.

"The people you've been so intent on watching. It's frustration you're seeing in them. Don't let it get you down. We can't all be as excited as you, now can we?"

"What are you talking about, Mona?" I seriously didn't know. It seemed a thrill ride a minute to me, and why anyone would see it any differently was beyond my understanding.

"Once you do this a few times the initial thrill loses some of its appeal, son. Trust me; you'll be seeing a lot more of it, this disdain on the faces. Airports can do that, but I won't spoil the fun. You'll see what I mean for yourself soon enough."

It was so weird to watch though. I had studied sociology, so it didn't seem like abnormal behaviour, especially in present-day society with the economic slouch and world problems. Poverty, climate disaster, religious upheaval, and war—it affected everyone, didn't it? It was one thing to read about it, however, and an entirely different thing to see it up close. It was everywhere I looked, people passing under the midday sun with heads down, eyes averted, no love between strangers.

I hadn't expected to witness the disdain on such a wide scale. Even in those who expressed sentimental joy to each other as they reunited—you could sense it was there, lingering ever still. They existed with walls around themselves that projected like a shield to ward off enemies. Fear of the unknown, not a healthy way to be. I immediately hoped Mona's critique on the airport was only that. A few uncertain faces I could take, but this was a little much.

"Remember to respect the personal space," Mona said. She handed me a small black bag. "Here you are then, this is your carry-on luggage. It can go on the plane with you. I want you to grab your kimono and put it with your wooden slippers inside the bag."

"Geta, it's pronounced geta. The wooden shoes."

"Yes, very well then. Just go do it."

I went back to the car and grabbed my getas and kimono.

"Oh, and you should know, my lad," Mona continued, "not everyone will be as friendly as you might like them to be. People have their own personal comfort zones, and they don't like to feel intruded upon. You don't want to come across as too abrupt."

I closed the car door and walked back over to her. "You are not exactly instilling me with a lot of confidence here, Mona," I said.

"I'm not finished. What I'm trying to say here is that it's a very diverse place, this earth, and you'll find upon your travels that there is a spectrum of perspectives to be had. See, you could say hello to a thousand people while walking down the street and get no responses back. But then again, you might."

I merely shrugged at the notion. If people didn't want to talk to me, that was their loss.

Mona gave me an exasperated look. "The point is, don't feel you must conform to social standards just because you think it's the norm. Always be yourself, and allow others the same kindness."

I was confused. "But I thought you just said I have to respect people's comfort zones."

"I did."

"And yet you want me to be myself."

"I do."

"By not being too abrupt."

"Now you're getting it," she said, as though it all made sense. Mona turned back towards the car. She grabbed another bag and gave the trunk a slam. "Look, son, all I'm saying is just do not be too quick to hand over judgment, okay?"

I simply nodded. "Okay, Mona." *Had I even said anything?*

Mona gave me another incredulous raise of her eyebrow. "Right then, shall we?" Without another word, she began to walk towards the terminal as quickly as I picked up my heels to catch up beside her, bag in hand.

And I thought the parking lot was impressive. Once through the revolving doors (which were enough to make my day), I was really at a loss for words. The terminal was an epic invention to behold, so far from anything I'd known before. The lights were so bright, and I noticed right away the sounds from the ceiling speakers, voices detailing flight information that rang out through the extended hallways. What stunned me ever more so was that, walking through the space, I did not cause a single alteration to any of the electric signals around me. I must admit, even with Mona's constant reassurance I was somewhat apprehensive. Soon, however, all my worries were put to rest. No lights flickered, no system shutdowns occurred of any shape or form.

I commented on the lack of disturbance, and Mona reassured me once more. "I've told you already," she said, "you have no worries here. The reaction you caused has been left behind you."

I so wanted to believe it…

But on to other things, starting with the latest sea of faces we were thrown into. They were a thousand fold more in spectrum than I had been subject to outside, and with that of a thousand more variants in individuality. What infinite styles to treasure! All far more distinct than the commonplace attire Mona had me put on. In fact, many of the garments held absolutely no resemblance whatsoever to my own featured attire. More to the contrary, I even found those whose donned orange robes bore something of a semblance to what dress attire I had been made to shed. I at once felt lied to and in need of a change.

"I know what you're thinking son, but I'm sure you've heard the term 'melting pot' before. Like I told you, it will all be very much different once you're outside such international facilities, once in your new home. Trust me."

"I'm sure that it will." *But that doesn't mean I have to like it.*

"Now come along, we can't be late for our flight." Mona then took up a brisk pace, headed towards some unknown destination. My, but she was fast!

Doing my absolute best to keep up with her, I watched my step and apologized as best I could to those who stepped in our way. As we marched through the masses, I noticed again that of a certain aura, one of disdain, coming off the people around us at any given time, now much more in extreme. I disliked this feeling, but what could I do about it? So I decided to take it all in stride and ignore the unpleasantries as best I could, rather than dwell on the fact. I instead placed all my focus on Mona, who was rapidly increasing her pace.

When at last we stopped, it was to observe a series of long standing lines of people waiting. Each line was separated by felted ribbon—to keep the cattle in check, which was only slightly hilarious. Many people waited while carrying multiple bags and large, wheeled suitcases, sometimes pushed on carts. I even saw a few animals trapped in cages, no doubt domesticated pets. Who really were the caged animals, I had to ask as I watched, trapped there myself, waiting for the end of the line.

I guess the line was needed though, as funny as it was to watch. For how else would there be proper structure to the system of baggage control? Fairness for those who waited their turn so once reaching the front of each procession, one could be attended to by the proper flight personnel. That's where the real magic was, at a series of lit desks where purple uniformed attendants stood behind a whole assortment of bells and whistles. Above them, a large monitor glowed blue with ever-changing flight information as each employee checked in passengers, taking bags and placing them on conveyer belts that moved the luggage behind black curtains where it would seemingly disappear. It was thrilling to watch the digital and mechanical wonder of it all, even from afar. My only disdain lay in that I would have to wait in this parade of zombie people for a chance at a better view. *Unless of course I just skip it all by running between ribboned sections for the front.*

"See the personnel in the dark blue uniforms walking between the lines? That's airline security, put there to keep order in case you were ever wondering," Mona said, sternly pointing to each one of the stationed guards. Boy, that woman could read me. I guess I would wait.

"Fortunately these are not our lines, Ambrosia. Our bags count as carry-on luggage, so there's no need to check them. We can take them right on the plane with us and skip this tedious process altogether. We only need to go through that gate." Mona pointed to an electronic doorway. Then, without another word, she was off again. I maintained a close pursuit.

As we stepped through the sensor gates that spread apart to allow us through (amazing to behold), we were led into another adjoining hallway and a set of stairs. These were naturally teeming with people. When we reached the top of the stairwell, we then journeyed through another narrow hall only to find ourselves placed before yet another adjoining pathway. I wondered when, if ever, we'd reach our planned destination.

"This is our route that must be travelled, Ambrosia," she said. "Buck up, our plane's on the other side of the airport. It won't be much longer now."

So I was told. But it was longer, and it proved to be quite the hike to get where we were going. Through so much zig-zagging, I had little chance to check things out for more than a passerby's view while making my way across the terminal. There were some marvels to behold too, but Mona skipped them all in the name of exercising participation, which did not sit well with me. Just the idea of speeding past these modern day inventions, built for the sole reason of transporting one to their planned destination, seemed somewhat counterproductive. So what if we were making better time on foot? I wanted to use the gizmo contraptions, damn it! Moving stairs, mechanical boxes driven by lift pulleys, conveyor belts, even motorized carts—it was all incredible, and I longed to play along. Mona wasn't stopping for anything though; it was all I could do not to lose her in the crowd.

However unable to partake in the fun, I marveled nonetheless at the everything that passed us by. Sheol, I even got lost in the precision crafting of the flight attendants' uniforms, and sometimes the flight attendants themselves.

When we finally came to a stop, it was only for a moment so that Mona could drop off the keys to her car at the rental office. Then, just like that, we were on our way again.

But to what end? To which way was this? Well, let me tell you, it was not to the Promised Land, and probably the last place I would want to end up at that particular moment. A direct kick back to the words spoken from my mouth earlier, but that's just Murphy's Law, I suppose.

So we found ourselves in a slow-moving line not unlike the one I jeered at only a short time before. At least here, though, the crowd was smaller. As I looked down at my half-empty bag, I wondered why some people felt the need to travel with all their possessions. It was evident that what I had read about humanity's materialistic inclinations had been no fabrication.

As I faced the line, I caught sight of Mona looking back at me. I read her features as saying: *Don't be so quick to judge others, the quest for perfection is a proposal of tyranny. You are no less than, and no greater.* Or was I channelling my Mothers, who most likely would have something similar to say? They were, it seemed, all cut from the same cloth. *Well, they can put all such worries to rest.* I wasn't casting judgment, not at all. It was more of an analytical observation.

As the line slowly progressed, I couldn't help wondering what it was we were waiting for. Still another line, perhaps? Maybe we were finally boarding our plane?

When at last we did get to the front of the procession, we were greeted by flight personnel who asked for our tickets. Mona pulled out two tickets from her coat pocket and presented them to the attendant, who readily looked them over before handing them back with a smile. She then directed us on to "security". On hearing this, I was not at all impressed.

"We need to go through airline security before they let us on the plane, Ambrosia. Such are the rules. Don't let impatience get the best of you," Mona said, scolding me.

I should have guessed this, as I'd read that tighter airline policies had been put in place and were a necessary part of travel since the hijackings of 2001. Once there, I went through the motions, answering a variety of questions about my luggage while personnel inspected the contents. They placed the carry-on on a conveyer belt (finally I got to see one up close) and ran it through a device called an X-ray. Pity I was on the wrong side of the machine for viewing.

We were then directed through a stand-alone door frame made to detect any metallic substances that might be on our person as we passed through. *Fascinating*. Mona went first without a problem. I was sent through next.

I thought I would pass this test without flaw. I was wrong. After three attempts and setting off the alarm each time, I was told to then stand with my arms held high above me as personnel passed a smaller, manual detector over my area. The man in charge was a burly, bald fellow, with an ominous look about him.

With my arms raised, he passed the instrument over me, moving down one side of my body and up the other. If the detector sounded during his routine, he would return to that same area again. When the device passed over my crotch, the machine sounded, if only for the briefest of instances. The man in uniform then asked me, sharply, "Are you carrying any metallic articles on your person today?"

"No sir," I replied.

You would think this would dissuade him. But again, he asked, "Are you sure you have no metallic items in your pants today sir?"

"Look, you got me sir, for I am packing, most definitely—has my long john silver set you off? I do so apologize for these balls of steel." How could I not? He had set it up so beautifully.

A natural comedian, I thought this funny. Something to lighten the mood a little, you know?

The next thing I knew he was shouting, and can you believe he pulled out his gun? I was told to keep my hands in the air where he could see them. Instead, I went to unbuckle my pants to show him I honestly wasn't concealing a weapon. And within seconds I had dropped it all and proceeded to show off the goods for the world to see.

That's when he shot me. Two to the chest, but it wasn't with bullets. Two miniature darts attached by wires to the gun, sank into my skin. As soon as he shot, I knew the intent of the weapon—a taser or electroshock weapon capable of disrupting voluntary muscle control, thus incapacitating its victim. It, however, did not work that way with me. *I guess in some ways my disruption factor still applies. Lucky me.*

Not that it didn't hurt, giving a pinch to the skin. Worried about what he might do to me next, I raised my hands and let him know I had only been joking. That's when they rushed me, as the main guard yelled for me to get on the ground. It seemed though, that I was already en route to arrive there, and I did not try to fight back.

So it appeared I had misread the directions. A hostile bunch of individuals, this lot. They almost didn't allow me to pass, instead wanting to press charges, talking about having me on indecent exposure and providing false information. Would they rather I had been really concealing a smoking gun?

I was thankful when Mona stepped in to sweet talk them down before they had the cuffs on me. I really wasn't sure on just how she accomplished this, but before I knew it I was on my feet again with the darts removed. I think she may have mentioned I was "not from around these parts", that I was "small town"? "Savage" would have been a better term. *Imagine, my first day away from home, and I land myself in prison?* I was going to have to start acting a touch more conservative from here on out, I thought.

And after all that, what had caused the kerfuffle? My belt buckle—I knew the minute I had it undone, and on hearing the clang as it hit to the floor. I really was lucky I didn't get actually shot.

So it seemed taking off your pants is the kind of thing that might stun some people; Me, I was just surprised at the speed at which I was able to remove my pants, and also the actions that ensued thereafter. I'd never felt such an adrenaline rush in my life.

"I see the spark in your eyes, son," Mona said. "Just remember, I could have left you there."

"Yes, Mona, of course...and thanks."

"I mean, honestly, what were you thinking?"

"I guess I wasn't."

"I guess not. You could have been shot, you know."

"Well, I sort of was in a way."

"Yes, and thankfully the electroshock didn't take."

"No, it didn't. Which means…"

"Which means nothing. You were lucky this time, Ambrosia. You might not always be. So from here on out, no more foolhardy actions. Got it?"

"You mean you're not even curious…"

"Ambrosia, this matter is no longer up for discussion!"

"All right, got it."

"Honestly son, you're incorrigible sometimes." I swore I could see a slight smirk on her face as she spoke the final words on the matter.

We ran to catch the plane.

Before boarding I was able to get a quick view outside to the main airway through the windows of the flight deck. I looked on as planes shuttled in and others positioned for takeoff. It was stunning to watch. The size of the airliners overwhelmed me, how they appeared gargantuan in proportion to all other vehicles in close proximity to them.

Soon we were called to board our flight, and we were once more made to line up with the other passengers ready to get on the plane. We were again asked to show our tickets and identification before exiting the terminal. Mona didn't seem at all bothered by the request and promptly handed the attendant what I assumed to be proper documentation, two little black books with our tickets. The flight attendant looked them over and handed them back. "Enjoy your flight," she said. I guess Mona had things handled.

If I had thought the airport was tightly woven, the plane itself was a claustrophobic's chimera. To say the corridor was cramped would have been an understatement, and I had never been in a more restricted space. A fair number of people were already onboard, shuffling down the aisle with more coming in behind us. Row upon row of chairs we passed, many occupied, with more people standing to the side, shoving bags in overhang compartments. For each row of chairs, a small window port could be found along the jet's interior wall and next to the furthest seat in. I hoped to be able to secure one of those seats.

So we made our way down the line, finally taking our seats at the ass back of the plane. As Mona stashed our carry-ons in the overhead compartment, I was fortunate enough to steal a place by the window.

It was astonishing to see the number of passengers they were able to fit on. I almost wasn't sure the aircraft would be able to lift off the ground. Before long, however, we were ready to go, and I could feel the plane start to move. Slowly at first, it pulled out of its hanger and headed to a spot on the runway. As I listened to the intense sound of the turbines, I suddenly picked up on a loud and muffled voice coming from a speaker above me. The voice belonged to the captain, who announced that the plane would soon be taking off. He actually said this twice, both in English and in French, and then the voice disappeared. A moment passed and again the captain came on, telling everyone to buckle their safety belts and to please pay attention to the attendants, who would soon be providing some very important information before taking off.

I turned to Mona. "Gama Mao, are we ever going to leave?"

"Patience is a virtue, my boy."

"Yeah, one I don't have time for."

I watched as Mona fastened a safety belt around her hips for takeoff. I did my best to replicate this; it was, however, still a learning experience for me, having never bothered with the seatbelt in the car. So it came to be that while struggling with the buckle in hand, I heard the most angelic voice approach me from the aisle.

"Sir, can I help you with anything?"

I looked up towards the celestial sound and saw there in its place a manifestation of symmetry adorned. She stood only inches away from Mona with one adroit hand placed candidly on the head of the outer seat. The measure of her body pressed inward, which provided me with a sharpened vantage point at which to take in the lady from all angles. I could see an elevated composure there, with subtle curves that traced along her hips and breasts. She was a woman of clarion complexion and carried an almost luminous hue to her. The shape of her face, a perfect oval, with an enduring fullness was accented by the height of her brow. Copious hazel eyes gazed upon me, and I could swear they carried a hint of violet therein. Crowning teeth gave way to an incandescent sparkle long laid behind flawless lips. Hair fell in thick and lustrous auburn locks that curled down to soft shoulders. Her purple uniform hugged the body tightly, or perhaps it was more of a magenta, but either way it looked beautiful all the same, from the V-line neck to the base of her rule, finishing somewhere before the knee. She wore her sleeves short and her boots high, providing a glimpse of pronounced thighs. A winsome appearance of hope and prosperity, was she. A true stunner.

"I'm…I think I'm okay, yes." *Don't choke on your words now.* I tried to smile.

"You sure?" She smiled back.

"Yeah…it's just this belt, can't seem to…" I continued to fiddle with the contraption.

"May I…?" She leaned over Mona. "Pardon me."

"Certainly," Mona replied.

The lady placed a hand on each side of me, grabbed hold of the belt, snapped the clip, and took up the slack.

"There, snug. Not too tight, is it?" She gave a tug towards the interlocking joint. Blood rushed to my face, filling the head.

"Uh..."

"Are you com-for-ta-ble?" Mona reiterated so that I might follow.

"Oh, yeah…it's good, snug. Thank you," I finally retorted, coming back down to earth.

She smiled back. As she stood upright, I saw the full measure of her prominence. Our eyes still held a connection, and I felt her warm tranquility wash over me.

"Then I do hope you enjoy your flight, sir," she said.

But I was already flying, and as she began to walk away from me I took in a behind view and felt as though I'd never come back down again. When she reached the front of the plane, she stopped and turned to face all the passengers before her. A voice came on the loud speaker to provide some form of instruction, but I wasn't listening. Where all else faded by an ambiance of shadows, she and she alone held the light, a light that moved like fire and dazzled the eye. With each series of hand gestures, an expression of pure splendour was made as she demonstrated things. I sat transfixed in the dance and imagined I was the mask that clung to the kiss of her mouth, the string on the life preserver that inflated about the chest with the breath of life's sweet oxygen.

So when she finished her demonstration and disappeared behind the curtain wall, I was ready to follow her wherever she bid I follow.

Until, that is, I felt a well-placed hand on the clip I was attempting to unbuckle. "And what may I ask are you doing?" Mona demanded.

"Well…just thought, you know, I'd go and…"

"And what? Were you not just listening? The plane's about to take off. No getting out of your seat."

"But…"

"But nothing. You have nowhere to go. So for now just stay there, sit back, and enjoy the flight."

Mona pulled a magazine from a small pouch in front of her and commenced to flip through its pages. "Honestly son, calm your hormones, the girl's only working."

Before I could contest, the captain came on to say that we were clear for runway travel, and the plane began to move ever faster. Soon picking up great speed, the corridor began to shake and I could feel a vibration moving through me. The enormous sound created a great swooshing in my ears, and suddenly I could feel it—we had lifted off into the air. The kiss of the ground that had once been our cradle had fallen away from us.

It was an extreme and surreal experience, hard to put into words. A large part of me was thankful that the plane was able to take off with me in it at all. Even with Mona's guarantee, I had still wondered if my condition would prevent us from being able to leave, and now a small part of me couldn't help but wonder if we would remain airborne.

I seemed to be experiencing other problems as well. I guess you could say that, upon being launched into the sky, my innards suffered from a queer disorientation. It was a snafu of a paradox, being carried by the wind while my centriole regions gave the impression that they had not yet left the ground.

The flight also began to take a toll on my auditory perception. A great congestion built up inside my ears, and the higher we climbed the heavier a burden it became. Trying my best to alleviate the situation, I wriggled a finger inside each ear and made some obscene facial expressions, my mouth stretching out wide in a feeble attempt to release the tension. I can only imagine how I must have looked, like some clumsy animal chomping down its chow.

Mona suggested I plug my nose while puffing down hard into it. The profusion in my ears excruciating, I corked and gusted. *Pop!* My ears took on a sudden burst as all the stress within them discharged. "Thank the Goddess," I said.

"I'm sure she appreciates your gratitude."

"What in the Sheol just happened?" I asked, putting a finger to my outer earlobe.

"Oh, that? It's nothing, just the ascension; sudden change in air pressure can cause rapid changes in the eardrum itself. Air pockets will often get trapped inside small folds in the middle ear and need releasing." Mona spoke as though reciting the words from textbook. She was indeed very knowledgeable.

"How fun." *But doesn't that mean the human design was never really meant for flight?*

With my pain remedied, I looked out the window and marveled at the images below, trying to ignore the sickness in my belly, the ringing through my cranium centre.

By the time we reached our desired altitude and the plane had leveled out, my offbeat senses had all but returned to normal. It was breathtaking to watch the earth beneath us, all its inhabitation slowly drifting out of sight, diminishing and finally dispersing behind clouds of white obscurity. And beyond there were the open airs of a clear blue sky, a euphoric state of being. I felt as a fledgling bird, wings spread, a great leap of faith taken, free falling away from the nest that had cradled me, my maiden voyage to embryonic discovery. An undeniable effervescence befell me, and I savoured it in all its glory.

The captain came on soon after we leveled out to let us know it was all right to unclip our belts, which I did with great enthusiasm. As for my newfound friend, my urge to run after her had somewhat subsided since she disappeared from my scope of vision. By the time she returned to serve those near the front of the plane, seeming far too busy to grant me the slightest of acknowledgements, I began to wonder what the cause for any such distraction was. *Pull for a stranger unknown...*

The flight was to be a long one, and Mona told me it would be at least seven hours before we reached our destination. As time passed, I sat in wonder of yesterday's end and of unknown tomorrows. My thoughts were scattered ones, and yet they continually found their way back to the heart of home, to that of my Mothers four: Xia, Isaura, Nasha, and Linnea... I pondered over how they might be doing without my being there, if they truly missed me and when I would have the chance to see them again. We hadn't been apart in my entire life since I'd been dropped upon their doorstep some twenty plus years prior. I hoped they were doing well.

Slowly time ticked away, and eventually it did chime for me. As again our flight attendant came back within reach, she had with her a wheeled cart carrying food and beverages. When she got to us, she very politely handed out our meals and let us know to find her if we needed anything. When she spoke those words, her gaze drifted my way long enough for me to think she was directing them only at me. Still, I had been wrong before (or so Mona had told me)—my own oversized libido had seen to that. So, desperately wanting to engage her in conversation but not willing to risk another blunder, I merely said, "Thank you" and nothing more. She gave me a show of her pearly whites and continued on her way.

I indulged in the meal presented to me—as much as one could—from a plastic container. Though, I must say, it was rather difficult in the beginning. Just getting through the plastic lining to the metallic container was enough to make a person not want to indulge. The contents of the meal did not improve upon this feeling. I wasn't even sure what I was eating at points—something that appeared as meat (it was not), a dried potato, some string beans… Mona finally told me to stop with the nonsense and just eat what was put out before me. So I humoured her, as I was taught never to waste food—*was this food?*—and put the ordeal behind me.

As our travels continued it wasn't long before a voice came on the speakers to explain that there would soon be a movie for our personal viewing pleasure and that we could find our earphones in the pocket in front of us. I had never been fortunate enough to have seen a film, and so it was with great enthusiasm that I grabbed the earphones and put them on, attaching them to the chair output as directed by Mona. Mona then pointed to where the film would be showing, a small panel positioned in front of the aisle seating. I took in the show with eyes wide open.

What a visual splendour it was, like a breathing work of art. This moving picture somehow seemed alive. The sights were enough on their own, but when matched by the awesome sound that thundered through my tiny earphones, it was like an eruption of flavour exposure to my entity. I was held in its grandeur for quite some time, but, as the saying goes, nothing lasts forever. The storyline was just terrible. I couldn't follow it, something about boy likes girl but girl doesn't like boy, but wait, then she does, or maybe she's unsure. Basically it's not clear how she feels. So then boy goes away, only to come back a man, but still he must prove himself, and still she's undecided because he's her best friend. She doesn't want to lose that bond, so she instead leads him on for the next forty-five minutes…

Mindless drivel. I strained to watch, and before the movie's end my eyes felt worn and tired. Where once they had been cast wide open by possibility, they now drew to quiet repose by want of curtain call, heavy with a need for further rest that would not remit. Taking refuge, I delved into reverie and drifted away from the exposé.

CHAPTER 4

◊

DREAMS IN HARTLAND

Obscure voices falling off a dead air, the sempiternal yearning of an ethereal sonancy. The susurrus of a name, esoteric marks enshrouded in mist. A sombre sheath of ominous decree reflects in the overhead, as the pierce of algid ensnares from within. A pain of despondency lurks in the core, the chagrin of an unsound enigma. Unclear visions distorted by haze, cast a beclouded taint to barren seclusions.

One's promised seams unravel, forsaken to a kiss sealed in the ruin of release. Ghost of a shadow lined in darkness, a plea etched in heartache goes unheard. The flash of a bewitching domain left to cinder in the ashes of the imbalanced. Naked in the dark, heavy roots' hold stagnate, no way to unearth the weight of this conviction. A scream of estrangement bleeds in the night.

I awoke with a start, still on the plane. The dream, it was the same as before, the same as every night. The haunting of a nightmare draped in the utmost confusion. What did any of it mean? Or did it mean anything? And why did these images of vexation continue to plague me so?

It all felt so real, yet how could it be anything more than an invention of my own devices? I couldn't hold any piece of it long enough to understand what might be going on. Too many perplexing questions, it exhausted me to linger upon them.

"Having trouble relaxing, are we?" I heard Mona remark from beside me. For the moment I had forgotten she was there, and she startled me.

"I'm fine, thank you." I didn't want to bother her with specifics. I turned to look out the window. But, facing the other way, I could still feel her stare like a knife probing my skull. I was sure of it.

"You sure?" she said. "Seemed a bit jittery there in your sleep I noticed, had somewhat of a rash awakening too. And you've broken out in a touch of a cold sweat. Just a few minor things I picked up on."

She was right; I was soaked. "Just a dream, nothing more," I said. "Actually…it was more of a nightmare. I can't make sense of it."

Why did I feel the need to mention that? It was something I did not enjoy discussing, as it only resurfaced disturbances better kept concealed, that perhaps scared me. I never was good at opening up. I rested a heavy head in my hands. *Try to keep it together now.*

Mona put her hand on my leg, giving it a faint squeeze. "In my experience, it sometimes helps to talk."

I looked up towards her, witnessing the reassurance in her eyes. "I've never been one to talk."

"Then it's a great time to start, don't you think?"

I paused to gauge the situation. Alone on a plane with a woman I hardly knew, a thousand miles from home and with all the time in the world. Would she be my confidant to which I could tell secrets I hadn't told anyone and didn't quite understand myself…? I didn't think so. *No, better I just keep these things to myself and …*

"It's so hard for me to explain, I don't even know if I can." It just kind of spilled out; I could feel a shiver rising through me. *Why am I saying this to her now?*

"Please try. Best that we start from the beginning, Ambrosia." Mona motioned in closer. "So when did this all start? Is this dream, something new? Or has it affected you before?"

For too long…"Why would you ask that?" The truth was that I'd been having it for some time but had never told anyone.

"I find that, in my experience, the troubling ones seem to stick around. So is it recurring?" She stared at me intently.

"Yes."

"I see…and for how long?" She was nothing if not direct.

"I don't know, six months maybe…" *To the day.*

"That is some time… And you're having trouble remembering it?"

"I am."

"Ambrosia, I want you to do something for me. I want you to try closing your eyes. I want you to concentrate on the dream while it's still fresh in your mind."

"Mona, I don't know." I really didn't feel comfortable talking about it, much less trying to understand it.

She put a hand on my hand. "Try."

With only a slight moment's more hesitation I gave in and did as she said. Closing my eyes in concentration, I did my best to shut away the outside world. Then, taking in a deep breath, I wandered through my mind before it slowly began to come on.

"There's really not much I can grasp onto," I said, as if from a distance. "It's fragments, to begin with. The moment I wake and attempt to remember, whatever was there all but disappears…" I spoke while still concentrating on the broken image.

"That's fine, and not at all uncommon. Tell me what you can," she urged.

"It's not what I can, but what I can't see that drives me to distraction. My memories of it are shaken; they lie in scattered remains mere moments after leaving the dream. It's such a frustrating feeling, this quickening state of amnesia that beholds me, a heartbeat away from having experienced it."

"But if you tell me what it is you do remember, missing thoughts may yet resurface. It's like I said, talking helps. Trust me."

Why was this so hard to talk about? It was just a dream, a hallucination and nothing more, wasn't it? No, it was absolute misery; I hated brewing over this thing because I did not fully comprehend it. It was like no other reverie I'd experienced because it felt so real and wouldn't go away. I could never speak of it before from fear of appearing weak, from fear of the acknowledgement—that I could not take care of this problem on my own. The problem was not going away. For the better half of a year it bewitched me, and always the same thing. The scabrous circumstance of a nightmare that vanishes on waking, dissipating like vapour leaving only shards of a scared memento in its stay. I no longer wanted to sleep, reality being a far more preferred substitute to such senseless detachments.

Very well then, Mona, you win.

"I...I can't tell you much. It's like I told you, my thoughts are incoherent at best, but…I know there's more to it than that, which I can now recall, it's like a veil has been placed over my mind." I took in another deep breath, one of exasperation.

"I know it's hard, Ambrosia, but you have to try."

I quietly continued, my eyes still shut, trying hard to relax them. "I remember feeling cold…but it was different than the usual feeling you would come to expect. I don't even know how to explain it; it's as if this bitter feeling resonates off me like a numbness that began from within."

"Numbness, yes, go on."

"I am naked, clutching onto myself in a fetal position. The ground beneath me is hard, a barren rock. I can hear something in my head, like an undertaking of voices speaking from the internal places of my mind. At least I think that's where it's coming from." I could feel my muscles tighten as they tensed harder, unable to find a release.

"Fragile vulnerability, sense of loss…yes, yes."

"It's a barrage of broken messages I cannot explain, and above these riddles still something else, a calling from within. The incessant hum of a word, hard to make out, but its title is familiar somehow? Yet the feeling is lost on me…I am drawn to it, must know its origin."

"Something precious you perhaps feel you have been denied."

"I am standing now, my vision is distorted. It's a fog I can't escape, as held under a cover of darkness…vacant silhouettes off a dead air give vague depictions to the true nature of my settings. Oddly shaped shadows drawn in the stillness, I reach out to touch one…"

"And then what?"

"Nothing. It quickly disintegrates to ash in my hand."

"Hmm…this could represent many things. Abandonment, confusion in the unknown… Don't stop now."

"The air stands dead, and yet there's a stench of decay that sits heavy on my cavity. It makes me question whether I am even alive." My voice rose as a shiver went down my spine.

Mona pressed in closer "It's okay, Ambrosia, you need not dread such suggestions. Death in a dream is often thought symbolic to lost opportunity."

"There's more," I hastened. "The voice, its beckon has moved closer. I can hear it calling out to me in ever-growing anguish. I try to move towards it, but my feet are so heavy I can't lift them."

"A burden of some kind, holding you down?" Mona answered by soft reply.

"Then I feel it. A presence is there, fixed on me. I peer through the smoke screen ash that encases my vision for any signs of movement, but I see nothing. My eyes, they start to sting, and I involuntarily close them for a moment of relief."

I felt Mona's hold on my hand tighten.

"The manifestation is now upon me! My senses are in a state of alarm as I stay frozen to the spot, a spirit no longer in control of his vessel. I can feel it there pushed against my body, embracing me with its warmth as a kiss is placed upon the outline of my mouth."

"Expressions of affection, tranquility, harmony," I heard Mona say.

"Harmony that comes to an untimely demise, for the second is seized by an ultimate fall. A kiss erased, the embrace unbound. I watch it happen, unravel and break before the schism of a shadow that dissolves into omission. It was a vapour dissipated on the wind, a solitary tear to run down cheek side, it was finished."

It was more than I'd ever been able to remember, and the moment it was over I felt a heaviness lift off me. Never had I been one to show this side of myself before, and though somewhat embarrassed by it, I was relieved to let it out. Mona said nothing, giving me a moment.

After a few minutes, I was able to put myself back together. Sitting up, I wiped at the dampness in my eyes. I looked at Mona, and she returned my gaze with a solemn smile.

"Thanks for, you know..."

"I know, and there's no need. I was happy to listen."

The plane was quiet. Over the next few minutes, I pondered over Mona's interpretations: abandonment, confusion, and denial. Denial—the word rang through me like the chime of a great bell going off in the deepest recesses of my mind. What could it be that I had been denied? Or denied to myself? And for that matter, for what reason would I repress such notions?

It was too hard to wrap my head around. The weight of the subject had made me restless enough already. I decided it best to ask the lady herself, let Mona decide what was going on inside my own head. "So, what do you think? I mean, about the dream."

Mona contemplated the question for a long moment before giving an answer. "Oh, my dear boy, I'm afraid I haven't the foggiest." It was not the answer I was looking for.

"Haven't the foggiest...?"

"No. That's not to say I cannot be of help to you, however."

Mona rose from her seat and moved into the aisle. She then reached up into the overhead compartment and pulled out her carry-on. Placing the bag on the unoccupied chair next to where she had been sitting, she closed the overhead and came back to rest beside me.

Mona placed the carry-on on her lap and began to rummage through it. I really had no idea what to expect, as she seemed very concentrated on the contents within.

"Uh, Mona...?"

"Ah, here we are. Please, hold out your hand."

I looked at her with skepticism. "Mona...?"

"Go on then."

"All right." I gave in and held out my palm, ready for what, I wasn't sure. She presented me with a folded up piece of red cloth.

"Well, go ahead. Unfold it," she said, sounding anxious.

"Oh, of course," I replied, as though it all made sense. Carefully I opened the folds, and there inside found the contents of a rather bizarre-looking instrument.

"Allow me?" she requested while leaning in towards the object in question.

"Oh, you go right ahead," I told her, having no real idea what I was looking at, much less what to do with it.

Mona put a hand on my lap and picked the thing up by a small piece of red twine attached to the top of the device. She held it there in front of me, letting it spin and dangle on the thread. I was almost hypnotized, unable to take my eyes off it as I became lost in the detail of the circle's twirl.

It was something amazing, but where to begin? I remember first noticing its colour, a colour beyond roses. It had the body of a cherry ring with the interior of a scarlet web that spiraled into a triangular blood red gem found at its center heart. An assortment of black feathers hung from the base of the ring's circumference, and other miniature semi-precious stones could be found within these feather's quills. None so bright as the red center, however.

"It's very beautiful," I remarked.

"It is. This, Ambrosia, is a dreamcatcher[i], your dreamcatcher." She cautiously placed the device in my palm, still holding the cloth.

"A dream catcher?" I was enticed to hear more. "Tell me, Mona, what exactly does a dream catcher do?" *How is this going to help me sort out my nightmares? And do you always carry this sort of thing on your person?*

"Well, Ambrosia dear boy, it's a device for catching dreams, naturally," Mona said with a smile, speaking as though I should have been able to figure that much out on my own. Which I had. *Naturally.*

"Yes, that much I've gathered, but there must be more of an explanation to it than that."

"Oh yes, there is. A fair background behind it, actually. If, that is, you wish to hear it?"

She was having fun with me, so I let out a sigh. "Yes, Mona. I believe that I would, if it is not too much trouble, thank you."

"No, no trouble at all, my boy. But might we want to get a little more comfortable first?" Mona pressed a button in the arm of her chair, which lowered her seat back into a more relaxed position. I was fine where I was, waiting…

Until finally she began, "The word in question has its origins buried in a thousand years of history."

Of course it does.

"It all started in a place called the island of Tortessos. This is where the great nation of Ojibwe[ii] resided. The legend goes that the Ojibwe people were, like yourself, harrowed by visions of nightmares. Medicine men did what was in their power to vanquish the nightly torture, but it was without remedy. Determined to put an end to this peril, the nation's elders sought out the aid of Asibikaashi, the 'weaver of webs'."

"Asibikaashi?"

"It means 'spider woman'. Asibikaashi would bring back the sun and distill the bad *bawedjigewin*, or dreams, as we have come to commonly know them."

"Right...so, how did she stop the nightmares? And what's this about the sun?" I think I was more confused now than before she began.

Mona's expression begged patience. "During nightfall, Asibikaashi built her webs to catch the harmful dreams that would perish with the first rays of sunlight."

"Ah, bringing the light to vanquish the darkness. Yes, it's very clear now." I rolled my eyes. How many times had I heard fairytale stories like this one from my Mothers? Rubbish they were, folklore of fantasy daydream believers. How was I supposed to relate any of it to real-life situations? There was not a world lesson to be learned in the lot of them. And now I was supposed to believe that a web could catch my unconscious thoughts, so I could, what, grab them later? *What a waste of time.*

Mona droned on. "It is further told that over the years the nation of Ojibwe eventually grew too large for the island of Tortessos. The people decided to break into tribes and dispersed to other areas. Finding it difficult to travel the distances between tribes, Asibikaashi decided to teach the people to make webs of their own by harnessing the elements found in nature. To this day people still follow her guidelines, and dreamcatchers are widely used throughout civilization."

"Okay...well, thanks so much for that brief and somewhat interesting history lesson, Mona." I hoped I hadn't come off as too disenchanted. "There's just one thing I don't get."

"And what is that, lad?"

"How come I've never heard of this Asibikaashi before now? Why, with all the many teachings I've endured, the telling of stories old, those legends of fantasy I've been made to hear throughout the years, and I have not stumbled upon this name. Not even once."

"My boy, are you so naïve to think you have heard every tale there is to tell? Legends are written every day…even now, somewhere something is beginning to stir, a new tale emerges, one to belong to the ages. Trust me."

"Sure, Mona, whatever you say." I then was caused to remember a story from my childhood. "You know, it's strange but, well, it's just that this character you describe reminds me of another I know, have heard about. There are definite similarities."

"Well, of course there are, son. She goes by many names; Asibikaashi is but one of them. Another would be…"

"Arkane: shadow weaver," I finished for her.

"You follow well," Mona acknowledged, rather proudly. "Your Mothers, they have certainly taught you the basics."

"Only a story, one of many. Their faith, not mine." I faced to look out the window to the cloud cover of skies soaring by.

"Yes, well…there are still a few things you need know about your dreamcatcher. See the thin branches of willow?" she said, surely pointing them out. "They were ideal for making a ring or hoop, and their leaves for the webbing. Other plants, including Dogbane, milkweeds, and sagebrush were also excellent materials for making cordage, the twine that forms your dreamcatcher's webbing."

I let out a small sigh before turning back to her. "What then about the precious stones and feathers, do they have anything to do with the filtering of dreams?"

"Well, of course." She looked at me as though I had seven heads. "They wouldn't be there without reason, Ambrosia."

What was I thinking?

"The feathers have their own significance. It was believed that by placing a feather on your dreamcatcher it was given the breath of life."

"I see." *Why not?* I thought. If a web can catch your dreams this shouldn't be too hard to swallow.

Mona went on. "There's more. The kind of feather held a certain distinction. Owls hold a path of wisdom, while the eagle shows courage."

"So what are mine then, owl or eagle?"

"Neither, they're crow."

"Crow? Well what the Sheol is the semblance in that?"

"That, my boy, you will have to find out for yourself, should there be any representation to be found out there. You see, we have a lot of crow's back home, crows and not much else, and the feathers appeared easy enough to find."

"Really, Mona?" I asked her. "Why would you even go through the trouble of telling me the importance of each individual feather if you have no idea what my own represent?"

"What do you want me to tell you, Ambrosia? I mean, really, do you think I have all the answers? Do I look like a library?" She was being somewhat snide now. "I told you what I know about the feathers holding significance; I think that's as good a start as any. You're resourceful, figure it out."

There was silence for a moment before she continued.

"Now, before we run off track again, allow me to explain the diamond in the center of the web."

The blood red diamond, it's what I'd been waiting to hear about. Something about it, the shine of its colour, the unmitigated brilliance, intrigued me.

"The stone at the center of your dreamcatcher is a rare one, the red diamond. It is the strongest of gems and was put there to give its dreamer the greatest allowance of understanding available."

"What do you mean?" I asked, not understanding.

"Just because a nightmare may seem like nonsense, it doesn't necessarily mean there isn't a message encrypted within it. Dreams, after all, are our thoughts working overtime, and we could, in many ways, be trying to tell ourselves something through a series of mixed messages. It can be hard to decipher, but it's important that we do." Mona's manner was as astute as ever.

"I'd be happier if the images would just stop and let me be at peace," I muttered.

Mona continued, "The diamond was placed where it was for a reason. The web catches hold of your nightmares that are drawn into the center by your stone. At this point, the dreams are filtered so that any important aspects may find their way to you. The strength of your diamond should be able to hold a great deal of the chicanery you are presently facing. When the web later catches the light, it too will be guided towards the centre, and as it channels through your gem, the trapped darkness will be dispersed and cease to exist."

I gave a slight laugh. "So what are you trying to tell me then, Mona? I need only use this once, and just like that I'll have all the answers I'm looking for, locked away for safe keeping inside this blood stone?"

"It's never as simple as it sounds, Ambrosia. With a dream as complicated as yours, it may take a series of different events to diffuse the situation. No one experience can give you all the information you seek. But if this dream does return, if it wants to be heard, you now have the means with which to listen."

She sounded so sure. I was a little more speculative.

"So, Mona, this dreamcatcher, you have one of your own?"

"I do; take it with me wherever I go. Travel a lot, you see. It isn't too uncommon a thing to find me off and away from home. No matter where I find myself, though, each evening before laying to rest I find a place, a window close to me on which to hang it."

"And so that's why you carry extras, in case you lose one?"

"Well, they make for a great gift too, don't they?"

"I guess they do. So, you're a heavy dreamer then?"

Mona let out a small sigh.

"I do have my own nightmares that haunt me, Ambrosia."

"Really?"

I was stunned. I almost asked her to expand but backed out before I could muster the words. Maybe it was the expression on her face. She panned away for a moment, pensive, perhaps a thousand miles away before returning back to me.

"So then, you find the dreamcatcher helps?" I decided to ask.

"Oh, Ambrosia, I wouldn't have it if it didn't."

*****

When the plane descended, it delivered quite the same effect as it did during takeoff. Again I suffered the drop in my stomach and pop in my ears before we hit ground. I say hit because that's what it was, or rather felt like, the sudden crashing thud resonating throughout the aircraft that signified we were no longer in the air.

Twilight had crept up on us, and I had the phenomenal experience of watching it transduce from beneath our haven's holding. Blue sky washed itself down in a cascade of yellows and pinks as the sun fell beneath. Hues of orange followed deep reds set over a purple haze that ended where darkness took up space.

Stars filled the night sky, and as we descended, they merged with the lights of man over cityscape. The atmosphere seemed in an eternal state of effervescent glory that swept the earth's channel and swallowed it whole in its unfolding.

When at last the aircraft touched down and we had come to a full and complete stop, the captain came on for the last time. He gave thanks for flying with the airline and welcomed us to the city of Hartland.

We were then informed to slowly disembark. We grabbed our belongings and began to shuffle down the line with the rest of the passengers. Suddenly, and terribly, I noticed I needed to go to the bathroom. Whenever the line slowed to a snail's pace, I came a little closer to losing it altogether. So when we finally did seem to be getting somewhere, my teeth were floating and all I wanted was sweet relief.

We were, as luck would have it, the last to exit, and as we made our way to the plane door, there she was: the flight attendant who had only hours ago stolen my heart away. Mona, who was just ahead of me, ended up walking past her without a word of thanks. *Strange*, I thought. I think the two may have exchanged a courtesy glance, a slight nod, but that was as far as it went. I, however, had other plans. Bladder be damned, I wasn't leaving the plane without at least properly introducing myself to the woman to which I owed so much. I had arrived safely, after all. So I walked up to meet her.

I immediately picked up on just how tall she was. Why, she even towered over me. *Must be the boots,* I thought. Her slender neck and proportional body made her the perfect image of grace. I said hello.

"Why, hello again," she responded with a perfect smile.

"I, ahem…just wanted to say, I'm really happy I had the chance to meet you." It was intoxicating to watch her, how her eyes passed over mine, drank me in.

"My pleasure, come back and fly anytime" She flashed me another shot of her gorgeous pearls.

I couldn't help but advance closer to her, and I could feel her body heat on me. I wanted to have her right there, just rip off her uniform and ravage her beauty. *All right, Ambrosia, take it easy now. Just get a hold of yourself.*

Knowing it was time to sink or swim, I decided to take things slow and choose my words carefully. "I…well, I live here now and I hope this isn't too forward, but I was just wondering if you'd like to maybe get together sometime, you know, just the two of us."

She stood there for a moment not saying anything, as though unsure of where to go with what I'd asked her. "Sorry, sir, but it's against airline policy to fraternize with our onboard clients." These were not the words I longed to hear.

Sink. Damn it. I'm sure my face went fifteen shades of red. "Er, sorry. Thought I'd take a shot. I understand if you're not interested." *Can't blame a guy for trying.*

"No, sir, it's not like that..."

Because it's exactly like that. "Look, it's okay. Policy, right?" I had never dealt with rejection before, and it seemed it didn't take so well. Still, even with the feeling of rejection pressing heavily down, and the ever-persistent pains in the pelvis, I did not want to leave the stately image placed before me. But Mona was waiting.

"Well, it was good meeting you," I said. "Have a great night, safe travels and all that, goodbye."

I spoke fast and turned to leave even faster, but just as I was almost out the door I felt a soft hand touch my shoulder. I stopped steadfast as she leaned into my ear and whispered, "I would love the chance to get to know you better."

I only wanted to pull her in closer. I stood there in silence, waiting, hoping that this was going somewhere, anywhere.

"It's just that…"

I hated to have to hear those words.

"…I'll be going back tonight."

Of course, what was I thinking? She's a flight attendant, after all.

She backed away, placing a hand out as I turned towards her. "I'm glad we got this chance to meet, Mr...?"

My name! I had not given it to her. Worse yet, I hadn't bothered asking for hers.

I grasped her hand, wanting to pull her in, to kiss her face on either cheek. "Ambrosia, my name is Ambrosia. And you?"

She smiled and pointed to a tag on her chest. A name as beautiful as the one who sported its attire. "Sadira," she said. How had I missed that?

Sadira—how flawless a word, a beautifully drawn symbol of delicate serenity. "Well, thank you, Sadira, for everything, I mean. I as well am glad our paths crossed."

"Then perhaps the fates will intervene, bring us back together again someday." She squeezed my hand before letting it go. "Take care, Mr. Ambrosia."

"Perhaps…" But I did not believe. "Goodbye, Sadira." I smiled and gave a small reluctant nod as I let her fade from view.

I found Mona waiting for me in the hanger that led away from our plane. She merely flashed a clever smile as I walked by.

"I need to use the washroom," I said.

"I thought you might. A cold shower too, perhaps..." she snickered. "Come, we will get you there."

We hurried through the busy east coast airport. Things here looked pretty much the same as they had on the west coast, although slightly smaller. The building design looked fairly similar, with plain walls stretching out over great distances, high ceilings with ugly square fluorescent lights. The gadgets were all there, display screens and escalators and conveyor belts. Announcements were sent out over the loud speakers.

We hurried past the restaurants and gift shops, currency exchange posts and baggage claim stations. Immediately I was thankful for not having checked my luggage prior to flight. The masses of people there bordered on insanity. Vacant expressions, heads bowed, eyes diverted to the conveyer belt. *Make a mad dash through the mayhem to squeeze through to the other side.*

On the other hand, I did see some things that made my heart skip. I saw other instances of reunions between loved ones, signs of sincere devotion that made me smile. It gave me hope.

But on a larger scale, people still seemed cut off. Not one person in the crowd was courteous enough to show me any consideration. No one ever looked my way or so much as even said a hello to me. I did no better, and it made me wonder if I was becoming conditioned to the feeling, or perhaps that my mind was on other things such as an oversized bladder ready to burst out on the floor. *Just where are you taking us, Mona?*

My pain had gone well to the brink and then surpassed it. Maybe Mona saw it, I wasn't sure, but when I could take it no more, she pointed the way to the public washrooms. As I dropped my bag and broke into a steady run, I thought I heard her say something about waiting for me there.

When I got to the bathroom, I decided to take a cue from the man who followed in after me; walking over to the wall next to him, I watched as he unzipped and began streaming his flow onto a stand-up porcelain container stationed there. *These must be urinals, what a fantastic idea,* I thought. Or perhaps I said it aloud. I wasn't sure, but either way the man I stood behind sure seemed to take higher notice of me thereafter. So much so that it caused him to half turn around, peeing on himself while tucking his unfinished member back inside.

"What the— Freak!" he said to me, storming out without washing.

What's his problem? I wondered. *The insecurities of some people.* I was only looking for some pointers, after all.

So I let the river out. And not a moment too soon, I might add. When at last I was finished, I closed back up, situating myself as best I could in the sewn up penal complex I was made to endure—really, how does anyone put up with wearing this?—and then I turned around to find my way to the sink for a wash up. There, I noticed my new self in the mirror for the first time. Mona was right; the clothes were a good match and I looked very debonair, perhaps except for the dirty blonde mess that was my hair and the dark circles under my blue eyes.

Yes, I could really use another eight hours of deep seeded sleep. It seemed I was a bit on the grotesque side of things.

Suddenly I became aware of what I must have looked like to others, what I had looked like to Sadira. With the former I could deal, but when I imagined the fool I must have appeared in the eyes of the woman I feebly attempted to woo… It was definitely a firm blow to the confidence meter. But there, alone in the privacy of the public lavatory, was also a certain level of relief that cradled my humiliation as I ran hot water down the drain, washing my hands of it. I needed that moment to put it all behind me, the look of idiocy that did not become me. *This was only your first attempt, you'll do better with the next. Now buck up, time to get back on that horse.*

Clean and ready for trial two, I turned to go when I nearly ran smack into a wall. I stopped with a sudden start at having found the living embodiment of a blockade stationed directly in front of me, in the form of a large man in uniform not unlike those of airline security.

"Whoa! Sorry, didn't see you there," I apologized as I looked up at the man. *Where did he come from?* He easily had half a foot on me, and I am not a short man. His stature was equaled only by his physique, which was alarmingly wide across his shoulders. Still, that wasn't what I found most disturbing about him.

He said nothing but only stared, stared right through me with his pale green eyes. Sunken in, dark and abysmal they were, and as much a reflection of my own frayed semblance. *Guess I wasn't the only one who had themselves a rough night.*

Well, if he wasn't about to stop me, instead content to just stand there in his discourteous manner, then I would just have to go around him. I wasn't much for conceding, but having had trouble in the area of security once already and with Mona still waiting, I thought it best to just sidestep the problem and get on with it.

He did not stop me as I went, only turned to look my way. I turned back and saw him standing there, watching me, a crooked smile traced over his narrow, pale face. "Damn those male superiority complexes," I grumbled under my breath, perhaps loud enough for him to hear. I felt lucky that he did not come after me.

As I found my way back to Mona, she handed back my bag with a raised eyebrow. "Did you fall in?" she asked.

"What?"

"Nothing, son," she said, giving a slight shake of her head. "Shall we be on our way then?"

As I picked up my bag and followed after her, I spoke nothing of my experience with the guard but instead brushed it off as ignorant bully behaviour. *She need not be bothered with such minor details.* So I wondered, was it possible that Mona had seen the officer enter the washroom after me? Not that his behaviour would seem abnormal, per se, unless of course he had reason for being there... Still, Mona did not seem alarmed. It didn't seem to matter anyway.

On we went, making our way through the rest of the building, exiting through revolving doors and out into parking lot. It was brisk outside, in the realm of eastern winds. You could feel a dampness in the air almost immediately upon entering this harbour town. It was something I wasn't used to, but I felt prepared for it.

Daylight had all but fallen to dusk, and the airport's exterior was lit up by a manmade brightness, vast by magnitude. Streetlamps sat high, raised atop tall beams that reached up toward the skies. Scattered throughout the airport's parking area, their vivid incandescence set the place aglow like beacons lit to guide the weary traveller home.

I followed Mona through the lot until we arrived at a space that, like so many others before it, held a vehicle. However, unlike the others, the car was one of sheer, refined magnificence. I walked around it twice to take in its full grandeur. Decked out in a crimson black, windows tinted to match, the windshield was a smoky grey. The wheels' rims were sterling silver. The layout had a sleek design to it, with a thin frame and fine, rounded edges. The top, a dome that ran down toward a capacious fin on its back spoiler. Perfectly spherical headlights sat erect off an arrow-shaped hood and flared front fender. Finally, sweeping wheel wells encased wide tires that sat low, hugging the ground.

"It's…quite striking."

"Isn't it? Glad you value the detail of its master craftsmanship."

I was at a loss for words. I merely nodded.

"I do so love my Porsche." She walked over to the passenger side and stuck her key in. She opened the door. "Well, go on then, get in."

Without argument I leapt into the passenger seat, bag in hand. Mona closed the door behind me, walked around the front, and entered through the front driver's side door.

"It's so good to be home, and to see you on this most wonderful of nights, Lenore." She made herself comfortable.

"Lenore?" I said. "You mean the car. You named the car?" I actually wasn't totally opposed to the idea.

"But of course. I think it suits her, don't you?"

I nodded. "You know, it does."

I think the first thing I noticed about this new environment was its feel. The seat, with its ~~leather~~ pleather outfitting, was so cushiony it was almost like it took the very mould of my body. The headrest was high and straight, so good for the spine, with lumbar support near the bottom. Also, with the frame as low as it was, I could almost swear I was sitting on the ground.

"Here, Ambrosia, let me take that." Mona grabbed my carry-on.

"Oh, thanks," I replied, still too distracted by the majestic linear attributes of Lenore's design to pay much attention. I ran my fingers along her lines, up the curve of her window frame, seamless.

"There should be just enough space in the back seat for them, I do believe."

"Huh…?"

"Nothing."

Mona inserted the key and turned the engine over. A humming purr issued throughout the Porsche. In an instant, the headlights rose and the dashboard lit up. Mona then pushed a small button below the dash and to the right of the wheel. Suddenly a blue screen flashed, and there upon it a working digital clock.

"A quarter past eight, is it?" she said. "Not bad. I'll have us home before nine, mark my words." Mona went for her seatbelt, then she turned to me. With a small sigh, I stuck in the clip and relaxed back into my seat.

That's when I noticed it, like the distant beating of a heart. It was faint at first, but with each successive tone the sound grew in unison. Soon, behind the drumming, there came on a clamour of commotions: a babble of voices, a tick tock of clocks, bells chiming and devices humming in vibration. The eerie bellow of a laughter in the air, a shuddersome roar whose direful din had risen to outright pandemonium. Oh bewailing outcry emerging from within, bring the stridency of an eruption unwrapping, extinguishing all—but the howl did remain.

A scream shot straight to the eardrum, piercing in alarm, its volume splitting the horizon. Then gone. And as the caterwaul broke, it was replaced by a tone both melodic and ethereal in nature. Washing in, its base centered in harmonious resonance.

"I like your taste in music, Mona."

"Ah yes, glad you think so. A little 'Darkside'[iii] is good for healing the soul."

Mona took her pack of cigarettes from her blouse pocket. She placed a stick in her mouth. Lighting it, she took in a heavy drag. Then, powering down the window (electric to enthrall me) and dispelling the smoke, I watched her melt back into her seat, her eyes closed, a small sigh of gratitude issuing from out her mouth.

"Looks like you needed that," I said as the scent found me. I too inhaled its redolence and found it to be somewhat satisfying to the senses. It was definitely not like it had been earlier, my stomach having since settled.

Mona opened her eyes again. "Yes, indeed."

I gave a slight laugh and looked out the side window. On the door I saw a couple of switches by the handle like those Mona had pushed. I decided to scratch my itch and pushed one myself. The window went down slightly. *Nice.*

"Shall we, then?"

I looked back towards Mona. "To the Hartland?"

"To Hartland." Mona placed an outstretched hand upon the stick shift and pulled us away from the parking space that had held us in its midst. Within minutes we were on the road and headed to city limits.

CHAPTER 5
◊
THE JOURNEY HOME

The journey that took us into the city and towards my new home was one of both wonder and amazement. The lights at the heart of the inner metropolis captured and transfixed me with their brimming spectacle of luminescence.

As the blinding glare of beams off busy vehicles flew past us and disappeared into unknown destinations of the night, the signs on the highway flew by with words that flashed rapid pieces of information my way, titles of locations, other areas that contributed to the makeup of this super city.

"We're close now, Ambrosia, this is our off-ramp coming up. Another fifteen minutes, twenty tops, and we'll have reached our destination." Mona cruised along the road with fantastic momentum.

"Happy to hear it." And I was. The excitement of the unknown brewed inside me, nearly bubbling over.

"Here we are then, the route to Hartland." Mona swung the wheel and veered over to the right, taking an off-ramp road that led us away from the main drag. She slowed her pace as we travelled down this road's semi-circular course. At its end we were met with a whole new series of avenues, each stacked with legions of automobiles. Mona had to slow down almost to a standstill while she merged in with the masses.

"Welcome to the bustling metropolis, my dear boy," she exclaimed.

We travelled along in this menagerie of machinery, where towering heights climbed the sky and streetlamps littered incandescent roadways as people moved about in all direction.

There were buildings everywhere, structures of so many shapes and sizes, scaling from petite dwellings to titanic tenements of architecture. Mona pointed out the parkways and billboard signs broadcasting images on every corner.

Ropes of wire connected by tall wooden poles ran along the street grids—power lines, Mona called them. I knew of their purpose: the process of electricity transferred and dispersed between places. So incredible to behold.

She went on to explain traffic lights, stop signs, and crosswalks. She described apartment complexes, office buildings, factories, restaurants, cafés, and shopping centres as we passed through. I heard about colleges and schools, walking trails, and graveyards in which to bury the dead.

Mona also spoke of ways to get around the city, the public transportation available to me. She pointed out the many buses as they went by.

I guess what I noticed most was how it seemed the city became larger the closer we got. The framework of the metropolis only rose and further developed into new heights; so many constructs towered over our heads like concrete giants. I immediately felt minuscule in comparison.

Lenore, she knew her city well, twisting and turning between roads as if it were natural reflex. "We're entering the downtown district now, Ambrosia my boy. Just a few more blocks and we're golden." Mona spoke with a tone of elation in her voice.

"Great" was the only word I could come up with to express my own spirit of jubilation at the fact.

Traffic began to thin as we continued around a few more bends, a side street or two, and an intersection that turned down a sloping hill. At its bottom we at last arrived at our final destination. Just like that, our journey was done.

"Here we are then, home sweet home." Mona took Lenore down a small ramp that led off from the road and delivered us to a dead-end. I watched as she then grabbed hold of a tiny device linked off her car keys and pressed a button at its center. Suddenly the entire side of a building lifted, revealing within a hidden space.

"The garage door opener," Mona explained, "electronically sends a signal for the door to raise." She must have noticed the bewildered look across my face. "It opens up to an area where I can store Lenore, called a garage."

"I see."

Mona pulled into the unit and the car came to a standstill. As the lights came down and the engine purred no longer, Mona unbuckled her belt and turned towards me. "Ready when you are."

"I've never been more ready for anything in my whole life." I was shaking uncontrollably.

"Well, let's get to it then, shall we?" Mona grabbed both our bags from the back and tossed mine over to me. The next thing I knew she had exited from the vehicle. I unclipped and followed her approach, saying goodbye to my black chrome beauty, at least for the moment.

We walked back towards the street, up onto a city sidewalk. I spun around on my heels, not really knowing where to look first. A number of lit dwellings held the street, brightening the night atmosphere.

"We're still technically at the back of the building. Let us move around and enter in through the front." We made our way to the end of the road and rounded the corner. What I saw next, I tell you, it sent me staggering.

There in front of us stood a solemn scene of breathtaking beauty. A gargantuan body of water. In the midst of its mighty bays was a great assemblage of ships. Beyond this mouth of the sea, and as reflected on the water's edge, sat the sum of a thousand shimmering stars. Stretching out across the vast waterway was stationed a booming platform of steel bridging the land, supported by strong, strapping cables that suspended between mighty towering pillars. From below the construct, these pedestals firmly descended down and disappeared into the depths. The luster of a long line of lamps hung over its entire extension in an emanation of sheer luminescence.

"I can see by the look on your face that the harbour has already gotten you under its spell," Mona said. "Trust me, lad, it hasn't been the first time I've seen it affect someone this way."

"It's remarkable, Mona. I had no idea…"

"That it would be like this? No, my boy, no one ever does, and then you see it." She put her arms out, welcoming the vastness of cityscape.

"And this is where you live?"

"This is it, right near the docks. Here you can get a full view of things." Mona stopped for a moment in contemplation. "I suppose we have time, I mean if you'd like to take a small stroll down to the wharf and then maybe to the end of that pier over there."

"Really?" The notion sounded fantastic to me.

"Come."

Mona stepped forward towards the direction of the pier. I quickly followed after her. As we wandered down to the waterfront, I noticed just how calm this area was. I remember only a handful of people dispersed throughout.

"It's rather quiet tonight, isn't it?" I said.

"Just the hour of the evening. It's a Friday, too late for those with little ones to be out, and too early for the nightlife to have yet appeared."

"Nightlife?"

"Yes, those who wish to experience the entertainment this city has to offer when the sun goes down."

"So what you're saying is that there's much to be had here in the dew of twilight?"

"Ambro, you are in for quite a time. I won't spoil it for you, though. You'll experience it for yourself, later tonight."

Later tonight? Just what was Mona planning, I wondered.

We sauntered down to the end of the pier, and I took in the whole spectacle before us. Scattered boats had docked here and there, some looking a little ragged and worn down after perhaps seeing too many bad days on the surf. Their bodies appeared a bit beaten, with chipped paint and splintered surfaces. However rough and tumble they happened to be, they still carried with them an eminence of distinction. Sheol, the equipment alone was an impressive enough feat. They held an assortment of ropes and meshed cages, poles, spears, chains, and webbed nets. *Looks like they're ready for a hunt.*

On the other side of the spectrum, a few of the ships looked quite dapper, their masts high with expansive salons and spacious decks. From V-shaped bow to sweeping stern, it could easily be said that a meticulous care had been devoted to the craft of these vessels. Of course, there were still other boats I couldn't see, thanks to the behemoth tarps cast over them. Judging by size alone, I guessed them to be spectacular vessels as well, their owners concealing them from prying eyes.

On regarding the wharf, it was made of a thick oak. Upon stepping out to the edge, one could catch sight of just how far it resided above the water. There on the docks came a border of large treaded tires tied to the wharf side.

"So that no boats coming into port are caused harm, a bumper of sorts. Any force when the vessel hits the tires will absorb its shock, within reasonable means," Mona said without my asking, as was becoming the custom.

We stopped at the edge of the pier, and I was able to absorb the view's immensity with a more ample appreciation.

"Well, there it is. Welcome to the harbour of the Hartland. Quite striking, isn't it?"

I was at a loss for words, so I merely nodded in compliance with her.

Mona pointed straight ahead towards the brightness that rested off the banks on the other side of the harbour. "There the region continues, and you'll be able to see it better in the daylight of the morrow."

Yet another face to the region. I had only just arrived and all I wanted to do was go across and explore.

"That long illuminated structure to your left is the Magian Bridge, which links the two sides of the city together. You can, of course, also go around using the road."

"Why would you want to?" Amazing, manmade structures that stretched clear across the body of water. The pass lit up with a shimmering brilliance. Just fantastic.

"Always there is activity to be found on these waters. A vast number of different vessels come into harbour and lay their anchorage here within these bays." Mona directed my attention to a long ship of impressive girth out in the middle of the harbour. "That ship coming in now is a freightliner; you see a lot of those here. The large steel boxes on its deck are used for the transport of cargo and supplies, pretty much its main use."

As Mona pointed at the ship's way, I could scarcely believe not seeing it before. Steam rose off the stacks of its colossal concoction of moulded metal, and a blast of sound arose from down its belly.

"Steam whistle. It lets you know when the ship's coming or going. Down in these parts you'll hear it most often, at all times of the day and night, in fact. Do not worry, as I'm sure that in a few weeks or so you won't even notice it's around."

"I'm sure." Although I couldn't see how this was possible.

I then saw, as coming out from behind the freightliner, and headed in the opposing direction, the emergence of what appeared a heavily armoured ship. "And what is that, Mona?"

"That is a naval frigate, fully armed, and with I would say about two hundred officers on board. At least that's what she holds."

"Really?"

"Yes, you will soon come to find that it is not at all unusual to see this caliber of ship often patrolling around. Hartland is largely a military port, with bases set up at points all along the dockyard."

"Interesting," I said as I watched the frigate go by, and thought about what it might be like to be in command of one.

Now, most of the other vessels that are out this evening are fishing boats, most likely coming in from a long day at sea."

"Fishing boats, like those we saw along the wharf?"

"Some of them, yes. There were also a few sailboats and yachts, I believe." She gave a glance back to the area we had just come from. "Most of those will have found their way back out to sea by the early hours of the morning, to return only when needed to."

"Long days…makes for a hard life."

"That it does," Mona said again, scanning over the scene. "Have you gotten the chance to catch sight of that odd-looking tub?" She pointed to a most unusual sort of seacraft. It had the countenance of a block, large and thick with flat sides. Hard to fathom how such a hulking mass stayed afloat.

"Mona, what is that?"

"That, my unbeknownst friend, is the ferry that runs between here and there. It's a form of public transportation, like the buses we drove by earlier. The ferry starts at 7:00 AM every morning and runs throughout the day. If you ever wish to ride it, the terminal where it docks is just over that way, to your left." She pointed. "Follow along the wharf and you'll be led to the ferry station where it makes dock, simple as that." Mona led my gaze to a region further down the way, where a square building jutted out from the wharf.

A ferry she says, to cross over waterway, I can't wait to go and see it for myself.

"Above the terminal there is also a spot for better viewing," Mona said. "Round these parts we call it the look off."

"Sounds enticing."

"You'll have to check it out sometime, I promise you won't be disappointed," I saw Mona check her watch as she had done so much the last night at the gazebo. "I do believe we should get a move on. We still have time to get in some supper."

"Supper sounds good." I hadn't realized until she had brought it up, but my stomach felt quite empty. Airline food had been too terrible not to decline, but it did nothing to curb the hunger.

"Let us be off then, the family will be expecting us."

"As you wish, Mona." The thought of meeting these others whom Mona called her children was both an exciting and particularly nerve-wracking one. My only hope was that they accepted me as one of their own.

"Trust me," she said, "they are going to love you."

In a few minutes we had made our way back to her building. Upon nearing a set of large black doors Mona slowed her pace, stopped, and swung her sights upon me. "Here we are then. Welcome to your new home."

I gazed up at the two-storey stone building standing before me. "It's …very nice." And it was, more than so. The building was wide, and it was covered with windows. Two lengthy bay windows flanked either side of the doorway, and several smaller ones were stationed evenly along its second floor. The entire body of the building was chiselled out of granite. The roof was flat with a protruding ledge, where idyllic sculptures of two stone figurines sat perched as guardians before a house gate. The statues were exquisitely detailed. They shared the image of a woman, alike in face and body shape, but only one appeared with delicate feathered wings on her back. The other had wings, too, but the reproduction was menacing, like the wings of a dragon. A pure representation of good and evil, fully exposed as carved out in the nude and measured to perfect symmetry which no real person could ever hope to realize. Two impossible objects cast in stone, so identical in form yet so opposing in identity born. How aberrant.

"Those statues up there, they're quite catching," I said, pointing to them.

"Ah, yes. Glad you think so. I'll have to introduce you to the artist."

"Fantastic." I was always up for meeting someone of such genius.

"Ready then, are you?" Mona said, taking a step towards the door.

"After you," I said.

She went to put a pull to the handle when I noticed the words inscribed atop the entryway. "The Nebula?"

"Why, yes, that is what we call it, the name of this place that is my home, and yours also, Ambrosia."

"You mean you named your house too?"

"Well, I run a bar and lounge where people in the city can come for drinks and entertainment."

How curious that she hadn't mentioned this before. "A bar, you say, like the kind that serves liquor?"

"That would be correct."

"I see…" How exciting, I thought, as I'd always wanted to take in the experience. Now I was to live within such an establishment? I wondered how this would work. "And so, you mentioned entertainment…just what type of entertainment is being offered?"

"It varies. We are primarily a dance club, but sometimes we'll have shows or live bands. Tonight is Friday, and we have our in-house DJ on the turntables."

"DJ? As in disc jockey, someone who spins records for a listening audience?" I was reeling with excitement at the thought.

"That would be the definition," she said, only slightly mocking me.

"And this is supposed to happen tonight?"

"Tonight and every night, my young friend," she said smugly.

"I see…so you live inside a bar then?"

"Certainly not," she said, pulling the door back. "I live above it."

I looked back up to the row of windows across the upper level of the building. "Ah, interesting."

"Yes, it should be," Mona said, as if talking to herself. "Speaking of which, I should really get in and see how things are going with the night's set up. We don't open for more than an hour, but time will be here before you know it.

"Well, it certainly sounds rather intriguing, doesn't it?" Hit the floor running right out of the gate.

"Son, you don't know the half of it," she said with a slick grin painted across her face. She disappeared through the door.

I made a grab for the handle to follow while the trail was still hot, but I got tripped up along the way. Happily, I managed to catch myself before hitting the ground. In seeking the culprit, I found that one of the shoes Mona had burdened me with had become unravelled. As a result, the laces had fallen under the step of my other foot, and in essence I had tripped over my very own self. *Faen.*

Mumbling about the advantages of my absent Geta footwear, I knelt down to remedy the situation as I heard the door close in front of me. I was about to tear my shoes off completely when suddenly I had the strangest feeling that I was being watched. It was like nothing I'd ever experienced before, so powerful a pull in fact, that I had to stand and gauge the situation at hand.

I turned to look around me, but there was no one there, neither could I find a person further down the way. Odd, I thought, for such a populated region. Even at the present time of night, one would think that at least a few people would be scattered throughout the locality, if only at farthest reach.

"Hello?" I called out, but my voice fell on dead air. The noise of the city had all but dissipated, as though fizzled out somehow, and suddenly on stepping out, I took notice of the unrelenting silence, gone to emptiness. Not the buzz of a car from some distant street, nor the whistles of a passing ship—nothing. Frantically I listened for signs of life, a far cry from some unbeknownst place, the slightest echo of footsteps approaching, or any of the thousand things left in between. The silence haunted me as sound it seemed had all but drifted to standstill, and died away save for a buoys bob on the bay.

Foolishness, I told myself. After all, hadn't Mona just said this time of evening was quiet around these parts? But then I just couldn't shake the feeling. *Get a hold of yourself.*

Doing my best to shrug it off, I turned around to head for the doors when a great shriek ripped across the sky. A sudden shiver of shock shot up my spine and spun me hard on my heels as I desperately searched around, attempting to locate the source of the shrill siren's caw.

There, overhead, as from the void of oblivion, a wild thing did fly. Like Black Death obsidian it was, piercing the night tide by a blade of dark stealth, it swept along the airs and came to perch atop a hanging wire. And where it came to rest, it sat and stared down upon the individual who beheld a backward gaze.

There steadfast we stood, fixed in confrontation, each bound to the glower of its other, I and this carnivorous bird of prey, this solitary crow. The thing was enormous, for what it was. I had seen ravens smaller than this crow in the forest around my home.

Was that all it was? I wondered. Had this bird been watching me from the periphery of a far off threshold somewhere?

The crow continued to descend its glare down upon me, and as it did I found that I could not look away. And I didn't want to—I liked looking at it and found it almost beautiful, like the dark hours before dawn, when the air settles and the waters grow still, where shadow takes you under its solemn wing.

I sauntered into its eyes, finding a twilight shimmering off an obsidian sphere. The site bored into me, keeping a hold without sway. To its dominion I walked, lost to the eye of the storm, moved by a prerogative of plenary tenure. I would have followed it anywhere.

"Coming, Ambrosia?" a voice called out.

What I heard was not from any part of the crow, however, but belonged to none other than the dearest lady Mona. The sound of her calling immediately shook me from my stupor, and I turned to find she who stood against the extended door, with arms crossed and raised eyebrows. "Or were you looking to be off somewhere else?"

"Me? Uh...no, just…" I looked back to where the crow had perched, but to my astonishment she was there no longer. "…heard something?" Up and gone, as if vanishing into thin air. Refusing to believe my eyes, I scanned the area.

"Thought you'd go and inspect? Is that right?" Mona spoke charismatically.

I gave a small sigh and drifted back toward her. "I suppose I did, but never mind that. The moment has passed."

"Good, guess you should come in then, hmm?"

"Guess I should."

I wandered back to her station and proceeded through the entryway set before me. Mona followed and the door shut behind us. Outside, I heard the call of a whistle, the song of a ferry sailing somewhere in the distance.

There, in a small corridor lit with red light, stood a man and a woman, waiting to greet us.

“Ambrosia, it gives me great pleasure to introduce you to Gany and Gliese,” Mona said from behind me.

“Allo, mon chéri. Pleasure to meet ‘ou,” said the man, Gany, with a peculiar accent. He followed with a customary embrace, a kiss on the cheek. The accent didn’t sound entirely unfamiliar, yet still it was decidedly different from those of my Mothers four. (Oddly enough, I myself did not adopt any such dialect, or so I had been told.) No, this was an altogether different sound, though possibly a derivative of the source. More than anything I noticed his tone, a greater pitch of intensity than my own voice.

“Pleasure’s mine,” I replied.

Gany took a step back, and I was able to get a better look at the man. He had a cool look about him, his hazel eyes emanating a mood of calm complacency. His facial characteristics were pronounced, and his complexion fair. He stood a little closer to the ground than myself and he had a sturdy physique. He wore blue shoes, dark blue pants, and an eggplant shirt with the collar unbuttoned. His head was covered by a grey cap with a distinctive crown and brim. His hair was kept short, and what part of it that wasn’t hidden beneath his cap appeared a sandy flaxen. He was a clean cut and handsome man, and I found his composure quite comforting.

Next to Gany stood the girl, Gliese. She did not waste any time floating over to close her arms around me, and I melted into the unyielding kindness of her warm reception.

"Welcome home. I hope that your journey was one of experience fulfilled." She spoke amicably, yet with an air of monotone hospitability, seeming at ease with the world yet not quite in it. I thought it was strange of her to have welcomed me "home", although I guess she was right, as this was to be my surrogate home.

"If you need anything, let us know," she said, easing away from me.

"Thanks, it's good to be amongst such hospitability."

Gliese was of a wiry stature, her body straight, her legs thin and long. Her arms and hands were also gaunt and lanky right down to the measure of each slender finger. It gave her the appearance of seeming taller than she was. Her skin seemed transparent, so that I could see a hint of the veins in her legs. She had a narrow face with a cleft in her chin and a hooked nose, her eyebrows sheer and drawn to form the natural contours of a seamless arch. Finely textured hair of darkened brown streamed down past her shoulders. The symmetry of her eyes transfixed me; they were large and bulbous with perfect delineation. Hazel, they almost appeared too big for the sockets that held them, as so faintly did the eyes protrude out of their borders. Somehow they seemed to conflict with her other characteristics.

Gliese wore a citrus blouse with a mustard skirt cut just above the knees. Corn stockings and peach-yellow loafers finished the ensemble. The colours made her complexion seem warmer than it was.

The monotone expression in her voice was almost impossible to read, yet I somehow still found a calming reassurance within it. Her presence seemed to float somewhere between darkness and light, and her body, long and agile, spoke a language of lively animation while also emanating quiet repose. The whole thing was a contradiction, seemingly out of place and somehow finding room to fit. She was hauntingly beautiful in a way, off kilter and offering me a certain sense of *je ne sais quoi*. Familiarity, perhaps?

This is what puzzled me the most, because she didn't remind me of anyone I knew. Though, as Mother Xia and Mother Isaura would have me believe, perhaps I was using my third eye or sixth sense. *Such delusion*, I thought. Yes, they would have me believing in fairytales of lives past when it could all be explained by coincidence. *Doesn't mean a thing, not a damn thing.*

Gliese's warmth was most likely, I thought, merely linked to my having left behind the only family I knew for the adventure of the unknown. She was no less than a total enigma, yet for some reason I could say I trusted her without doubt, feeling close to her from the very beginning.

"Gany and Gliese help with running the club." Mona spoke quietly. "Gany is our resident DJ, and Gliese plays barkeep."

At once my ears picked up. "So you tend the bar?" I asked her.

"I do allow for libation," Gliese responded with what I took to be her way of saying yes.

"Yes, of course you do," I said. *I could use a drink now,* I thought.

"So, chére, 'ow was the trip?" Gany asked.

"It was fine," Mona said. "I'll tell you all about it once we've had the chance to settle in. Tell me, Gany, are you the only ones here?"

"Summer, she is upstairs, and Stars is out somewhere, I do not know. The rest 'as yet to arrive," Gany said.

"Good. That means we can give Ambro here a chance to breathe before the night takes hold." Mona gave me a wink. "Well, I think we've stood in the corridors for quite long enough. Come, won't you?"

Mona led as we followed. We travelled through another set of doors and down a small hallway that led out into the main room: an area strictly obscured under cover of darkness, yet seemingly both vast and spacious all the same.

"You haven't begun with the setting up yet, I gather?" queried Mona whilst still in motion.

"We were just about to get the things in order when we 'eard you come in," Gany explained, somewhere from within the black.

"We have less than an hour now," Mona said.

"There are only minor details to resolve, then we will be ready," Gliese said.

"Good. And you, Gany?"

"It is all good, madam. The turntables are lit up with the set list ready."

Beyond the shadows of objects cast amongst us, showing but shapes of things gone heavily unseen as the silhouettes of bar room fixtures, I followed in the sound of their footsteps onto the edge of somewhere. It was here that the light filtered in, allowed through a crack opening of yet another doorway, that led to a return of red revealed before us through that of a stone stairway heading upwards. We stopped there a spell before going further.

"Well, if everything is being taken care of, you won't mind if I steal Ambrosia away for awhile," Mona stated. "I want to show him to his room and around the homestead, get him familiarized to the surroundings."

"We 'ave it covered, mademoiselle. Take the proverbial load off," Gany said.

"Yes, freshen up and we will again see you," Gliese said.

"Bless your hearts," Mona replied most sincerely. "Ambrosia, are you then ready?"

"Most definitely," I remarked, taking that first step.

"Oh, and Ambrosia?" I heard Gany's voice call out.

"Yes, Gany, what is it?" I said, turning and catching sight of him in the shadows.

"J'aime ton air."

From behind me, Mona said, "It means he likes the look of you, in French. Do you know it, the language?"

"Obviously not as much as I would like…" I said.

"Thanks, by the way, I guess," I replied to the Frenchman, not sure how to take the remark. I didn't sense a malicious tone, yet the remark could have been directed toward the matted-down fro.

"Anytime, mon ami, anytime," he replied, disappearing behind the shutting door.

CHAPTER 6
◊
THE FOUR CORNERS

At the top of the stairs, we came to yet another door. Opening it, we entered into a small and dimly lit foyer.

Mona removed her shoes and threw them into a closet filled with a half dozen or so other pieces of footwear. I did the same, and it was nice to get them off. My feet were more than a little sore.

"Take off your coat and stay a while," Mona said as she removed her own jacket.

I handed my coat to her. She took mine with hers and hung them both up inside the closet. "Good," Mona said. "Come, allow me to give you the tour."

We left the foyer and continued up more stairs that ended on a second landing, in front of an entrance. "This would be the main floor," Mona said.

"It's...nice," I said, staring blankly at the rosewood barrier in front of me.

"There's more to see than that. Take a look around."

I turned my gaze to the left, to what appeared to be a long, dark hallway.

"First, allow me to show you to your room." Mona walked a few paces into the darkness, and I followed as closely as I could. As she came to a stop in front of a door, she turned the handle and it creaked open.

I walked towards the blackness, unsure what to do next. Then, from behind me, I heard a snap. In an instant, the darkness lifted to reveal my reflection staring back at me. I jumped, still not used to seeing myself in my new clothes.

Moving past the mirror, I took stock of the scarlet hue of a bedchamber laid out in its glory before me. There was a fair diameter to the confines of the area, square with a high ceiling and hardwood flooring beneath my feet. On the back wall beside the mirror, a window rested near the left corner, and an ample-sized bed frame stood to the right. The bed itself occupied the support of a dark oak frame with an arched headboard. An amaranthine veneer lay over its spread while twin pillows took position atop the comforter's surface.

Abreast the framework stood two incarnadine bedside tables, and upon them each a cinnabar lamp. Over to the corner of the room was a chestnut bureau that displayed a mark of divine craftsmanship as seen down to the finest detail of its design. Equally as pleasing, a chair and table sat to the left in front of the window, a pen and pad placed across its surface in asking for the mark up of a blank page. I was sure I would have a lot to write about. Finally, next to the desk stood an open closet door, fashioned to the brim with assorted articles of clothing.

"They're for you, in case you're wondering," Mona said, coming up behind me. "I had two of my brood plan a proper wardrobe for you. If you don't like what you see we can always change it later, but I think you will. Summer and Praesepe, they have an eye for these sorts of things."

"Summer and Praesepe, hmmm..." I brushed my fingers through the hanging attire. "My would-be fashion consultants. A lot of red, I'm seeing…" It almost seemed on purpose, this sea of burgundies, auburns, and sangrias. Fortunately, I was not at all opposed to this. "And will I have a chance to meet and thank these two fine-natured individuals?"

"You will, absolutely. In fact, Summer should be kicking around here somewhere now. More than likely in her room; she spends a lot of her time there hidden away."

"Quiet type is she?"

"Sometimes secluded, yes," Mona said. "A little shy, maybe, but nothing wrong with that, is there?"

"No, nothing."

"Exactly. It just takes some time to get to know the person, but when you do..."

"You discover something truly remarkable."

Mona looked at me with a soft smile on her face.

"Yes."

My attention returned to the closet, looking for a possible place to hang up my kimono.

"You can just leave your carry-on in here," Mona said. "You'll have the chance to settle in a bit more later."

"Right." I set my luggage down beside the bed.

"Oh, and over upon the bureau you'll find your room key."

"Great, thanks." I went over to grab it when I remembered something more important.

"Just one second," I said, bending toward my carry-on. Opening the bag, I removed a red cloth. I carefully opened the folds and picked up the red twine from which the dreamcatcher dangled. "No sense leaving this in the bag while there's a perfectly good window to hang it in, is there?"

"I suppose not," she agreed.

I walked over to the left-hand corner of the room, where I found a hook at the top of the window-sill. "This is where it is meant to take up placement, correct?" I asked.

"It certainly would be, my boy," Mona confirmed, proudly.

It did look particularly nice there, the blood-coloured diamond shimmering in the starlight. "Well, that's that. Should we be off, then?" I asked, turning back towards her.

"Okay, let's move on." Mona disappeared out the doorway.

When I stepped out into the hallway, I found it alight. No more did the shadow cast its plate of caliginosity on me, but neither did it so appear to reach the sights of any other neighbouring region. In looking past my door I could plainly see to where the hall ended and led into some other area of design. And no longer were the walls adorned by a guise of rosewood, instead blending to falu and further down to amaranth. Beyond this an array of colours continued, alternating throughout the passage. A wide transition of magentas translated to rich golden hues down the way. Mirrors also hung in succession along each adjacent wall, and the outline of a few other doorframes could be seen spread along the hallway's path.

"We'll visit those places soon enough. At this moment that is not the direction for which I will be taking you," Mona said, gesturing for me to follow her. "Come, for there are other things I must show you."

I turned away from the mirrors, where I was fixing my messy hair, and followed her to the beginning of the hallway, past where I first entered, that reached to the stairs and the foyer below. Darkness had all but burned away, laid to waste across any visible distance. *She must have switched on some main line to all areas of the house.* I was happy, and still a bit surprised (though at this point I really should not have been) that none of the lights showed signs of flickering as I passed.

"Here is where our journey begins," Mona said, moving toward an entrance. "Here, at the north end of the house, is the common room."

I approached the opening and poked my head through the aperture to address the space that preceded me. What I observed was something quite extraordinary, that took my breath away. I moved further in. It was like nothing I'd ever seen before, a place of visual marvel, extensive by design and formed to the shape of a triangle. The room had high ceilings and an expansive floor space, all done in hard oak and glossed over with a fine finish. The crowning chandelier that hung in the center of the room elicited a low glow over its quarters below, complementing the wine-coloured walls and salmon borders. All of this was, however, of little matter when compared to the canopy beacon that governed over the room.

Red-stained, enameled architecture poured onto a palette of glass that held to ceiling space and stretched over much of the room, its cascade casting a glow of radiant allure. Within the glass, depicted by flawless delineation, were three signs of deity: head of the Ram, Feline, and Archer. Icons I knew all too well, each a symbol representing a devout figure. The root of these images, I knew, lay within the first or oldest order, long forgotten by modern society. They represented the same belief system my Mothers governed under: the order of the Goddess.

I had a fair understanding of each symbol's original representation. They were stories I'd heard more than a thousand times before, stories that, intriguing though they may have been, were merely that, works of fiction.

What real bearing did these stained glass icons place on me, then? Absolutely none, save for perhaps a benign though nugatory feeling of nostalgia. The beauty of them made me yearn for home.

Don't even ask about them. If she's anything like your Mothers four, you may be here all night. Still, so beautifully rendered... I've never seen such use of stained panels.

Moving on, at the far corner of the room was a v-shaped burgundy sofa. Within the couch's confines a triangular table was placed askew, and to each end of the settee a large zanzibar aloe stood, planted in stylish maroon vases. I also caught sight of a dracaena, some bay laurel, even hyssop. This plant life clung to the walls and even dangled from pots suspended off the ceiling. As for windows, there were two for each outer wall, trimmed in crimson. The inner wall was home to a beautiful brick fire-place with blood-red mantle piece.

With the dim light, warm colours, and a hint of rosemary in the air, I would have been happy to col-lapse fast into the room's clutches right then and there.

"You like?" Mona asked, but it sounded as though she already knew.

"It is very inspiring." I stood in awe.

"Yes, it is. And that, my boy, is only the begin-ning. Let us move on."

Turning away from the parlour, we walked back through the colour-coded hallway. Four doors stood out along the way, two on the same side as my bed-room and the other on the opposite wall, set at the center of the pathway. With the exception of this one door, each was numbered. The other doors, however, held no sequence. The number five was placed on the second door; on the third, a nine. Mona offered no help, hardly taking notice as she passed. Naturally, I never asked.

At the east edge of the house, we entered into yet another room, identical in dimension to its predecessor.

"I'm afraid you'll find much the same at both south and west corners. Makes for good *feng shui*, you know," Mona explained.

Clever Mona, she had read me like an open book.

"I bet it does."

I walked throughout the room, examining it. The walls were a steel blue, polished with a lapis lazuli wash.

"You are now viewing the lavatory." Mona moved out into the center of the room.

As in the common room, a ceiling canopy palette blended in brilliance created a picturesque depiction of porous divinity. Here laid the four, those governing spirits of the tides, water numen, each portrayed immaculately through a symbol burned into glass. Aquatic Vertebrate and Crab Crustacean idols sat handsomely on either side, while a pair of serpents wound around each other at the center. One devoured the head of the other, while to their either side stood the Araneae and the Scorpio Maurus facing off. The image depicted a transfer of power between the two signs. The original serpent holder having fallen to oblivion, relinquished all authority. So it was decreed that the title, along with everything that came with it, would be passed back to the one who came before, as written onto the sign whom did precede the soul of the dreadfully departed. Therefore a second serpent holder came into being, taking that which was given as birthright.

Only a story from my childhood, but also one of my favourites. My Mothers would sometimes tell this bedtime fable before they laid me to sleep. It made my skin crawl every time, as it did now to remember it.

As for the rest of the room, below me a cover of white linoleum stretched clear across the floor, plain and thus the perfect antithesis of simplicity against the ornate scene overhead. Venetian blinds and baby blue curtains framed the windows at the centre of each outer wall. I saw a concave marble sink with silver faucets shaped in the likeness of dolphins. The sink's body, a voluminous ovoid, was done in a dark blue granite with ivory rock cabinets.

The room had two doors, the one at the corner through which we entered and another at the far end of the room that led elsewhere. At the room's forefront corner was a triangular, royal blue Jacuzzi tub pointing outward and that ran beneath the surface of the flooring. Like its sink counterpart, it shared the same style faucets. The throne and shower were also a blue granite. Long, fitted fiberglass panels squared off an enclosure around the shower stall behind a navy blue curtain.

The room's foliage nourished an awareness of pure rejuvenation. Roman chamomile and white flowering gardenias flourished over the furnishings, their rich aromatic fragrance carrying divine odours over the airways. Indeed, standing in the room seemed to cleanse my mind, body, and soul.

"Like a breath of fresh air, isn't it?" Mona declared.

"Yes, it is." It was slightly too warm, like the other rooms, but I agreed with Mona. I suspected the whole house would feel this way, not unlike the warm pocket of air around my mountain home.

"You good?" Mona asked.

"Very."

"Good. Let us take our leave, then." Mona exited through the other door, and I quickly followed.

Once again we were at the start of another long hallway. Mona, who never stopped moving, was silent while we moved through the space, which contained a similar mirror arrangement, and progression of colours along its walls. However, in contrast to the last hallway, the colours were more diverse, beginning with white, then silver shifting to black, then a return to wine and amaretto, byzantium, azure, aquamarine, celadon, and, in closing, tea green.

Here too, the path led us to several doors on the outer side of the hall, with a separate solitary unmarked door near the centre on the opposite side. This new passage, however, held not three but four outlying doors. Three of the doors were marked with the numbers four, eight and twelve. I did not catch the other number before Mona stopped and turned around.

"You know, I think I'll show you over to the west wing of the house before venturing into the south. Always a good place to finish."

I didn't question her motives, as I guessed it had everything to do with keeping the right *feng shui*. Mona then backtracked a few steps to open up the solitary door located towards inner center, and we stepped through into another hallway, dimly lit. Here, it seemed my reflection looked back at me wherever I set my eyes. It startled me at first, seeing this silhouette over and over again from each side and even from beneath me. It seemed indeed that mirrors played a pinnacle part in the house.

"Mona, what is this place?" I asked through the thick silence.

"A bridge between areas, my boy. No more, no less." The voice came from somewhere ahead of me.

I was going to ask more but the light came in, blinding me. I stumbled and nearly fell against a wall. What had I just walked into?

"Allow me to present the northwest corridor," Mona informed me as I struggled for balance.

I looked around and saw that Mona wasn't joking; we had in fact landed in another adjoining hallway, a shortcut through the center of the house. Electric blue branched off the walls only to be swallowed up in a sea of verdant green to the left and green-black to finish off the right.

"Please follow, Ambrosia, we now journey to the western corner," Mona said without waiting for a response. She led us down the verdant path.

Like that of all the other doors along the outer wall of partnering hallways, these too had a placement of distinctive number arrangements. There were three in total, with the number six marking the door in front of me, which was stationed at about halfway down the hall, and another coming up on the way, marked with a two. I was starting to see a definite pattern emerge, and so I was able to guess what would appear on the door at the other end of the hall, opposite to where we were headed. As for the reason why, I was still in the process of trying to figure that out.

At last we emerged from the echo…

"Here we have our dining area, a great place for the family to gather and break bread." This was the third triangular room, in a forest green scheme and equipped with its very own canopy radiance, stained to code.

Sure enough, as depicted in the pigments, an ensemble of earth numen held to the form of three divine emblems, the Innocence set between the Bovidae Longhorn and Hollow-horned Vertebrate. At the room's center, as set below the subtle burning of another crystalline chandelier, an immense adornment of armchairs took shape around a great table. The entire set was made of solid pine, skillfully hand-carved with refined accuracy. The chairs were fitted with dark green padded veneers, plait backings, and scalloped heads. Upon the round table's surface a line carved in an 'S' curved through its center, stretching end to end to form two tear drops; the taijitu symbol. I knew it well.

Acting as supplement to the round table, another masterful piece of woodworking sat on display in the corner. It was a cypress china cabinet, exquisitely executed with glassed siding and cabriole-carved legs, intricately cut to take on the presence of some hoofed creature. Beneath a raised top, and above a bowed bottom, brass handles took on the appearance of hilts. The dishes lining the cabinets were emerald plated and encompassed a fern-like illustration that entwined over the measure of their surfaces.

Shamrock drapes opened up over jade window frames, while a series of paintings hung on the wall with the same forested scene, and bestowed in its impression a fetching portrayal of each of the four seasons. Twisted honeysuckle vines fell from olive-coloured urns. The base of windowpanes were laced with jasmine; the taste of its perfume in my mouth invoked memories of early morning wanderings through our garden, where the air was cool and the dew clung to the courtyard below, soaking its surface with unadulterated rejuvenation. Where the rays of a sunbeam touched down, I could feel the grass between my toes...

Finally, under the table a Zen garden lay beneath a triangular, transparent section of the floor, framing the dining area within a state of heightened bliss.

Mona was on the move again, we left the room behind and entered a fourth and final hallway, continuing along the chosen path. It was mirror-lined like all the others, with three doors placed sporadically along one wall and a lone door to the center of the opposing side. This time, the numbers on the doors were eleven, seven, and three, presented in the order to which we passed them by respectively. *An odd series of numbers, spread four apart. How curious.* And so, the plot thickened. But what of the other extra door placed on the southeast side? I paused to ponder outside door seven before moving on.

In this hallway, the colour change was more extreme, as ample as a twilight array. Tea changed to yellow-green, which led to chartreuse, maize, lemon cream, champagne, cerise, violet, indigo, cerulean, and electric blue. The aria of its wheel knew no bounds, and it made me feel as though I were journeying towards something greater than the sum of all my parts combined. When at last we arrived at the south corner, saporous emanations of an unknown origin delighted the senses, teasing my taste buds out into the open aroma—we had entered the kitchen.

"Mmmm, something's cooking," Mona stated, picking up on the scent.

Sheol, I hope it's ready soon, whatever it is, I thought as taking in the sweet aroma and hearing my stomach gurgle.

As Mona moved towards whatever stirred inside the oven, I looked around the room. In keeping with the house's design, the room was triangular with a chandelier, hardwood floors and two exits on either end. But here was something altogether different…

The room's design was simple, yet the placement of each piece within played its own intricate role, tying the room together in euphoria. Yellows and blues conceded to a sea of green bursting through a flame of white translucence. The room looked as if it were lit through a pane of glass, hit by the sun and spread apart into an array of shrill iridescence, a lucent thing of unabashed aesthetic refinement. It was marvelous.

Beneath the chandelier, towards the room's hub, stood a triangle counter that ran paradoxically with the angles of the room. Pans hung high from a board that rose from the countertop, along with a mishmash of other assorted cooking utensils. Past that, other articles hung on the walls, including a domed clock with long pendulum near the entrance and a carved spice rack on the opposite side of the room. The clock seemed broken, for no sway did its pendulum keep, its motion stilled from the mouth. It was not unlike the one clock I knew, there in my Mothers' house with hands stationed at 3:33, as forever frozen in time. Why does one not fix a stopped clock?

Countertops of holly with elm cabinets set out below them spread along the length of each wall. Several broad washbasin sinks were stationed within the counters' makeup, which held on either end appliances and additional cabinets and shelving. It seemed all items, be it the fridge, stove, or waste bin, shared a coat of lemon cream. Additional cabinets lined the walls. Between them, windows were stationed on each outer side of the room, while to the innermost wall stood a solitary abstract painting, exquisitely wrought with an epic field of cream hues, an amalgamation of colour I thought not able to be spun by human hands, but there it was all the same.

The place was covered in vines hanging down in brilliant tresses of yellow sand verbena with touches of peppermint and lavender flowers. A few eucalyptus plants were also dispersed throughout the room. The scent of citrus hung sweet on the air, combining with the smells of cuisine simmering in the oven.

But beyond all of this, there was still something more, something that could only be touched upon after all other things were described and so pushed out of mind. For you see it demanded my full, unequivocal attention, where in a house full of treasures, it could surely be said that here lay the crown jewel. I am of course speaking of the skylight canopy.

So what then of its cycloramic pageantry? Simply to gaze upon it was not enough, you almost wanted to reach out and touch it just to see if it was actually real, and would have had it not been placed so very high above your head; the quality of its majesty commanded the room. I must say, the full measure of its beacon nearly blinded me as I stood there, marvelling its rich integration of golden, sun soaked oxides. Brilliance streamed through its opening and manifested the glass to an iconic shape of air numina: signs of the Twins, Scales, and the Carrier.

I recalled the divinity of each symbol then and as I looked on high, it seemed I finally understood them—immortality was theirs to have, if only to carry on the legacy of their creator. For in this state of composition, they truly did belong to the ages. Shining down like Venus before us, they began to stir something within me, something I hadn't felt for some time—I found myself lost in the fantasy of the myth.

But this re-established faith proved fleeting, merely a symptom of finding oneself before a scope of beauty so beyond that which is to be believed. Such a thing can cause one's mind to accept almost anything, no matter the lack of credibility. I struggled with my doubt alongside the scene that held my eyes to heaven's scene.

"Very capturing, isn't it?" Mona said, breaking the silence.

"Yes, Mona. It's all been very…enlightening to take in."

"And you find it quite appealing, I'll bet. A cordial reception of sorts, would that put it best?" Mona smiled as she did whenever it appeared she knew what was going on in my head.

"Yes..." I replied, searching for an elaboration.

"It's all a bit bewildering, how strongly a place you've not seen can affect you."

"That it is… So then, you feel it too?"

"Well, it is my house, and you know what they say, don't you? There's no place like home." She winked, a small grin fixed upon her face. Then, with her hands folded behind her back, she began to drift across the room. As she approached a set of top corner cupboards, she stopped and opened its doors.

"Really, when you think about it, it's not at all funny," she said. "I mean, that you perceived an affinity for this place so instantaneously." She rummaged through the cabinet. Then, turning to face me once more, her soft eyes focused on mine. In her hands which she held slightly above her waistline, were a couple of moderately sized wine glasses.

"Still trying to get my head around it," I declared, glancing back to the stained glass mural above as she placed the glasses she carried on the center countertop and walked over to the fridge.

"But of course," Mona said before disappearing behind the fridge door. She emerged with a sleek, long-necked black bottle. As she walked towards the triangular island with the bottle in hand, she gave the slightest tone of a whisper. "Wouldn't be the first time someone felt overwhelmed by the sheer weight of it all."

"Really? How do you mean?" I sought with further intrigue.

"I've seen it before, through the eyes of others, others who, like you, sustained an immediate impression upon entering this place." She stated this as a fact that should come as no surprise, and maybe she was right.

"Seriously?" I said. I watched her pour a thimbleful of cloudy liquid into each glass.

"Quite." Mona put the bottle down and grabbed up the glasses.

"So, why do you think—"

"—it happens at all?" Mona finished as she made her way towards me. "Well, this place is a lot to take in.

"That's very true." *But why this room specifically?*

"But I'd like to believe it's more than that..." she said, handing me a glass.

"What do you mean?" I asked.

"You are of course familiar with the theory of dimensional coalescence... " she said. "I seem to remember your Mothers telling me that you had been well practiced in the craft of invocation."

"The act of invoking a presence by way of a supplementary dimension, in conjunction with our own realm that creates yet still another domain, unsighted and to be had all around us..." I rattled it off like textbook. "Yeah, can't say I ever really believed in it, though."

"Ambrosia, you surprise me." She didn't really sound that surprised. "But did you not partake in the ritual?"

"Yes, well … we did perform the incantation over several occasions. though I can't say I ever felt any effect from it." Where was she going with this?

"Ah, I see, I see… But if not that, what then of your astral body?"

"A supersensible substance that can pervade all space, escape the human body, and survive beyond the cadaver?" You'd think it was permanently etched on my mind. "And you're asking if I believe…? I mean come on, Mona." It was not my intent to mock, only present my point.

"I see." Mona kept a cool smile, taking pause to look down at the liquid swirling in her glass.

Had I gone so far as to insult the woman's belief system while a guest in her own house? Again, that had not been my intention, but that was very well how it could have been taken. Yet she didn't seem upset…

"So then, my young skeptic," she said, "might I be so bold as to ask how you came to such solemn conclusions? What with your upbringing and all, I mean…that is, of course, if you don't mind."

"Not at all," I said. I paused to choose my words. This was, after all, the first time I felt I didn't need to hide my true feelings—I wasn't quite sure how to go about it. I gently swirled the liquid in my glass.

"One unmitigated truth," I said. "That is, there really is nothing out there, save this one life, this sentience of living reality. It is the be all, and end all of human existence. Mona, I've made more than my fair share of attempts to include myself in the practice, and time and time again, I've found nothing that would serve as an antidote to the contrary, nothing so concrete as to give but the slightest notion of a reasonable doubt. Sorry, but that's just the way I feel."

Mona didn't seem bothered. "No need," she said as she tilted her head and widened her smile, exposing a minor yellowing of the teeth. I hadn't noticed that before. "Please continue, for I'd very much like to know, to a greater extent, your thoughts and conclusions on such things."

"You wish…for only that my cynicism may continue?" I was surprised at both her request and my gall, that she would express such a genial want for my opinions, and that I would actually give them so freely to her. I was generally of a decidedly reserved proclivity with expressing my opinions on such personal matters. Never did I divulge anything of the sort to my Mothers, always suspecting it might break their hearts. Now here with Mona, I spoke out without need for reservation. It was a both terrifying and strangely liberating occurrence.

"But please," she said, "grant this old woman the chance to hear in deeper detail the meticulous method behind your reasoning." She traced the line of her glass' rim with an outstretched finger.

"Well, it's just simple logic, isn't it?" I said. "Never having seen a sign of apparition manifest itself before me, nor feeling the presence, nor knowing that which I would claim as being the resounding glory of a supernatural emanation … I have to say, what is there to believe in?"

"And you felt nothing during the rituals?"

"You're speaking of blind faith. Look, I know that should be all you need, and maybe it is enough…for some. That's just not me. You know?"

"I'm sure that I do," she replied kindly.

"And you're not at all angered by this?" I wasn't ready for her understanding—or, if not understanding, acceptance? Was I looking for a fight?

Mona walked in a step closer and put her hand on my shoulder. "Ambrosia, never fear to speak freely the matters of the heart. Even if I choose not to necessarily agree with your side of things, that doesn't mean I do not respect it, or you. You're entitled to your opinion, after all."

"I'm glad you think so."

"Don't ever feel you can't talk to me, son. About anything. I'm not one to judge, and I'm not one to preach. I always say, 'Hold no taste for any such dictation that would hold a person under a rule of persecuting persuasion.'"

"Hmm, I like that."

"You trust in what you think is right, and that's good. Just don't ask me to believe in it."

"Oh, Mona. I would never!" I was floored by the notion.

"I know you wouldn't, child. But remember, no one has that power. Don't ever try to take something so sacred from someone. Give respect, so that you too will be respected."

"I do, and I won't. I mean, I—it was never my intention to..."

"I know, and you didn't." Mona looked down at her drink. "So, I presume your Mothers don't know any of this."

"No, you're the first I've told."

"Well, my boy, I am honoured to be that confidant. But why is it that you waited so long? Why not tell the four people closest to you?"

"You don't know them, not like I do." The thought of revealing this part of myself to them was too crushing to fathom: to have their son abandon the single most important value they made every effort to instill in him? I had played it out in my head so many times, coming out to them, and the result was always the same: my Mothers devastated to find out their only child was a traitor to everything they held sacred. A family torn apart, all because I couldn't keep my feelings to myself. I wouldn't do it. I couldn't.

"No. I could never. Not to them, their faith," I said.

"Really, Ambrosia, I don't think you give them enough credit. But why me then? Why now?"

"I don't know, it just seemed…right. Maybe it's because I haven't known you all my life. Anyway, it feels good to get out. Thanks for that."

"You are welcome." Then, looking directly into my eyes, she said, "Let me tell you something, son, I am not so unlike your Mothers. We may have only just met, but we are family now, as much a family as you've ever had. And because we're family you should never fear telling me anything, as I want you to feel that you can share with me anything that is on your mind. That goes for everyone in this house, as you too will find that, at some point, someone will undoubtedly need your help, if only to lend an ear. You always support the ones you love, Ambrosia. Don't ever forget that."

"I know, Mona, and I won't."

"I know you won't, child," she said. "Remember, in this world you may sometimes feel alone, but that is not the truth. Just give people a chance and you'll see. Both your Mothers and I care for you deeply and want only to see you find happiness in your life. That's why I brought you here. And whatever you choose to believe, whomever you choose to become, nothing will change that fact. We will always hold you dear to our hearts. Know that my love for you is unconditional."

Unconditional? The woman only just met me... "Thank you. I mean, again, Mona...for everything. I know what you're saying here is genuine. And I really appreciate your listening. That, and taking a chance on someone that only yesterday was a stranger to you. I can't tell you enough how grateful I am, for all that you've done and continue to do. I extend my eternal thankfulness." I raised my glass, giving something of a salute.

"Why, Ambrosia, how generous of you to say so," Mona said, also raising a glass. "Cheers," she exclaimed.

Happy to finally have the chance to wet my lips and quench the thirst that stirred from within me, I let her glass meet my own. They made an audible clang as they came together.

"Cheers," I said, swallowing the tiny amount of liquid in the glass. It went down smooth and tasted like nothing I'd ever encountered—a savoury blend of spices, rich in flavour with a peppery zest that stewed on my tastebuds, leaving in its wake a torrid swelter that seared through me in a flush of heat so pointed that my every extension was cast aflame. For a moment I was engulfed in ecstasy—but, like most things, this rapture was not made to last and soon the blaze began to simmer and finally subside. The remnants of a glory lingered still in clement afterglow.

"Well, that was well received," Mona sighed. "So what did you think?"

I honestly thought it fantastic.

"Mmmm… whatever is the beverage made of?" I asked.

Mona gave a sort of shrug, tossing a hand to the air in an expression of opaqueness. "Search me."

"Oh."

"You'll just have to ask its creator, I guess," Mona said, taking the glasses and making her way back over to the counter. "Her name's Heze, and you are just fortunate enough to be living under the same roof."

"Oh, well, I guess I will," I said, making my way over to her and resting my elbows upon the countertop, hands folded.

"I'm glad you feel that way." She too rested her arms on the counter. "So, child, I guess that only leaves me with one more question."

I really wasn't in the mood for any more questions. But what could I do? "All right Mona, ask away."

"Well, let me review for a moment, if I may. You tell me that, according to your beliefs, there is no such thing as the astral body."

"Yes, that is correct." Why this again?

Mona let out a small incredulous grunt, as if pondering the notion briefly before persisting further. "And so you also have doubts about the existence of spirits, those who stand lost between realms. For how can a spirit exist, but not the astral body?"

"Fair enough." I couldn't believe she was continuing. Maybe I had been wrong about her understanding.

"To you, there is no such thing as Dimensional Coalescence."

"Indeed."

"So then, would it be wrong to say that you've demonstrated a level of impertinence towards the Goddesses' teachings?"

I stood up straight. She hadn't conveyed hostility, but then she didn't have to. Had I crossed a line? I had always been taught to be polite and respectful. In that I believed.

"No, Mona. I don't think…I mean, don't get me wrong, I still do have nothing but the highest of respect for the teachings that have been instilled in me, and I always will. It's just the more fantastical aspects I hold in contempt." *Too strong a word? Perhaps.*

I began again, "Allow me to re-phrase. While I hold the lore and the mysticism in high regard, and I see the fables to be powerfully engaging, I do find them to be just that, a story; in other words, an act of fiction—perhaps the greatest ever written. And although filled with life lessons, I would have to treat them as more a philosophical guide than a testament of my faith." I hoped that was good enough for her.

"Very good answer. I could not agree more," she replied amicably.

Excuse me?

"A guide through which to live by, absolutely. That is all I was looking for. We should, I think, gain something from all our teachings."

Oh.

She looked coy as she grabbed the bottle. "Can I interest you in another?"

"Please," I acknowledged. It was then, as I watched her again pour a small portion of the cloudy liquid into each glass, that a thought crossed my mind. "Mona, would you be so kind as to answer a question for me?"

"Why yes, my boy, whatever is it?"

"Well, we've covered a lot of ground since beginning this discussion."

"We have, we have." She spoke softly as she returned the bottle back to its place upon the countertop.

"But it's just now, during your recent recap of the subject matter invoked by our discourse, that I've taken notice of something."

"Please do tell. May your notion keep no further in abeyance; do relieve me the pang that is my perennial unease." Mona disposed the slightest suggestion of chaff as she passed me my glass.

"Yes..." I took the glass and sent a somewhat unimpressed look over her way. I'd answered all her questions, the least she could do was humour me in mine.

"You wish to know why I haven't yet asked you why you think the room pulls at you," she said.

"Well, yeah." This woman, she had me all figured out. "I already know what you believe, that I feel some sort of connection to whatever energies linger in the abode; that here your affections for the Goddess Mother, they transcend beyond these walls, the flowers, or even the glory presented in this canopy."

"Precisely right, she is as much the earth as the effervescent mountain, whose bedrock when penetrated by shifting plates beneath the crust erupts, sending a spurt of molten magma through the atmosphere, rushing down the surface until it comes to rest, collected to cool by the voluminous oceanic body that surrounds it. She is the very elements that govern us, the spirit of this world and all coalescent realms."

"Good enough," I said, again humouring her, "but do you want to know what I think?"

"I believe I already do know."

"Do you? Well, would you be so kind as to enlighten me then?" I challenged her.

"You've speculated that perhaps something in the room itself set you off. That is, a stimulus found in the environment; perhaps more than one could have targeted a memory that in turn elicited this change in your behaviour. It would most likely have been something that is familiar to you."

Well, she hit the nail on the head with that one, didn't she?

"Familiar in the sense," Mona continued, "that it triggered the thought of something of likely comparison, which is not at all unlikely, I suppose. What with the lavish variety of floral arrangements found in your home garden. And let's face it, much of the home décor is reminiscent of the tales you've grown up with. Of course, the familiarity doesn't necessarily need to come from this lifetime."

Whoa, wait a second. "You're talking about reincarnation?"

"Take it with a grain of salt. Seriously, son, you need to relax." She gave me an encouraging smile and continued. "You know, I bet even the layout of the room itself has a part to play here. The placement of each and every object is poised with specific accuracy. It's all to give the area an appeal of equalization, so that no matter where you stand the room gives off a radiance of near perfect harmony.

I took a second glance around the room. At once it became blatantly obvious to me. Most everything here matched its other, from side to side to, well, side. Tit for tat, measure for measure. By the Goddess, it was incredible—it made me wonder if I'd missed it in the other rooms, too. Yes, Mona had hit it on the nose. With the smells, sights, sounds, and essence of all around us, how could one not be drawn into the serenity of the room?

Speaking of smells, I wonder if that mystery dish had finished cooking?

"And then, it could be the aroma arising from the…"

"Okay, Mona. I think you've made your point."

Mona gave a small chuckle. "Seems nonsense to think otherwise, I suppose. You not believing in those sorts of things."

"I suppose it does."

Raising her glass, she said, "To new homecomings, then?"

"And new friendships made." I raised my glass a second time to meet hers. They clinked as they came together, and then we tipped the drinks back into our mouths. I savoured the moment. The same familiar rush hit me, but with a double in impact this time. I brought the glass down hard onto the counter and exhaled a sigh of satisfaction. "I have to say, Mona, that really hit the spot."

"Glad it pleases you, my boy. It's not for everyone, you know." She grabbed my glass and made her way towards the sink to my right. "Not me, though. I find a drink like that at the end of a long day to be most satisfying."

"Yes, I'd have to agree." The drink did most definitely satisfy every pore of my character. My body melted as I sank back onto the surface of the countertop, in a state of total serenity.

It was then at that most peaceful moment, with a mind of sang-froid, that the dinging off a loud chime sounded by way of the stove.

"Ah! Soup's on, my boy. That would be the sound of the dinner bell; she's music to this old girl's ears. Just hold that thought another moment while I rustle us up some of what's been cooking."

"Yeah, no problem." *And what thought would that be?* I wondered.

Mona grabbed a pair of mitts hung up beside the stove as opening the oven door, reached in and grabbed the contents within. She placed the steaming pan upon the instrument's surface.

The perfume of the meal's juices rang off the dish and into my nostrils, filling me with comfort. At once my senses were uplifted, and that to which had become dormant from familiarity again blossomed fully inside me. My hunger rose, boiled to points unsustainable as my mouth was drowned out by sweet salivation.

"Mmmm, smells delightful, doesn't it?" Mona's head wavered over the heat.

I could think of nothing better to sink my teeth into. And that's when it happened. The doorway I had but only recently passed through stirred to catch the eye. It arrived in my peripheral, a sense of something, or someone…

I turned to look, and what I found there, with all of me I swear I could never have prepared myself for, not in all my life.

CHAPTER 7
◊
SUMMERSTAR

My breath stilled, as though seized by a moment, a moment without time and where space faded to lethe. All manner of undertaking was thrown to ruin, and my body escaped me as I floated to the places where heaven stirred within, delivered by the light of her eyes. And I could see only one, just she who warranted my whole life's reason, who presided over those dreams of mine by a presence of resounding order. She made me never so much want to believe in the ways of the Goddess, if for no other reason than to know that she belonged to eternity. Meaning that with each life's passing, coming to journey's end, she would continue on to be born again, so to live forevermore

Seized by a moment of disbelief that a mind's mere creation could not handle a hope to meet, I asked myself how she could be real. She looked the same.

"Child!" I heard a voice exclaim. I was torn away from the vision and pulled back down to earth. It was an end to the enchantment we held on to, along with any hope of trusting that momentary lapse of reason I suffered at the hands of a celestial enterprise, the delusions of a lust-stricken fool.

"Mona!" the girl cried out. I watched her as she broke into a run, appearing as a swan in flight, her wings spread wide. Mona threw her arms out to receive her with warm embrace. I longed for nothing more than to be a part of it.

Mona gently expelled the girl and met her gaze, holding her tenderly by the shoulders. "Summer, dear, so good to see you. Allow me to wish you happy birthday!"

So this was Summer, and it was her birthday. The name fit, clearly enough. Her clement disposition reminded me of sun-soaked afternoons, where the gentil flux of a balmy breeze blew in off the waterways, bringing with it a sense of unsullied refreshment that carried forward over the physique.

"Thank you," Summer said timidly. She blushed, her eyes meeting no one.

Mona smiled kindly in return. "Summer, I have someone special here that I'd like you to meet." Mona ushered Summer to look my way, guiding her with a well-positioned hand on her shoulder.

Summer flicked a glance my way, and I immediately felt another sudden rush of intoxication take me. My chest pounded and my stomach churned as my palms grew sweaty. A mess of crisscrossed emotions raced through me and I could no more tell up from down. It was wonderful, yet at the same time it scared the living Sheol out of me. Not ever before had something caused in me an effect quite so strong as this, yet never had I before known beauty as she so readily possessed. And perhaps before that night I knew not what beauty was. Ethereal comeliness in its truest, most natural form, unscathed by taint of any kind. Her face, although having turned another seven shades of red since following our addressed greeting, was an impeccant pageantry of allure. A complexion of vitality complemented the freckles of her already faultless visage. From the finely streamed guise of her brow to the gently peaked prominence of her nose and her tiny dimples found by both cheek and chin, Summer fell under one harmonious act of equipoise and seemed as if at a level beyond symmetry.

Her grey-blue eyes fluttered between the floor and me. A shy smile found its way onto the subtle continence of textbook lips. As succumbing to that of a skittish shake, a few wisps of her silken textured titian hair fell in front her face.

She wore a baggy shirt smeared with dried paint (something I knew and so took great interest in) and loose-fitted jeans with rips at the knees. I could imagine that underneath that bulky exterior there was a hard and able-bodied frame waiting to be let out. She was sublime.

"Summer, this is Ambrosia, the boy I told you about, who I went to pick up."

If ever a higher potency of blush were attainable, Summer had just exceeded it. She said nothing but continued to make contact through a flicker of her eye, mesmerizing me.

"Well, go on, child, don't be shy now. Say something," Mona urged her on.

"I…happy to meet you," she whispered.

I looked back at her in awe, taken in by her voice's soft brilliance that beckoned me onward.

Spellbound in silence, I stood and gazed upon the beauty that had me undone, and for all the things I longed to say, could think of not a word, clever or otherwise at which I might address the fair creature. My mind had gone a complete blank. Panicking, I did the only thing I could think of doing and repeated back verbatim the exact phrase that she had dispelled upon me. "Happy to meet you." What else could I say? She had me in a daze.

Then suddenly it came to me. "Oh! And happy birthday." *Nice save there, malaka.*

"Thank you," was all she said as her lips turned up the shy smile.

"Pleasure's all mine."

Summer stood silent and gave a slight nod, as though not really knowing where to go next.

"So, uh, how old are you turning?" I wasn't sure if I should ask it, but really, where else was there to go?

"Twenty-one," she said softly, looking at me momentarily before shifting her gaze.

"Twenty-one? Why, that's my age." I was more than a little ecstatic to hear it, but I did well to keep my composure.

"Really?" She couldn't hide another shy smile.

"Yeah..."

"Well that will do, I suppose." Mona broke through the silence like a barrage of thunder stealing away the good night. "Summer, darling, if I may so inquire, are you or are you not planning to join us for the evening's festivities downstairs?"

"Oh, well, I...hadn't really decided as of yet," Summer responded as she turned her attention to Mona, brushing her hair out of her face.

"Well, look, I know it's not your thing, but it is your birthday after all. Hate to think of you up here all by your lonesome. It would be a shame for you to miss all the fun."

Summer gave a small sigh. "How's tonight to be different from that of any other erstwhile night?"

"Well, I suppose to that I would have to say: mere chance alone may be swung solely by how you seek to bring about its change, and to stray from such reaches is to espy nary a change to be won."

My, but she was good with turning things around.

Summer gave no response but her mouth turned a slight pouted frown—still beautiful.

"In other words, child, you won't know until you try. And I think you should at the very least make an appearance. Try to have some fun tonight, dear. Ambrosia plans to be in attendance, and he barely knows a soul. You should go, keep the boy company if nothing else. Do it as a favour to me. It would be nice and the polite thing to do, really."

Summer dropped her line of sight to me again. "You too, will be going then?"

"Yes, I…ahem! Sorry. I do think that I would very much like to see more of the downstairs and this Nebula that Mona speaks so highly of. I must admit I am a little tired, but not ready for rest just yet. And so I do believe that I am up for going down, if only for a little while...to see what it's all about. You should come too."

"So, child, to what do you say to that? To what rebuttal then do I find you with?"

Summer looked up to meet Mona's eyes. "Yes then, I suppose that I will go, for a little while."

"Ah, grand!" Mona clasped her hands together. "Well then it's decided. So I will leave you two to it. Dinner is done."

Dinner! It had totally slipped my mind.

"But are you not staying?" Summer seemed at once alarmed at the thought of the two of us alone. I was nervous, too.

"No, daughter, I'm feeling a bit spent from the journey and so I think it best if I go and put my feet to rest awhile."

Well, that certainly came on all of a sudden. Or if not, she had hid it quite well as I had no idea she was feeling this way.

"But, Mother, you've only just got in. Are you not hungry? Have you had the chance to eat anything today? You should have something. I made more than enough pizza to go around."

Pizza? I turned my head to glance towards the stove to take in the picture of aroma that filled the room and brought my taste buds to boil. I'd never had pizza before.

"And I'm sure it tastes delicious," Mona said. "I left it to cool atop the stove. You will save a piece for me, yes? For now though, I really must be off, and so I give you my leave."

I watched as Mona made her way across the kitchen and through the door from whence we came. I wondered where she was going, what room was hers?

Summer called to her as she went, "You will be coming to the club tonight, will you not? Mother?"

Resonant silence followed from where Mona had just exited.

"Oh..." Summer uttered as she took her eyes from the door and directed them to her feet. It made me sad to see her like that, or anyone for that matter, but especially one so lovely as she. "It's, um, quite the stunning place you've got here," I said. "I mean, this, it's...well, it's just beyond, really..." I raised a hand to the shimmer of glass stained in the overhang.

"Thank you," she said.

And silence prevailed.

"Yes, well… So, pizza then…?"

"Why, yes, of course dear. I wouldn't miss it for the world," Mona's voice came back into the room.

An unexpected shock to the nerves, Mona peered back through the door, crashing through my tepid attempt at conversation. In a way, I welcomed the unwarranted invasion.

"Oh, and Summer, I meant to ask you—your planned attire for this evening, what is it?"

"Well, to be honest … I really hadn't put too much thought into it yet."

"Right, then might I implore that you wear that lovely dress I picked up for you during my last travels?"

"Eh, Mona, I don't know..."

"I wouldn't ask, except I haven't been given the opportunity to see you in it, and apart from tonight, who knows when I'll get you out again. Unless, perhaps, you plan on making this into something of a reoccurring theme?"

"No! No, that's all right… I understand. If it means that much to you." Summer did not sound at all impressed, nor did her body language hide it well.

"It does. Thank you. I suppose I'll see you both downstairs soon enough then. Should—" She was cut off by a violent coughing fit. "Ahem, sorry… something in my throat. As I was saying, you should think about getting ready soon, things should be starting to get underway any minute now."

No sooner had she said it than a beat pulsed from underneath, streaming distant sounds carried on a steady bass that hinted off the floor, measured between the walls where we stood.

"Ah good, seems Gany's already hard at it."

It must have been somewhere past ten o'clock by then. Had that much time passed already? It seemed I'd only just walked off the plane. I turned to look at Mona, but she had again vanished.

Summer looked sad, her gaze fallen. Lament for the dress, perhaps? There were so many things I wanted to express to her then, questions I longed to ask, to know the precious things that made up who she was, those thoughts and aspirations she kept close to her heart.

My nerves were shot, and I felt at any instant I might shatter into a thousand tiny pieces should she deny me any small answer. It was all I could do to look at her to keep from falling apart, and I didn't know why. My chest beat as if it were ready to burst. Weak in the knees, I felt ready to collapse, as though the only thing keeping me up was her hold over me.

"Would you like some…?" she finally asked.

"I'm sorry?" The excitement rose in me like a rocket ascending to space.

"Some dinner?" Her face again reddened.

"Oh...yes, I think I would like that," I replied, wondering what she made of my wandering mind, worried she had caught sight of my perverse misconceptions.

We made our way towards the oven, where the pizza lay cooling. My mouth watered. I leaned down to take in the fragrance. "It smells delectable, Summer. Did you make this?"

She put forward a small gesture of satisfaction. "It was the reason I came into the kitchen. I knew it was about ready to be taken out of the oven."

"And you had no idea we were here?" I asked her, wondering if she hadn't heard us roaming the halls.

"I had my suspicions when I saw the hall light on, and I thought I heard voices when I was walking towards the kitchen. But I had no idea who the person might be...well, maybe I had. " She looked at me a second more with that same lulling gaze that sent me into a dream the first time our eyes met. Just as quickly, it was gone again.

"I see," I responded with the hope she would continue.

"I mean…I was hoping it could be Mona, but I didn't know, not that she had returned…or I knew, that she would be coming at some point, only I wasn't sure when that sometime would be, and…what I'm trying to say is—"

"You were not yet aware she had made her way back," I said, saving her from her fluster.

"Yes."

"Got it…and you didn't hear us at any time before that?" *We must have passed the door to her room*, I thought.

"I was listening to music in my room."

Funny, I thought, that up until just then I hadn't heard a sound since we'd entered the house.

"Must play your music rather low; I wasn't able to hear anything." *Unlike now when I can feel a resounding beat from the toes of my feet to my chest cavity.* "Not that I'm implying you weren't."

"I use earphones," she said.

"Oh," I said. "I've never had the pleasure, always wanted to though. Well, I did use some on the plane I guess, but… So what was it that you were listening to?"

"Me? Just you know, stuff."

Too personal? It was just music, after all, and I was a connoisseur. I pushed a little further. "And what does this stuff sound like?"

"Uh, it's all a bit random, really."

Yeah, too personal. "Okay…but you enjoy it?" Kind of a stupid question. Who listens to music they don't like? Too late to take it back now. There should really be a way to edit conversations with pretty girls.

"I guess." She shrugged.

"Right, right." And with that we ended discussion attempt number two. "I suppose we should maybe eat then?"

After cutting the pizza pie, each of us grabbed a slice of the flat-breaded, uniquely topped creation and journeyed over to the triangular counter that had so recently been mine in drinks and conversation. I had hoped for the rekindling of such activities; however, Summer stood silent, pulling as far from me as she possibly could, doing her best to make the least amount of eye contact possible. Mixed signals? But I was not swayed.

"So, how long have you been here? Living with Mona, I mean?" I asked, in another effort to make conversation.

"Oh…for a little while."

"So…a little while, then?" I hoped for more.

"Yes."

So much for the brief passing of that conversation. But I had managed well enough so far, I thought, in that I hadn't spontaneously combusted during our exchange of words.

While conversation wasn't easy, I knew she wasn't being purposely aloof, just that she was apprehensive. I saw no rejection in her eyes (when I saw her eyes), only reluctance to show certain parts of herself too quickly. At least, that's what I believed. While her guarded body language and distance did clout my spirits some, I had to remind myself that Summer had, after all, only just met me, and so this was probably more an understandable act than I first realized. *They are not you; they do not come from the same place. Not everyone is so outgoing.*

From what I had remembered hearing, Summer was given to being somewhat skittish around others too. *Don't take it personally, remember that first look she sent your way. You just have to indulge her a little...* I also could not forget the perfect smile that came to her face whenever her gaze met with my own, and that gave me confidence in a way I couldn't hope to explain. Who's to say she didn't shy away from me for the same reason I shuddered in my approaches towards her? The possibility of rejection is a powerful deterrent for anyone, but it is nothing more than an idle fear based on the limitations one sets out for their own self. *Keep telling yourself that.*

Still, I couldn't help feeling a tad silly about the way Summer had affected me so quickly after having met her, like a frightened fawn mesmerized by the spark of a forest cast aflame. If I wished to know her at all, I knew I had to shake the disease that was the source of my hesitation and realize she was just another person and had no desire to strike me down. I had done nothing that would cause her want to do so.

As I nibbled at the entrée she had prepared for me, I pondered further. It was Summer who had opened communication between us when she asked if I wanted dinner. Someone who didn't wish to speak wouldn't make the initial effort to address you, would they? No, she wanted to talk, but was just somewhat shy about it.

And then what if I could be the person who helped her open up? I loved the thought of experiencing the bloom of her flower, nourishing it so that she may allow that I, and I alone, become the roots that bury down and dig deep into the furthest recesses of her catacombs.

Maybe the magnitude of my intent did extend a touch too far. *Meh.*

I needed only common ground with which to engage Summer and gain her confidence so that she might open up and share a part of herself with me. And therein lay the trouble: I knew less than zero about Summer. The silence between us was reaching a boiling point of discomfort, so I needed to act fast.

"Mmm, I must say, Summer, this is a choice meal you've prepared. I've really tasted nothing like it. This here is cheese, right? I've never tried cheese before, but I've always wanted to." *Good, that's good. Now keep going.* "Tell me, what's it made of? I mean, besides cheese?"

"Oh…it's hardly worth mentioning. I'd probably bore you with the details. But thank you."

Like taking blood from a stone. "No, really, I want to know."

"You do? Really?"

"Of course."

"Okay…but just don't begrudge me if you don't find it at all interesting."

"Oh, I don't think there will be any worry of that."

Surprised by my interest but happy to oblige, Summer began to describe the steps of making the pizza. She left nothing out, explaining what went into the dough and which spices she used in the sauce to get it just right. She clarified that the main topping was not in fact a cheese but a cheese substitute called Veganrella. She moved on to the different peppers, onions, and other vegetables she had decided to use for ingredients. I was amazed at how much went into it: mushrooms, olives, lentils, zucchini, cooked squash, spinach, broccoli. As she went into further detail, she became ever more enthused, and although I was amused to see this I was unable to keep from imagining the delicate person set before me taking the dough in her supple fingers and beating it into submission before giving it a good drag through the garden. The thought of it made me chuckle to myself—maybe not a good idea.

"I'm sorry, is something funny?" Summer stopped to ask me.

"What? Oh no, it's…it's nothing. Really." Again I found myself defending my own act of idiocy.

"Looked like something to me."

Damn, and things had been going so well. "Honestly, it hadn't anything to do with you."

"Really? Something just caught your mind while I was talking then? What was it?"

Wow, she could change with the tides.

"Look, I didn't mean to offend," I said, scrambling. "Just something you said, it reminded me of something else, that's all."

"I hate it when people laugh at me," she said, sounding hurt and looking away.

Now I felt really terrible. What could I do, though? I couldn't tell her what I was really imagining, could I? So I decided to cram a large piece of pizza into my mouth, which gave me time to think while I chewed it down. By the time I was finished and able to talk again, I still had little to go on, so naturally I winged it.

"Uh…look, Summer, it's personal, you know?"

"Personal?" She was not understanding.

"Yeah, you know, personal."

"Okay…"

She did not sound okay, so I had no choice but to keep going. Going nowhere, that is.

"Look, it's just I heard the word 'mushrooms,' and it just got me thinking was all."

"Mushrooms? Got you thinking what? How does me bringing up mushrooms have anything to do with what you were snickering about?"

"Well, now, allow me to finish. I was thinking about mushrooms, but in another way—a different *kind* of mushrooms." Lies! Oh, such a lie.

"I'm afraid I don't follow."

"You know…" I did an impression of a person under the influence. Now I only hoped she wouldn't judge me too harshly. I did so love to partake in all the goodness the land provided.

"Ohhhh..." Summer giggled. "Of course."

"Right?" I laughed along with her in sweet relief.

Like that, her whole disposition changed for the better. *Dodged a bullet there*. Did all young women have this effect on the men they attracted—numbing the mind, tripping up thoughts? Although perhaps it was a good thing, great for breaking the ice.

We spent the next few minutes in silence, absorbed in our meals, my mind frenzied for another conversation starter. Trail number two (or was it three?) had had its bumps, but at the very least I'd given her a laugh, and learned what not to do in conversation. There had been a definite glimmer of light when she spoke so enthusiastically about the meal she had prepared. If I could somehow provoke the nature of those emotions again, I might see an even broader awakening.

I needed to be careful though, and walk the line without crossing it. *What else should I ask her about?* Then it came to me like a sledgehammer across the head—Summer's shirt. She'd arrived parading stains upon her garb. I noticed a colour blotch on her sleeve and could not believe I'd displaced the thought until that moment. Perhaps she had a talent for painting, and that was something we could definitely share.

"So, Summer, tell me, do you happen to have any other hobbies of personal interest, or is this it?"

She gave me a puzzled look.

"I, err…just thought that, you know, with your passion for cooking and all, that maybe it extended to other places, other things." I panicked.

She shook her head as though not sure how to respond.

"Because I paint," I blurted out.

"Oh."

"And I just thought, I mean, what with your shirt there…" *Get it together, man!*

"What's wrong with my shirt?" She started to look it over.

"Oh, nothing! Nothing whatsoever. It's great, really. Just thought it looked, maybe, like there was a touch of paint on the upper sleeve is all, and—"

"You thought that perhaps I painted also?"

"Well…do you?" The question begged to be asked.

Summer fell silent, looking down to the counter and clasping hold her right arm with her left hand, in what could only be considered a guarded position. "Painting…it's not so much a hobby for me, at least not like cooking is..."

She then looked directly into my eyes. "No, to me painting is more of a passion."

Now that's what I wanted to hear. "I know exactly what you mean."

"You do?"

"Oh yes, for me it's a way of life. It's a driving force, the need that lingers on, still hungry…"

She looked at the stain on her shirt. "This is what nourishes me."

This is great news. "I couldn't agree more."

"So, you feel the same then?"

"Of course, and you have no idea how good it is to hear from someone who really gets it, who understands the sting and the rapture that goes towards the method. The process—we are wont to its pull."

I had no clue where I was going with this, but it felt right. It sounded as though Isaura—my Mother and the teacher of fine arts—were speaking directly through me.

"I understand..." She sounded like she wanted to say more but didn't.

But did she really understand? It was now she who sounded a tad bewildered. Perhaps she was intoxicated by the chance to talk about art with someone who loved it as much as she. This, I had heard, was known to happen when two people of such commonalities came together. Or maybe I was reading too much into things in assuming she felt as I did.

So then, what was with this girl? She appeared all over the map. Closed at the hilt...but find the right key to unlock her, and she breaks free like a captive thing let fly—flying until finding another cage for falling into; a prison of the mind's own making.

"And what is it you paint? The medium, I mean." I only hoped I wasn't being too forward.

"Me? I mainly use oils."

"Ah, just like me." I wondered if she made them the same as I did. "And style?"

"Style? I have no real style, I guess. I do enjoy both forms abstract and impressionistic, however." She seemed to want to delve further into the conversation, even as her sights spent more time on the countertop than they did on me.

"Really? Because you know, I rather consider myself an impressionist of sorts, and I enjoy the visual language written in the abstract."

Summer's eyes lit up as she drawled out a heartfelt sigh.

I continued, "What is it you love primarily, in and of this movement?" I leaned in closer towards her.

"Oh, everything... I guess if I really had to pinpoint it, it's the amount of freedom one can adopt in the composition. No need for rule, where brush strokes lay as visible to the naked eye and angles come as inscribed by a contrast of ordinance. Oh, and the added movements of its characters! How they build a relationship between the art and observer, each perception being unique, dependent on the personal experiences of its viewer..."

She spoke as though no one had asked her before. Clearly, Summer had a vigor for the trade, one that showed no signs of stilling.

"And the emphasizing of light. So powerfully does it alter the various qualities found in each and every element the artist creates within their world…"

By this point, hand gestures had been introduced alongside the words. She gazed at a distant point, as though seeing the very thing she described. *Magnificent.* There was no stopping her.

"But then, I do so love the movement of surrealism as well, how it draws on aspects of unpredictability, elements of surprise. Though for some it may appear absurd at first glance, one only needs take a deeper look and fall into immensity..."

I did not want to interrupt her, but I broke in during a momentary pause. "Yes, a work of such non-sequitur rule, that sets out to demolish all sentient mechanisms and chooses to instead replace them with answers beyond reason—thought without cause. It brings about effect, the super-real, a dream without need for boundaries."

Was that over the top? I didn't think so.

She looked at me. There was love in her eyes—I saw it there, I could swear. Oh, she was lovely. Never had I been more enthralled. With her I could construct an ebullience of nirvana—together there was nothing we could not do! A rhapsody played betwixt our hearts to the spell of fortunes found. Just, how to make her see it? Perhaps she already did. *Take this slow…*

The sad truth was that I didn't think she saw me the same way. No, even in this heightened state of cogent elation, I thought she would fail to read my signals. For fear of too recklessly exposing her heart, she'd repress her emotions. That was fine. I didn't want to move in too soon and risk damaging the bud before it bloomed.

But then, maybe I wasn't giving her enough credit where credit was due. Summer had shed several layers since our meeting such a short time ago. That, at least, was something. A foundation had been laid, a common ground had been established, and now I needed only to build from there. Like anything worth shaping, the key to making it perfect was all in the planning and patience.

The principle behind these two fundamental rules went against the true nature of any man—I wanted to have her immediately and without putting forth any of the effort required to woo such a fair creature. *Oh, what a world that would be.* I took another bite of pizza.

"You know, I suppose I also have quite a fondness for the abstracts. Might I get the chance to see one? Of yours, I mean." A bold move.

"Sorry?"

"Your paintings. Might I be given a chance to see one of the finished works? That is, if you have any here with you. I know it's common for artists to sell, or even give their pieces away. But if you do have some of your work here, even one still yet to be completed, well, I'd consider it a privilege if—"

"You know, it's getting late." Summer's disposition changed back to that of a frightened fawn sent running into the thicket. Her body closed in around her, and her eyes pitched down to the floor. "We should really think about finishing up here. They'll be expecting us downstairs soon."

It felt like a door had been slammed shut in my face. It was obvious I had stepped over some boundary, screwing everything up the minute I'd asked about seeing her work. Was she really so insecure that the moment someone asked a personal question she closed up like a lotus blossom at the dawn of evening? On the other hand, I should have known such a shy girl wouldn't respond to prying. *Faen! Think with your head, man!*

"Well, if you think that's best," I said. "Probably should get the show on the road." I watched as she grabbed her unfinished plate, crossed the counter to pick up mine, and deposited both in the sink.

"I'll clean this up first thing tomorrow morning," she said, proceeding toward the door. "Are you coming?" she said softly.

"Oh, a—yes!" I darted towards the doorway to follow her. On exiting the room she threw a switch and all that was left behind us turned to black.

Down the hallway, we stood in front of door number seven, the second in a series of three doors. "This is my room," she said. "I will leave you now and change into my evening attire."

"That sounds fine," I said, though I would have liked to help her with that. "You get things together and we'll reconcile after."

Summer turned for a second to look in my general direction and see if my prying eyes weren't far enough removed before going any further. Then opening the door no more than a hair, just enough to squeeze through, she as quickly shut it behind her.

Alone now, I listened to the steady flow of the beat that emerged beneath me. The pulse of sound coursed its way through the floorboards, penetrating the air with its rhythmic melody. Funny how I had all but put it out of mind while in Summer's stay.

I waited there for what felt like a long time: standing, toe tapping, sitting, and eventually standing again. It's when I began to pace that I knew I could wait around no longer.

So I decided to explore the region while I waited, and come back periodically. I made my way down the remainder of the hall, through the magic and wonder that was the dining area and down the next hall, until I found myself again surrounded by the salmon and wine of the parlour. Before getting there, I managed to pass by a door I had missed before, which true to my assumption, had the number ten placed upon it. That left only one unknown door number remaining, though I did not know how exactly it would fit in with the rest, a door seemingly out of place.

As I made my entry into the main living space, I again marveled at the glory of the stained glass. It called out to me. Further into the center of the room something else caught my eye. There, mounted atop the fireplace, was a large rectangular black screen—most likely a television. I hadn't seen one like that before. Given my history with electronics, I wondered if I could even get the thing to turn on. It was as Mona had said though, and it became increasingly clear that the makeup of my "condition" had more to do with my surroundings and my position to the electromagnetic field than did it just me alone—a great relief. *So I suppose in this case I should be all right, and willing to chance it anyway. If only I could locate the power button...*

"Ambrosia?" I heard a soft summoning of a voice, which caused me to stop what I was doing and turn around.

There she was, an angel clothed in tepid pink. What beauty was this set before me? Like no construct of the wildest mind's creation, a starlit dazzle drew on this dream. She was merely a few feet away, purely clean, hair flawlessly straight. Her sleeveless garment flowed down to the very ends of her and formed to her body like a second skin. Her shapely angles told a story of health, and the cut of her, inimitably precise, betrayed a hidden placement of hard-pressed abs resting firmly atop smoothly sculpted hip bones, a prominence of unbridled specification that cohered to the curved trim of her thighs and gave chase to the lithe descent of everlasting legs.

If words could yield a value of emotion close to what I felt upon seeing her, still you'd not be able to capture it. *Oh, patron saint of the heart, let me discover you.*

"You are...ravishing." It came out before I knew it was being said.

Body language continued to indicate closure, tightening even as the compliment came to rest upon her. A shot of red coloured her face, and the streak of her eyes crossed the floor. Yet the makings of a kindly smile came through this wave of diffidence.

"Thank you," she whispered.

"My pleasure."

An instant of soft silence befell us where I might have liked to stay forever: there, watching her. It was a moment to be broken all too soon by the sowing of even softer words.

"You are good?" she asked, breaking through the veil obscurity.

"Me? Sure, definitely…"

With her head down, she waited as though for something to happen. So it would be that I took the initiative.

"Well, shall we then? That is, if you're ready."

"I suppose that I am," she answered, but she did not sound the part.

"Right, right…" I said. "Let's get to it then."

Upon a passing's hesitation, Summer moved to depart, and I who followed after couldn't help but take in the look of her...gait. The lady's sway seemed somewhat limited, and on further inspection I could see why. Her footwear, slippers of slightness that, though pleasingly suited to the fit of her delicate structure, provided a lift to foundations that would do better if secured more solidly to the ground. Indeed Summer stood near taller than me now, and was showing some difficulties in her step. It was clear to me that she wasn't used to wearing this style of shoe. It reminded me of my own unwanted trade.

Together we progressed towards the foyer, with Summer flicking light switches off as we went. I wondered why Summer didn't just do as Mona had done and thrown the main switch.

In the foyer, I found my way back to the footwear I'd left behind before entering my new home. At least Summer would not be alone in suffering, I thought as I placed the sneakers back on my feet. I was in no way partial to the snug fit of these entrapments. Rather, the free breathing space offered by my getas was a much missed and preferred alternative to the devices of suffocation I then donned. They squished my toes, hurt my heels. Not that I'm prone to complaining, but why put oneself through such ordeals when you don't have to?

Leaving the foyer, we exited through the principle door and proceeded down the red stone staircase that led to the club below. Upon entering, I realized just how soundproof the upstairs in fact was. While not entirely insulated from the noise blasting terrifically through the small space, the living area was sheltered a great deal from the penetrating sound.

Summer stood at the final gate; when opened, it would lead us both into the jowls of the Nebula. She glanced up at me, and I could see the terror in her eyes. That's when I realized I was really going in there, to experience something I'd never experienced before—and I wasn't going alone. I would be accompanied by the most engagingly gorgeous person I had ever known. The thought made me go fervent with desire and I wished for nothing more than to get the evening's events under way. My feelings of overtiredness had all but been erased, and as the second wind began to rise, excitement erupted from within and darted through me like a rocket burning out of control. This was a night of infinite possibility, and I was ready to grab it fully by the reigns. Just the fact that the music hadn't gone haywire on my approaching entry was enough to tell me as much. It was a sign.

With a simple hand gesture I encouraged Summer forward while making a promise to myself to keep close beside her. She took a deep breath and set the door ajar, at once disclosing us to a flood of lights and sound—and what sound! The elevation in the assonance with its great surge of vibration forced its way through with such an immense impact I nearly lost all bearing. I was blown over.

Nothing in my experience, not through the articles I'd read or the pictures I'd glimpsed in magazines, could have readied me for what I found on the other side of that door. It was as though I'd entered into an alternate reality stripped of mediocrity, stripped of the predictable conventionality consistent with the ordinary world I knew. A blast of sound rushed past our eardrums as a massive domain opened up before us, swimming with life and elusory activity. Under an envelope of darkness, the scene exploded with flashes of fluorescence that cut the night. The shutter of strobe lights and blaze of lambent streams disintegrated the opaque, as though a spark of wildfire were sent cascading over the range of our compass, casting the black asunder.

The place played host to a sea of patrons scattered throughout its vicinity. These scantily clad individuals mingled in groups, standing or sitting amongst the tables. Yes, the skin was in and out in the open, showing through the everywhere of a community growing up around us, wandering this way and that, brushing past me on their way towards who knew where. It was so that in this legion of sexual innuendo the room seemed itself alive with the feeling of magic, and the party wasn't letting up any time soon. I could see that a steady stream of people were pouring in from the other end of the bar, most likely the main entrance where we had first come in earlier. I wondered just how packed it would get before the night was through.

Stationed in the center of the club between high wooden pillars stood a field of movers and shakers, drawn to the sway of the pounding music. There, at the forefront of these lines and placed atop a highrise plane, stood Gany, mixing his electronic din. Absorbed in the moment, he jived hard to the aria of song he laid down. His hands worked over what I trusted to be turntables, devices with which Gany spun his records and developed his signature piece of melodic styling. Wearing his headphones on one ear, he listened to the song on deck and, with the other ear, focused on his present feature, waiting for the ideal second for a solid transition. He seemed to prefer frantic tempos and repeating tones, as he manipulated electronic signals into a series of build-ups and break-downs throughout each track. If he was good, the audience should scarce be able to tell where the disintegration of one track fell apart into the ascension of another's new beginnings. I had faith that he was.

Amid where Gany set up shop, a pair of enormous audio speakers stood to either side of the dance floor. I watched amazed as each boomed and jarred in position as the tempo lifted out of the system. I was sure they would blow if pushed any further.

Beyond the dance floor was a doublet of stairs that led to a second landing. The space was smaller with a few tables strewn about, giving a person right admittance for viewing the exhibition below. At its back was a window that stretched along much of building's infrastructure, allowing for all inhabitants the perfect view of the night sky and the harbour underneath, its waters cast aglow by the city light.

This is the world I'd come into, and what a world it was to behold—grand celebration, hearts beating, feeling alive, the thunder clap of electro-house turning through a vivid lightshow. It was there within those walls of unanimity that a cool collection of characters came together under one name.

A voice called me back from the ties of captivation. The voice was unfamiliar but beckoned the title of the angel by my side.

"Summer, so good to see you've decided to come out!" The projection of sound sent me spinning around, where I took sight of a young woman tucked within a tight embrace of my dearest Summer love.

"Good to see you too, Nashira," Summer signaled back, barely audible.

Nashira removed herself from the clinch, falling back. "Let me look at you. Summer, you are radiant this night." Again she projected her voice, though in this crowded room it was rather necessary.

"Thank you," Summer responded humbly.

A lady of smaller stature, Nashira was thin yet well-shaped. She seemed to carry a rather austere quality, rigid and standing straight as a board when removed from Summer. To say she wasn't attractive would have been to do her a disservice, but she looked so damn stern I could hardly see anything else. Deep-set, serious eyes lay behind narrow glasses, and her nose was sharp and long, her forehead narrow between lined temples. She carried a look of forlorn emotion with seldom a trace of a smile. The woman had frizzy ebon hair, which may have played to her strengths had she let it down. Instead it stayed pulled back, as cold and controlled as the rest of her. Yet her hairstyle revealed a slender neck, her skin bare and raven in all its earthy beauty.

Nashira wore a long-sleeved, black button-up shirt, which she had fastened right up to the collar, and straight brown pants—surprisingly conservative attire considering most of the crowd were half-naked. She did not seem to care however, and seemed oblivious to the people around her, people such as myself, standing right there in front of her. Since Summer wasn't making any leaps to provide introductions, I took it upon myself to extend a proper greeting.

"Hello there, I'm Ambrosia. Pleasure to meet you," I said, taking a step forward and opening my arms out in welcome.

My approach wasn't met with in kind gratitude. She chose not to meet me halfway but instead sent little more than a cold gesture in my direction. Caught off guard, I stumbled around inside my head for what to say next. I did well to try to turn my attempt on embrace into a handshake, almost tripping over myself in the process. I repeated my greeting, this time a little louder, worried it may have gotten caught in the measure of song. "I said, it's a pleasure—"

"Yes, I know who you are," Nashira snapped back, looking straight at me, still not moving. "The one Mona left us for, for whom she journeyed cross countries to acquire."

"Um, yeah, that would be me, I guess." I really hadn't been prepared for this, and I was at a loss for words. Did she resent my being there? She didn't even know me.

Nashira turned back to Summer. "And might I inquire as to just where Mona is keeping herself presently? I'd very much like to talk to her yet have not been allowed the chance since her arrival."

"Oh, Mona went to lay down for a bit, said she'd be down later," Summer answered.

"Feeling a bit tired, is she?"

"Yeah, I think so."

"Right, that's only natural. It was a long journey she was made to do."

I wondered if that last statement wasn't directed at me, as though it were somehow my fault for her present situation. Nashira did cause me to think back however, to Mona and the moments leading up to her departure, namely the coughing fit. She hadn't seemed too tired until then, but then it had been a long day.

"Well, don't let me keep you," Nashira said to Summer, "It is your birthday, after all. Please, go get yourself a drink, relax." Then, looking to me, Nashira gave the slightest passing of a nod. "See you around, Ambrosia," and with that she was gone.

See you around? That's it? I didn't know what to think. I turned to Summer. "Uh, Summer … what the Sheol was that all about?"

"Hmmm?" She looked at me as though completely unaware of Nashira's behaviour.

"Don't tell me you didn't see that. The way she just treated me! So what, am I just special, or does she act in that manner with everyone!?" I shouted over the music.

"I'm not sure I know what you're talking about," she replied. I scarcely heard her. Maybe she didn't want to talk about it or didn't like confrontation. Or maybe she genuinely had no idea what I was talking about. Really, did it matter? Nashira was gone, so I thought it best to let it go. No point in turning an otherwise perfect evening into a dramatic ordeal. Perhaps Nashira really acted this way with everyone.

It occurred to me that Nashira very well could have been an occupant of the house I now lived in. Did one of the room numbers upstairs belong to her? I hoped not. My questions resided on the sharp end of distraction, and I did my best to push them to the ends of cognition. *A beautiful woman waits here for you, so go on.*

"So, what about that drink then?" I asked.

"Um, okay…the bar's over this way, if that's what you'd like to do."

"I would very much like that."

Together we journeyed to the site Summer marked out for us, not particularly far I noticed, just a little further down from where we'd come in. Abreast of her, weaving between the faces, I walked through a great entourage of identity. Taking in the surrounding sights, I couldn't help analyzing the scene and further ponder the images already playing over in my head, images of a company of which I had now become a part. A wide assembly gathered there that night, male and female, young and old alike. While most did appear rather youthful by nature, there were definite representations made for the other spectrums of age also, including, shall we say, mature bodies circling the masses. The best example of this came when I crossed paths with the senility of one sexagenarian, clad in leather strapped across his mostly bare chest. He was not alone in his excessive debauchery, though I must say the acts of exhibitionism were far better embodied by the more youthful appearing individuals in the crowd. Slinky halter-tops and tight miniskirts pulled down over G-strings filled the room, as did mesh suits and long-sleeved teddies, rubber gauntlets and silk leggings. I saw wet-look vests, latex shirts, leather chaps, and platform boots. I spotted the hosiery of whole body stockings, suspender tights, cami-garters, and belted thongs. Some were decked out in chains and studded belt buckles, and others wore collars and carried leashes and tassels. I saw a masked mystery man, complete with a zipper across his mouth. So much skin-driven exhibitionism, like a feverish love brigade making ready the lady paladin's arrival—Bilancia, divinity of sirens.

If this was the night's chosen attire, I wondered why Mona had not made mention of it sooner. I felt oddly out of place in my new shirt and jeans. And while some did choose to dress more conservatively, and by that I mean more similar to the like of what I was wearing, they weren't nearly as fun to watch. The eyes chose to wander. It was easy to lose yourself in the flood of ecstasy here, and I felt almost unable to keep my head above seducing waters.

I, however, had been granted the perfect antidote against the mounting precipitation of sexual innuendo: Summer, my lifeline to keep me high above the crushing undertow of distractions. She was the saving quality of a body to reach for and a hand to hold onto. Now if I could only grab hold of that hand…

Our destination, a well-lit oblong counter made of wood, most commonly referred to as "the bar". It was abuzz with lively chatter and revelry as we took up a space along its border. And though I found it difficult to understand the ritual of waiting to be assisted when I could just as easily serve myself, I obliged to Summer's silent request and stayed steadfast to my post. I took in my new view, noting vivid hairstyles highlighted in green and intense yellows, pinks and blues, colours I never knew could find themselves on people's crowns. I saw immense spikes stuck straight in the air, frizzled puffed-up fros of gargantuan size, lengthy tails hanging off the back of the head, hair twined and matted in a series of ropelike locks.

I was amazed to see elaborate designs inked upon the skin and rings of sterling pierced through a series of holes along the many different regions of exposed bodies. I wondered what else could be found in those areas that were not visible. Thoughts better left behind.

I turned back to Summer and the bar. Just beyond the wooden divide stood a series of lit glass panels, each showcasing several rows of bottles, all similar in size. To the right of the panels was the onset of another selection of bottles: wine and other assorted beverage containers forming a pyramid. Also behind the bar and in front of the glass were two faces moving with haste, serving drinks to the many stationed there in wait. I recognized one of the faces but did not know the other.

The latter, a young woman of average build, moved gracefully throughout her area, finding drinks and attending to the thirsty people waiting patiently (some not so much) to be served. She had clear-cut features and seemed at first inspection to hold a bearing of sophistication. She seemed discerning when she surveyed her setting, her eyes large and softly beautiful as they deeply absorbed her surroundings. Yet she also seemed to be having fun, the satisfaction shown by her bounteous smile that displayed her unmarred teeth, brimmed and straight. She carried a sense of purity through a fairness of complexion, fine eyebrows, and soft shoulders. Her hair was black with brown highlights that streamed down to touch the dominance of her back, which crept into view from a smart light green dress that flowed off her body. On angular hips the cloth clung and descended to her knees, revealing the lissome curve of calve muscles supported on suant ankles covered in a shell of bistre. Her footwear, not unlike that of Summer's, relied on a higher cut of heel with an intricate design conforming to its overlay. I peaked behind the bar to spot those last details. But it would not be by this girl that we ourselves were served, but instead by another to whom I had been already introduced.

"Interest you in a libation?" the dreamy voice called.

"Gliese, good to see you again," I addressed my greeter. "A drink, yes. That is, after all, what we're here for, right?" I turned to Summer, waiting for an answer and the inevitable search for reassurance that would follow.

"I'll have a beer," I heard a voice call out—but no, wait…it sounded like Summer, but her lips, they did not move. Moreover, she wasn't looking in

Gliese's direction. The sound, it came from the other side of me…

I turned around. Nothing could have prepared me for what I saw next. Had I fathomed it possible for one to be in two places at once, I would have sworn she was the very same, yet augmented in every way possible.

Summer, it seemed, had a sister.

CHAPTER 8
◊
OPPOSING FORCES

Not only a sister, mind you, but a twin. Identical by order, yet somehow it seemed this new wonder to behold was something of an entirely different force of nature.

Suddenly my taste turned to an insatiable hunger, one that drove on to starve the very heart of me. So deep was it that I knew a spoonful alone would never be enough to quell this lech of a relentless yearning that so fervently burned within. The mere thought of her consumed me, and I could not be satisfied without the gift to drink in her wine. Its want pined away inside my mind, driving me, forging its way to the center of my being so that soon it became all that I could think about.

Her hair was wild and free, coloured in blue-black ersatz. Her face was made-up in splashes of rose carried over the cheeks, and purple lined her eyes. Those piercing green-grey eyes…with lush lips coated in deep red, wet in the light that glistened upon them. She wore a Persian blue, long-sleeved teddy netted over navy undergarments with a lace-up bustier and buckle thong. Spider-webbed anklets and sapphire spiked heels donned her feet. So much skin of her bare body showed, the symmetry of angles running a motion of perfection, a fluid streamline drawn in the direction of everywhere I wanted to be.

As she leaned in closer over the bar counter, I could see a shape of things to come, running far beyond a list of her curves and angles found from front end prominence to backside bend.

I found myself unable to stave off starving beast no doubt clawing its way out of me to reach her. I could have died inside those eyes, only to be reborn and made to live on forevermore within her being.

"Hey, blue eyes, nice hair," she said, her voice the spirit sound of an empyreal order. She smiled at me, and I lost my breath.

"The fruits of your asking," came the otherwise chimerical voice to my right, now cutting through me like daggers, a nightmare severing the seams of this, our newly made affiliation.

The girl who rapt my heart in spades faltered from the grip of my gaze, and in her wavering she seemed jostled from a trance. She then turned her sights on the sound and grabbed the brown bottle that had seemed to materialize in front of us on the bar.

"Thanks, Gliesnis, you're a doll," she said.

Oh, but what grace! So confident, she grasped the bottle's neck and tossed a look back as she shot me up with her aphrodisiac. Yeah, she was a woman who knew what she wanted. *Take me.*

"And you, dearest, have you settled on anything?" Gliese spoke, but I wasn't seeing her.

My angel answered for me. "Yes," she said, flirting with her eyes. "I'm sure there's something you'd like, hmmm?"

Was this real? How could this be anything but a trick played on the mind? Perhaps I had simply imagined what Summer could become if only she were able. I thought to look between the two sisters to confirm I wasn't dreaming, but my eyes, they would not falter.

"I'll have what she's having, thank you," I said to Gliese without needing to think, never taking my sights off the magic before me.

"Mmm...excellent choice," she said, whilst giving me the proper run down.

"I thought so," I added, doing the same.

"Your drink, Ambrosia," Gliese said, returning quickly—perhaps too quickly—and placing the glass bottle beside me.

"Ambrosia?" my love said. "Surely, you know your name means 'true gift of the gods.'"

"I do, thank you." I was somewhat taken aback. "Know something of what's in a name, do you?"

"I make it a point to know what's important." She dangled her hand out for me to receive it. "Star," she said, and I was drawn to her like a magnet. "*Enchanté,*" she added.

"Star, is it? Meaning, 'heavenly body, stationed high above stratosphere, influencing humankind and planetary Earth.'"

I thought I saw her blush, but it could have been the lights flashing across her skin's surface. Yet she was just as quickly able to come up with a response of her own.

"Well, you tell me. Did you or did you not just get the sense of something occurring, like feeling the earth move beneath your feet? Call it a kind of natural phenomenon."

My, she was a brazen little thing.

We examined each other's faces, the music surrounding us.

Gliese gestured suddenly then toward someone else, one whom I am sad to say had become somewhat ignored. "Summer, love," Gliese said, "the usual glass of red wine then?"

I spun around to see her still there, waiting for something but not looking back, not to me, not to Gliese, not to anyone or anything. Her eyes presented only to the floor. I felt instant shame.

"Yes, Gliese, that will be fine," she whispered.

"Oh, hey sis, didn't see you there," Star said. I thought I detected there too a trace of contempt in its send off.

"Hi, Star." Summer issued an equally daunting reply. I supposed there was always some struggle between sisters, as my Mothers could attest.

With Gliese gone again I stood between them, in the middle of two points of eternity, and I knew then what nirvana looked like.

Star turned to me once more. "So, you're the one then? The Ambrosia Mona's been talking about, whom she went to go pick up?"

"Must be."

"Well, I suppose that makes you family then, doesn't it? And we always make time for family, don't we?" She beguiled me, pressing a finger to my chest and letting it drift down upon my solar plexus before falling away. I felt my muscles immediately tighten in reflex to her touch as a shiver raced over me and awareness rose in those specific places of my own anatomy. "Shame on you for not granting me the pleasure of a proper, more suitable greeting," she said.

"Well, I'm sorry, it's just..." What was I supposed to say?

"Luckily, it's something that can be easily remedied, after all."

"It can...? Yes, it can."

I knew what she was seeking; I looked for it too. She wished that I would embrace her in welcome. *So waste not another moment's hesitation.*

I quickly turned my body towards her and moved in to receive her open arms. I never made it there though, even with Star being as close as she was. My efforts were thwarted as an arm appearing around my shoulder pulled me back. Gany had somehow managed to push his way between Star and me. His intent, seemingly unmalicious if not totally oblivious, was still unwelcome.

"Allo mes amis, and 'ow are we on this fairest of bonnes nuits?"

"Hey, Gany, how's it going?" I tried to come off as enthusiastic but knew I didn't sound the part.

"Bien, bien. And what about 'ou Star? Doing well on dis glorious nuit, hmm?"

"I'm fine. Shouldn't you be up on stage right now?" She asked him outright. She too did not sound the least bit impressed by his ill-timed arrival.

"Yeah, who's in control of the music, if not you?" I asked.

"I 'ave it covered, mes chérs. Eh, a friend is filling in for the moment."

I briefly turned my sights to the stage and saw that indeed another took his place. A young blonde man I did not recognize.

"Sure that's not all he's filling?" Star remarked. I wasn't exactly sure what she meant by it.

So only good den, mon ami?" Gany turned back to me, letting go of our shoulders. Then, before giving me the chance to respond, he added, "Well, 'ave to do something to make it better, repair the situation, no? I believe I have juss da, how you say, da t'ing?"

"Oh, and what would that be?" I asked, crossing my arms. I didn't think the evening could ascend any higher than it already had.

"Yes, do tell..." Star came in, sounding suddenly interested.

"All in good time, chérie. All in good time." Gany spoke with a calm satisfaction then changed his focus to other avenues. "Summer, si belle, you are most gratifying dis bon nuit."

I turned around and watched as Gany left us and took up Summer's hand. He laid a soft kiss upon it.... *Just as I had done to Star. I'm seeing double.*

"Oh, Gany, thank you." Even in the dim light, I could pick up on the flush of her skin.

"We do not clean up too bad, non?"

I watched as Star took a step towards the two, not yet finished with the limelight. "But then, how good can anything be when left so long to collect dust on the shelf. Right, Gany?"

And so I was seeing another side of Star, an ugly side. I didn't like it. Why she felt the need to attack her sister like that was unbeknownst to me, and I thought it unnecessary.

"Ah, Star, always so full of compliments. Better is it to keep such things to oneself, non?"

"Oh Gany, do us a favour and shut it. Or at least learn to speak the language, instead of butchering it so." Star threw back her drink before slamming the bottle on the bar.

"Ah Star, always joking..." Gany said, ignoring the jeer. "So, we are good den, all of us? Shall we maybe venture to a less exposed place, en grande pompe*?"*

"Grande pompe?" *Gany, where are you implying we go?*

"Sure, why not?" Star uttered her acknowledgement, without once ever looking his way.

"Bah oui." Gany turned around. "Gliese, 'ou are coming?"

"This is true," said the yellow-endued tapstress, returning into view with a half-filled wine glass. "Is your potation, dear sister," she told Summer as she placed the crystal glass in front her. *Fancy.*

"Ah, oui. Très bien." Gany thanked her before Summer had the chance.

As I looked upon she who I had met in the upstairs kitchen little more than an hour before, who I felt I knew much longer than that, I saw a vision of melancholy standing there, and that sorrow stretched down to the floor. Again I felt shame for having ignored her.

"However, you may wish to seek refuge without me," Gliese said. "I shall come after, when time permits that I do so."

"Do not take too long, chérie, or we will 'ave to start without 'ou," Gany said before turning back to us. "Come then."

Before Gany could lead us away from the bar, Star took charge and grabbed her sister's reluctant hand. "See you there," she cooed at me. With that, Star whisked Summer away into the crowd, drinks in tow.

I turned to Gany. "Well, are we going or aren't we?"

"After you, mon ami." Gany said, gesturing towards where Summer and Star had fled.

"Uh, except I don't know where we're going, remember?" I said, not understanding him.

"To the south corner, of course. Straight dat way."

"Oh, all right then." Hesitating not another moment, I made a grab for the bottle on the bar counter and journeyed into the sea of faces before me.

"They're very different, aren't they?" I projected my words behind me so that Gany could hear.

"Summer and Star? Non, non. Just, ah, opposite ends of the same pole."

"Because they're twins."

"Because they are twins."

"Like night and day, they are."

Through the faces, together we made our way across the floor until at last arriving at the southern corner of the room, an area covered more in shadow than light. Even for the bar being dark as it was, every part had some colour spectrum illuminating it, but not here. It was like a light had burnt out. It was also more secluded, and the boom of the music seemed to dwindle somewhat, though it was still a substantial force.

"So where are they?" I asked immediately, looking to either side, hoping to catch sight of them. I was about to double check when something bumped into me from behind. I immediately spun around. Only Gany was there.

"Did you just bump me?"

"Pardon?"

"Nothing… So where did Summer and Star go, you think? This is where we were to reconvene, in this dark corner?"

"I am sorry, but I am not sure that I quite understand."

"What's not to understand? We're here and they're not."

"Ah, but they are here. Look closer." He ushered me to turn my full attention back towards the area I was facing.

I looked into the darkness, standing near on my toes for a better view. "What do you mean they're there? I don't see anyone." I tried adjusting my eyes to peer though the black.

"You only 'ave to open your eyes to see."

He walked past me towards total darkness, last touching the brim of his cap with a tip of his finger then pointing to shadows that proceeded to swallow him whole.

Like that, gone. *What in the House of Dao?!*

I jerked my head around to look for others who shared my reaction, but no one seemed to take any notice. It was as empty of people as before, and the few passersby did not give the faintest of acknowledgement.

So what had just happened? Obviously the darkness went further into the corner space. Yet the walls didn't seem to allow for it. Then perhaps a room, hidden behind the corner? I didn't know. What I did know, however, was that wherever he went, two others were most likely there with him, waiting on the other side. That was enough for me to proceed.

So I took a walk, my arms sprawled out ahead of me, ready at any second to hit a barrier. Yet nothing came but the swell of darkness.

For a moment that's all I saw: an extension of black, by a barricade of none. Then it happened—my sudden blindness began to clear, and I emerged from the fog. I found myself in a place I knew as impossible to be, yet there it was just the same. Somehow, I had ended up in what appeared to be a long, stone-covered corridor, dimly lit by a series of burning torches staggered along its walls. Down at the end of the hall stood an arched doorway shrouded by shadow.

At the forefront of this obscure channel did Gany take poise, alongside another, more covered in shadow—the two of them, watching me.

"What in the—"

"Ah, you made it. Merveilleux."

"Gany, what…is this place?" I stammered.

"This, ah…it is just another piece of la maison, no? It leads us to the main foundations."

"Right. So there's more, then?" I tried my best to get my bearings and take it all in. I then looked behind me to where I once was and saw what only confirmed the bizarre nature of things.

"What is problem, hmmm? I mean, is it really so difficile to wrap your 'ead around? 'Ou can still see the club, no? You can still 'ear the music, yes…? Are we then not still in much the same transition of space? I believe so."

"Space or time…?" I whispered. He was right. I could clearly see into the club. I could hear the music too, although it was now more than a little muffled. Indeed the whole thing, it seemed somehow different from being there and felt like I had emerged from outside the scene, placed on the outskirts and looking in. The place, alive with light and sound and all its droves of people, legions of bodies fluxed to the surge of a pounding beat in the distance, seemed to me within another world.

"They can't see us? None of them can, none of them know where we are?" I inquired.

"Oui. And so privacy is granted."

I ripped myself away from the ongoing picture show playing out before me and looked back to Gany, needing more answers. "Why? How is this place kept secret?"

"Is it not enough that it is?"

Not enough.

He sensed my answer. "It is too dark between spaces. It's in the way the light is positioned. People, they are blind to see."

"Like an optical illusion."

"Mais oui, an optical illusion."

Still, I wasn't sure. "I don't get it. Even in the darkness, you'd think one would be able to see the firelight rising off these torches."

"Well…" He walked closer so that I could see for the first time since arriving in that corridor the whites of his eyes. "Could 'ou? Could 'ou see the light?"

He had me there. "No. No, I couldn't."

"See." He smiled. "And what people often cannot see as fact—"

"—people won't believe," I finished.

I let out a small sigh and returned to the club scene. "Just seems like looking in on something I'm no longer part of. Surreal, really, like it's another place."

"Or plain of frequency channel," the stranger with Gany spoke up as stepping out of the shadows.

I had nearly forgotten she was there. Slightly shorter than Gany, the girl carried with her a buxom and full-figured shape. A faint complexion worked well in making other attributes that much more striking. Her face seemed to shine, even in the dim light. Her hazel eyes drew you in, and the thick cinnamon hair that fell just shy of her shoulders emitted a certain radiance of allure. On her feet she donned a set of emerald heels that glittered with only the most minimal of movements; knee-high stockings of viridian followed up to a long-sleeved dress of what appeared an iridescent blue-green.

"Where are my manners? Ambrosia, please allow me to introduce the lady Alrisha."

I directed my gaze toward her. "Alrisha. And are you another one of Mona's house guests…?" How else would she know of this place?

She merely nodded, coming towards me with a warm embrace.

"Nice meeting you," I said once she released me. Again she gave a slight nod of acknowledgement.

"Alrisha, she does no say much. Do 'ou, Rish?" Gany said.

"I can see that," I said. "But, Alrisha, if you don't mind me asking, what then sparked in you the need to speak up moments ago? What did you mean by the words you said?"

"Only that people can see just that what is set before them," Alrisha explained without, I thought, any trouble.

"Yes, yes. It's too dark to see." Not sure if that's what she was getting at.

"Now, you are 'ere to see Summer and Star, no…?" Gany said.

"They are here then…?" I said, looking around me but not seeing them,

"But of course. So let us go see them." Gany clasped his hands and began to head for the arched doorway, bidding that we follow. "Come, the others will be eagerly waiting our arrival."

Suddenly all priorities changed. My heart was racing as I made my way in pursuit.

Together we descended down the stone passage and through the threshold. We reached a spiralling staircase, also lit with torches, and, making the journey further below, I listened to the sounds of the club fade away as we reached the foot of what appeared to be the bottom level. We then passed through the arches of yet another open portal, where the music finally disappeared completely.

As we passed under the marble structure, seemingly more grand in size and appearance than the last, we were brought to a place of grandeur, far greater than I could have ever imagined.

"Gama Mao!" I lost my bearings as I gazed at the spectacle before me. Stretching long and high, a princely cathedral bore its foundations deep within this underground shaft. Entirely drawn in marble like its archway, the everywhere of this room shimmered so that it caused an image of oneself to be reflected upon the surface stone. Like the spaces that led into it, this room used fire as a source of light, but with so much the greater a source for inspiration. Here, the torches were presented by raised statues; I counted twelve, intricately patterned and towering on high. Each one an icon and beautifully rendered. The torches protracted from hands held aloft, a light that stretched out over the scope of the room, reaching up to epic ceiling enclosure. The statues themselves, located to either side of us, stood in two rows six deep, evenly spaced along the chamber's length.

"Spectacular," I said.

"I think so too, mon ami," Gany replied.

Past the statues, the back of the room was shaped like a half-sphere, and within it a raised semi-circle held position. Two girls were seated there on its either side, one dark as midnight's serenade of moonlit overture, the other as light as dawn's sun-beamed canzonet. As we descended towards them, I noticed something else also, a dodecagram insignia etched upon the floor space. It was held inside this raised three-quarter ring that they sat upon.

I greeted them ecstatically as we all gathered there within the horseshoe. I sat across from the twins, and Gany and Alrisha sat beside and between us, as taking up position to the either side of me.

"So glad to see all of us here," Gany said. "An offering to the bir'day girls, then?" He fished a small glass pipe and lighter from his front pocket. He then deposited the contents of an unknown substance into the mouth of the pipe and passed it Summer's way.

Summer gave her thanks as she held the pipe, studying it a moment before putting the tip of it to her mouth. It was an instrument I held an envious want of replacing.

As Gany flicked the lighter and held the flame to the pipe, Summer took a long breath inward. She held it then, getting a steady stream of smoke before letting go. The smell was at once familiar, foliage I'd spent years within my sanctuary indulging. It invoked my hunger for it almost immediately.

"Très bien, chérie. Star, you will indulge, s'il vous plaît?"

The smoking pipe was then passed from Summer to Star's hands. She took the lighter to reignite the flame and soon expelled its measure, handing the pipe to Alrisha. “That’s some good skata,” she said.

Alrisha followed suit, and soon it was to be my turn. I took the pass with great appreciation. Looking at the pipe, smouldering from its hollow cylinder, I couldn’t help but be excited for what came next. Putting down the untouched bottle in my hand, I took the lighter and made a few awkward attempts to light the bowl before I succeeded. In taking a long haul off the pipe, I drew the contents down into my cavity and felt its intoxicating hold as I kept it there. When finally I expelled the smoke, a flood of anxiety went with it, relieving me the burden of all manner of pent up vexations. Muscles freed themselves of tension, melting away on serenity’s stream, where my vision deepened exponentially. So it was that I felt utterly at ease with myself and the world around me. “That is good. Where’s this going next?”

“To moi, garçon,” Gany said.

I handed the pipe to Gany, and as I did, caught Star studying me. I couldn’t help but engage her. “You know Star, I never got a chance to wish you happy birthday.”

“That’s right, you didn’t. Bad boy. But I’ll forgive you.”

She had me in spades, but then she said something that grabbed me off guard. “After all, the beginning of atonement is the sense of its necessity.”[iv]

“Byron,” I said back to her, immediately recognizing the quote as written by a poet of the romantic period, the early nineteenth century—a personal favourite, arguably one of the best writers of his time.

"Ah, Star, our petite poet. You brighten up our darkest nights with your ability to woo us with words."

"Whatever, Gany, you only wish you could," Star bit back.

"To the contrary, I could never, 'ow you say, be able to create something so palatable," Gany said in jest of Star's rude remark before looking my way. "It sounds, 'owever, that our friend might know a thing or two of the issue 'imself, no?" He let a puff of smoke billow into the air from the pipe before passing it along.

"Yes, I believe he does," Star said, taking me in with great interest.

"I am familiar with the work of the poet you speak of, yes, as I am with many poets of the time, and times other. I was lucky enough to have had the chance throughout my upbringing to study much of the finer forms of literature," I said.

"Seems 'ou two share a common ground, hmmm," Gany said. "Much to talk about, I think."

"Well, I'm all ears," Star said as Gany passed the pipe to Summer. I couldn't help watching as Summer nearly dropped the pipe during the exchange, unable to see it from lack of looking anywhere beyond the floor.

"Gany turned back to me. "So, Ambrosia, that is, if I may so ask—" Gany said.

"You may."

"Merci beaucoup, monsieur. It occurs to me 'ou still 'ave yet to tell us anything of your story. Come, tell us something about Ambrosia. It, I think, will benefit our modique collective if 'ou share a bit, oui?"

"I might say the very same of each of you," I replied. "The only one I've had the pleasure of getting to know to any degree is Summer here, though I must say the experience was a rewarding one." As I grabbed the pipe once more from Alrisha, I sent a smile in Summer's direction. It was not returned.

I thought I heard Star mutter something then before talking. "Yes, Ambrosia, do tell. I'm dying to know more about you."

"Yes, well, there isn't much to tell, really, but I'd be happy to divulge if you're so inclined." Taking in a deep breath, I then proceeded to attempt to summarize the first twenty-one years of my life, a life spent entirely within seclusion.

I spoke of my abandonment, and how I had arrived at my new home. I described the garden, the forest border, the seemingly endless lake. Summer seemed dazzled by the description of the garden especially, as she gazed upon me for that brief moment with wide eyes and fixed attention. I spoke of my Mothers four who raised me, and of my learnings, an elaborate teaching of the world's workings, with knowledge of today and yesterday. I mentioned the faith I was immersed in, that which likened Mona's own. And I told them of my extensive training in self defense and the art of samurai. Finally I described the clothes I had become accustomed to, and how truly odd it felt to be in this new attire I'd been given.

I spoke nothing of my condition, something I thought best to keep to myself, lest they think me mad. For as natural a thing as it had been to me in my everyday life, it was, I knew, an odd circumstance to be plagued with all the same. From what I knew about the world outside my home, history had shown that at times difference was met with hostility and fear. Even with my affliction not being a danger to anyone, it could be perceived by many as anything but. And even though I didn't see that as happening here, I needed to practice caution. Also, the problem had been remedied, so I thought there really was no need for mentioning it.

The pipe continued to circle around us for another few turns, Gany filling it as it went. Until at last, while coming to my story's end, the foliage was finally spent. Pity, I thought. It was good herb.

"And that about brings us to now," I finished, and could not help an involuntary glance over toward where Summer was sitting, who at once did her best to make it look as she was paying me no attention.

Catching sight of this, a pain touched over me. I couldn't let go of the guilt I felt for having paid her so little attention since her sisters arrival on the scene.

"Well, that was a waste, wasn't it?" said a voice from the other side of semi-circle.

"Excuse me?" I said. I swung a head to look at Star.

"Malaka…" she said. "That made absolutely no sense to me whatsoever."

"What didn't?" I exclaimed, staring at her in disbelief.

"Your story. There are so many holes in it; I don't even know where to begin!"

"Really, you think so?" *The nerve of her!* She didn't even know me. "I'm sorry, but are you calling me a liar?"

"And a poor one at that, I mean come on, you actually expect us to believe even half of what you just said? I think the smoke must be affecting your mind," Star asserted as the others in the circle sat in awkward silence.

I felt my face heat up with anger.

"You think I'm making this up? Makes no sense, you say? Makes no sense—And this does?!" I yelled in echo, gesturing with my arms to the magnificence of the room.

"What the Sheol are you even talking about?" she said.

"Star," Gany interjected, "we are 'ere to 'ave a good time, no? There is no problem far as I can see. Can 'ou no let things be?"

I put a hand out in his direction. "No, no, it's all right, Gany. I'd like to hear this." And oh, how I did.

Star continued, "Okay, so an orphan is somehow delivered to the middle of nowhere by who knows who. But wait, it's not nowhere—it's some huge mansion run by four women, who live in the middle of some immense secret forest cut off from the rest of the world, on the edge of some epic, un-crossable lake that seemingly has no end. Oh, except you can see the mountains that are surrounding it, but they're impossible to get to. And somehow these unattainable rocky mountainscapes seize warm pockets of air, that are ongoing and funnel down your area, creating a seemingly never-ending Chinook that sticks around, like, forever! Isn't that remarkable! Maajiidook…" she cursed.

"Now just wait just a second—"

"Yes, totally secluded from the world, not another living soul knows about the place, save for the one who dropped you there and of course Mona. Yet it's readily supplied with everything one ever may need, including heat and electricity."

I stared at her, my mouth agape.

"Not that I have to defend myself, but I believe I already told you—we lived off what the land provided. We gardened, we hunted. As for the electricity, it was completely renewable; the entire house was powered by solar panels. We also had access to geothermal energy generated and stored in the earth. And wind power. It was all very sustainable."

"Not to mention state of the art," she said. "And how did these so called 'Mothers' of yours happen to come by this land again?"

"I don't know that, I told you. Obviously my Mothers have some pretty important friends, friends that helped them in times of need, probably even had a hand at building much of the house. That much I could tell you simply from my own deduction."

"Humph," she indicated her disbelief.

"Look, my Mothers, for whatever reason, never told me anything, wouldn't ever allow the past to be brought up. I don't know why, but the subject was always taboo. So obviously yes, others knew of our existence. Wait, why am I even explaining myself to you? I have nothing to prove!" I was fuming.

Star wasn't listening to reason though, and she certainly wasn't about to just let things go. "So you are saying that there *were* links to the outside world? Well at least that's a start, but it doesn't take a scholar to understand how much of this story still isn't on the level."

"I don't have to take this, and certainly not from you," I shouted. Her eyes were so cold, like icicles, her tone so hateful. I was without words.

"Don't you…? Well then, what about this: you tell us you're an educated man, but just where did all that new literature of yours keep coming from? Oh yes, the internet, way out in the wilderness. Right…"

"What's not to believe? The signal was strong, driven by satellite." Not that I ever had the chance for accessing it, or even to see a working computer up close, only benefiting from the knowledge they had extracted for my lessons.

She ignored me. "And still you keep to this fantasy world, kept from all outside human exposure, where you were protected and never permitted leave; where no one ever came or went and so had no chance of ever again leaving you. Sorry, but it just doesn't add up. Why don't you just tell the truth? Why don't you just come out with it!?"

She then steered her attention to the rest of the circle. "There's absolutely nothing special about him, he's an orphan just like the rest of us, but not one with any special past, living in some secret palace all this time. He's just some loner, likely discarded and left to fend for himself or die trying. And bravo for surviving, but that doesn't change the fact of what he is, still a nothing, forsaken by those closest to him." I almost thought I saw her fight back a tear.

At once I could see this was no longer about me. It was so much bigger than that, and I had no means of stopping it. *So let her rage against that dying light.*

Yet some of her words hit home, and I couldn't shake the fact of it. I often wondered how much of my life had been kept from me. Still, it was all true, and Star's rejection of my telling of it stung.

"I mean, give me a break," Star muttered, once finding that no one had responded to her little outburst.

"Okay…anything else?" I decided to ask.

"Don't patronize me," she snapped back.

"How is that patronizing you?"

"Star, please!" Summer, to my esteemed surprise, actually spoke up in my defense.

"Oh, come now, Summer! You can't honestly believe anything he's telling us, can you?" Star said.

"It's the truth," I told her.

"Save it," she said, taking a gulp from her bottle, reminding me that mine was still quite full beside me.

"No, Star," Summer said, "I will not let you insult him a moment longer! What you're saying, it's…it's hurtful. If this is what he tells us is true, we should believe him."

My would-be redeemer—it was no easy feat for her to stand up to her sister like that, I was sure. But I wondered, did Summer herself have doubts about my story? Or was it that she too felt a sudden need for extending disbelief? Did she, in fact, only speak what she thought was the right, polite thing to say? Were they all only humouring me, and if so, didn't that make Star the only one with enough courage to tell it like it is? *Don't give respect where respect isn't given.*

Why, though, would my words be taken with a grain of salt? Did the pieces of my life that I chose to present in most intimate detail have no bearing on belief whatsoever amongst these people? Was no one here under the opinion that the things I was telling them were in fact true!? What reason did they have to disbelieve me? Because their lives had been so different?

Wait, calm down, you're jumping to conclusions. No one's saying that. She's got you questioning things you don't need to. Don't let it get to you.

"I believe you." The whisper came from beside me, spoken out of Alrisha's mouth. Somehow that seemed to help.

"Oh, Summer, poor deluded little girl that you are, playing with your paints and doing your best to hide away in your forever broken shell of an existence. It pains me to have to tell you this, but sometimes you're just about the saddest thing I've ever come upon. You seriously can't believe him," Star mocked.

Summer looked as though she had got the wind knocked out of her; I don't think she could have replied if she wanted to. I felt the same, so stark was Star's language.

But then she did respond, "I do."

"You know what I think?" Star pointed straight at me. "It's just like I said, you're probably just like the rest of us here, only worse—a runaway—one who likes to create elaborate stories, stories he'd rather believe in than have to face the truth. And maybe you do believe them, have been telling yourself lies for so long they've become your reality, so it's the only thing you've got left. Me, I think you're compensating for something."

"Now just a minute!" I demanded of her.

Still she persisted, "Infant child driven deep into the heart of the mystic forest and left there, only to be delivered into the arms of strangers. Strangers who are more worldly people of scholar, experts in their chosen fields each, who decided for some unbeknownst reason to move to woodland realm. This is where they come upon the child and decide to raise him as their own, to self-school him, and to train him in the ways of the samurai? Because, why not?"

"I fail to see what you're not getting here."

"And were they swordsmiths too? I'm thinking so. Tell me, you bring your weapon of choice along with you? Of course you must have. But where are you keeping it now?" Star asked me.

"No."

"No? No what?"

"No, I don't have it," I told her, and them all.

"So you won't show it to us?"

"That's correct, because it is not here."

"Well, why not?"

"It's not permitted."

"Not permitted?"

"What you are talking about, it's something sacred to the place that I come from. The place and its people whom I left behind and stopped being a part of when I chose to pursue ambition. For that reason alone I am without," I said.

"Convenient answer."

"But the truth."

"Yes, and you always tell the truth. It is, after all, the path of the righteous. And you are righteous, Ambrosia; disciple of the four seasoned sensei of the House of, what was it again?"

"Dao. The House of Dao."

"Right…Faen me, but you really do believe that, don't you?"

"Of course, it's the life I lived!" I yelled back at her.

"Yeah, sure," she continued. "But not really, is it? So let me tell you another story, one that's easier to believe, and then we can choose which one we'll being going with, okay…?"

I was too angry to dispense a response. To show such disrespect, I couldn't believe.

"So here it is. I'm guessing you've probably been in your fair share of homes along the way—none of them like that which you describe—likely thrown out on your ass too each time they got tired of putting up with your lies."

I was up and on my feet, seeing red. I could near swear a sense of the overhead torches rising up with me in the flame. It didn't stop her though, not for a second.

"And where did that leave you, growing up with life on the street, stealing to survive? Did you end up doing time in juvie? I bet."

"Star," I heard someone call out, but the rage in me was too great for deciphering whom.

"So many wrong paths to take along the road to nowhere, hey Ambrosia. And now you managed to graduate to full-gone gonzo, hiding out in whatever shelter they put you up in before Mona was able to swoop in, scoop you up, and bring you here for reasons I couldn't begin to understand, let alone care."

"Star."

"Just another project for Mona to have her way with, to mould in her image and show the way. Another soul for saving." She scoffed.

"Okay, you know what, we're done here!" I told her.

"I'll tell you when we're done!" Star bit back.

"Chérie, calm yourself," Gany intervened.

Summer then again spoke up, "Star! You know that Mona told us she was going to see some very dear old friends of hers, who kept in their care a young man, a man named Ambrosia, whom she would be bringing back home with her."

"So?"

"So…why can't you just let it be?"

"You know why, Summer. Because this here, it's complete nonsense, and it makes me sick to have to hear it! You know it's not true, so why listen?!"

"But…"

"But nothing! What Mona told you, it was only that she was going to meet up with some people she knew, who wanted to dump their problems off on her because she's a sucker and they were sure she'd say yes. It was likely more of a business connection than ever friends."

"That's not what she said and you know it!" Summer exclaimed.

"So what? Maybe she just told us what she thought we wanted to hear. And for that matter, where does her list of associates extend to anyway? The friends she keeps…makes you wonder just exactly what kind of a place she ended up going to…hostel, safe house, asylum maybe? I mean, these so called 'Mothers' of his, they could have worked there for all you know."

"How dare you!" I screamed.

"Star, chérie, please, let us speak courteously" Gany said rising, trying to calm me as putting a hand on my shoulder. "We are, after all, all adults 'ere."

"Too true, Gany." She came back.

"Then can we no act civil?"

"Well you tell me, as I was under the strict impression that civil was a term reserved for the sane only.

Gany's hand tightened its grip on me.

"Mademoiselle, you mustn't say such things. Whether 'ou believe that what he is saying to be true or no. He is 'ere with us now, and is deserving of our respect, a part of this place as much as anyone. Remember, he is not the only one with baggage, juene femme.

"An ode to the permanently broken, then." Star gave a raise to her bottle.

I should have let it go there and then. But I couldn't stop myself from starting in again.

"What gives you the right?"

"Excuse me?" She said, once finishing her swallow.

"You heard me. To just go off and call me a liar like that? I mean, where do you get off? You have no idea who I am or where I've been—only what I've told you—and to spit on that, to show such disrespect to not only everyone here, but my Mothers, and yours. I find it utterly disgraceful, and for that I pity you." I said, again taking my seat alongside Gany and Alrisha.

"You pity me?" She seemed at once taken off guard.

"But beyond it all," I continued, "how you talk to her, your own sister. I mean, who the Sheol do you think you are?"

"Her sister!" Star suddenly snapped back at me before turning on Summer the very same. "And really, it comes as little surprise. Dearest faithful Summer who would gladly swallow up anything Mona dare push down her throat only so that she may regurgitate it at a later time. Which is exactly what any good puppeteer wants from her puppet—no strings attached. Well, you know what, I say ay-gamisou," she said, cursing everyone.

"And you know what I say…?" I did my best to break in.

Star then focused sights back on me. "And another thing, if Mona and your 'Mothers' really were such old friends, then why wait until just before a few days ago to mention their names, why not tell us sooner…? I mean, we've been living here for some seven months now and I never heard tell of these women before a day ago."

Seven months, is that really all they've been living here for? "Seven months? Try twenty-one years."

"Instead she decides to spring it on us whilst sipping her morning tea like it was nothing. 'Oh, by the way, I have these friends of mine I'm going to meet, with which I share a special bond and great deal of history and whom I would do anything for. I'm sure we can trust the man we're taking in won't do anything that would cause us any mistrust.' Well, I feel safe…be lucky if he doesn't slit our throats in our sleep."

Well, she was definitely in full form; it was not a pretty sight to take in.

"No, Star, it wasn't like that at all. You know that," Summer disputed.

"'Oh, and yeah, I'll be leaving today, shortly following breakfast.'" Star did her best to mimic Mona.

"Well, why not? Just get up and go, go on and leave us, travel to who knows where, off playing saviour!" Star spoke back to her mimicked Mona, "Act like it's nothing at all! And if you don't come back, well hey, it's not like you're ever here for us anyway. So don't worry, we'll get along just fine without you, as we've always done."

"It's a need-to-know-basis, love, in that 'ou didn't need to know," Gany finally said, trying his best to bring about reason. It was reason that fell on deaf ears. "Really, would it 'ave made any difference if you 'eard about the existence of these souls, their relationship to Mona on times prior? Non, I do no think so."

"Faen yeah, it would've," Star objected.

"Really, and 'ow is that? What do 'ou believe knowing these things would change? Nothing."

"Trust!" she shouted back at him. "I mean, if she can't be honest with us about her past, then what else is she possibly hiding? Malaka."

"Enough! I won't have you slander her good name like that any longer! I won't have it!" In a move that came as a surprise to us all, and most certainly her sister, Summer now jumped up from her resting place, putting herself right in Star's face. I guess the questioning of the mother figure was a touchy subject all around.

"When have you ever given a care about her past anyway? Hardly make an effort at all! Try asking her something sometime! Try finding out the things that might allow you to get to know her, on some level—any level whatsoever! I mean, can you give me one instance, just one instance when you did that!" Summer shook with emotion.

Star said nothing.

"That's what I thought," Summer said, looking away from her twin with what can only be described as shame.

"You calling me a hypocrite, sister?" Star finally spoke back. She was now also up and on her feet, meeting Summer's challenge before she had a chance to fully pull away. Eyes pierced as daggers drawn, the sting ready to lash out in tongue. They both cast shadows on the room's back wall, flickering with the flames.

"Oh, Star, I've no need to. You've already gone and seen to that yourself. To think, after all she's done; taken us in off the street, clothed us, nourished, and sheltered us."

"Yeah...which was more than I could do, right? Isn't that what you're really saying, sister?" Star said.

"Star, you know I didn't mean—"

"Save it!" Star stopped her then turned to break from the group as she made strides to walk away.

"Wait, where are you going?" I asked as quickly as she made way.

"Going to dance!"

I made to again get up, but Gany got there first, with another well-placed hand on my shoulder.

"Let her go."

Down the long line of the cathedral she moved wildly, until the archway shadow clipped her wings completely, expelling a Star from our company as we sat there, silent.

I looked back at Summer, who had sat back down with her head hanging towards the floor. And I, left wanting, wished only that I might console her, if only I could reach out to touch her hand, tell her that everything would be all right.

"I…I'm sorry. Didn't mean it to go so far, I…" She was broken.

"It's all right, chérie. We understand." Gany walked over and knelt before her, put his hand on her lap, and gripped her palm in his own. "No worries, eh?"

"Yes," she whispered back through tear-soaked eyes.

It wasn't all right, though, not for me anyway. I wanted answers. What had set her off so? Nothing short of an August gale was she, unfurled in the fury, unremitting, as unleashed before an unsuspecting follow of abashed onlookers.

"So…anyone mind telling me what that was all about?" I looked for answers, but got none.

"Is nothing…she is not so bad, really. All about the highs and lows, mon ami. Is much like a crazy roller coaster ride, no?" Gany tried giving a small chuckle, but it didn't help make the situation any less uncomfortable.

"Crazy, huh? I can see it."

It wasn't long thereafter that we all decided to take our leave of the sanctuary, putting the pristine palace architecture in recline as we climbed the spiral to return to the sounds of nightlife outside surreality.

It just so happened that I found myself walking next to Summer through the torch-filled stone hallway, with Gany and Alrisha trailing somewhere behind us.

It was the first real time we had been alone that night once having come downstairs, and I was still feeling guilty for paying her less attention since having met Star. Seizing the moment as best as I could, I tried, once again, to engage her in conversation. Just what to say?

"So, this place, it's pretty amazing, don't you think?"

A mere nod is all she gave, and ill at ease I was quick becoming. Starting to fumble for where to go next, I was about to say something stupid concerning her sister, when at last she broke silence.

"No more than any other."

A bit delayed, but all right.

"So yeah…about what happened down there, I swear to you it's all true, every word of it. I mean, why would I lie about it?" I don't even know why I brought it up, but she put a stop to it before I could continue further.

"Please, Ambrosia. I really don't want to talk about this anymore," she said as we reached near the end of the hall.

"That's fine."

It wasn't. I felt ever the more apprehensive about what things I could reveal to her, or anyone for that matter.

"Going in, mon ami?" Gany said, coming up behind us.

"Um, yeah, was just waiting on you," I said as we approached the forefront looking in. "Where's Alrisha?"

"She'll be along, chéri. Shall we then? You first," Gany said as he ushered Summer.

Summer took her leave then, walking through the dark perimeter and back out into the club area. Seeing her there from where I stood only further added to the hypnagogic nature of the experience. It seemed like she wasn't real, or faded from reality into a kind of living tapestry. *Just an optical illusion.*

It was my cue to exit. Walking through the space and back onto the scene, it felt like the coming out of a tunnel into the light of day. I suppose it wasn't so different, really, the club's colour spectrum hitting me like an exploding prism on entry.

So I found myself again within the increased sounds, before a sea of faces and beside Summer. Instinct then told me to look back to where I'd just come from, if for no other reason than to confirm the illusion, when unexpectedly I was struck in the shoulder, nearly knocking me off my feet.

I spun in the direction of the hit, only to find Gany.

"Sorry, is hard to see when the light hits," he apologized.

"That's fine, Gany, I understand," I said, turning back to Summer. There she stood, eyes down. Yet I thought I saw a small grin upon her face. Was that in accordance to my near casualty with the floor?

"Liked that, did you?" I said, laughing in spite of myself.

"So back to the grind, oui?" Gany said, placing his arm around my shoulder, his other on Summer's. I was suddenly reminded of the way he had initially come between Star and me. "You two should go find a place, make yourselves comfortable." He then let go of us and headed towards the stage, quickly burying himself within the busy crowd before us.

Standing there, with the music pounding down upon me, it was almost more than I could handle with my already heightened senses. The lights were near blinding. I thought I had sobered up since smoking the herb, what with my chance brannigan with Star. Fighting will do that, take a good kick and nullify it. I was mistaken however, and upon re-entering the club, I again recognized the full effect that the foliage had delivered on me. Funny what a different ambience can make. At that moment I just wanted to grant myself some ease, hang loose, and let it all sink in.

"Maybe we should take up Gany's advice, Summer," I proposed to her.

"Oh…um, yes, I suppose."

"Well, after you then," I told her, gesturing that she move forward so that I may follow. With that, we were on our way, drinks in hand.

The pickings were slim, but Summer did eventually find us a small table to sit at, its location just over and to the side of the dance floor, on a high rise slightly removed from the crowd below us, where the action was.

Gany was back up on the turntables, and the floor was alive with music that was especially loud where we were, being so close to floor speakers. Not that I minded, but it would be, I knew, difficult to attempt any kind of conversation over the punch of the audio. Sheol, it was hard enough to sometimes make out what Summer was saying under normal circumstances, so I couldn't fathom what new difficulties might ensue while locked in among our present contextual listening sphere. Of course, this wouldn't stop me from trying.

"Yeah so, how do you feel about this music?" I shouted.

She looked confused. "I'm sorry, what?" I saw her mouth out the words.

I made a second attempt, louder this time.

"The music! It's great, right?"

"Oh! Yes, it is!" she yelled back. She turned to look at the empty wineglass in her hand.

I looked down at my own brown bottle and realized I had not yet taken a sample of the inward nectar for as long as I had toted it around with me.

Tipping the bottle back, I took in an ample swallow. It wasn't bad, aside from being warm, not at all like what I was used to, which was closer in comparison to the wine Summer consumed. No, this was something else, smooth going down with a full rounded flavour, slightly bitter aftertaste. So this was beer, was it? Would be better served cold, I thought, which of course it had been.

"Would you like another drink?" I asked Summer.

"Pardon?" she asked, leaning in closer towards me.

"Another drink! Would you like one?"

"A drink? Um, okay…I mean, I guess so, if you do."

"Okay…just let me finish what's here, and I'll go up and get us another two of the same! Unless you'd prefer something else?"

"Some…would be fine, thank you." I thought she said.

"White?" I asked, not hearing her.

"No, red."

"Sorry…?"

"Red…red wine." She hardly raised her voice, but at least she had no problem in repeating herself.

"Right!"

"You don't mind do you? I mean, if it's a bother."

"Sorry, what?"

"I said, if it's a bother!"

That's more like it.

"No, no bother at all! Be my pleasure!" I said, and then threw back the bottle, doing my best to consume as much of it as I could before getting up to make my way to the bar. Another smash of the cream-soaked ale, and there'd be nothing left.

On my feet I suddenly felt a sweep of dizziness engulf my brain so that I almost fell. I quickly grabbed the table.

"Are you all right?" I heard Summer say.

"I'm fine, just got up too fast. Made for a bit of a head rush," I said, trying to regain whatever composure I lost along with my pride. "Let's try this again."

I never got the chance, however, as on turning to go I ran straight into the very person to whom I was making the venture.

"Interest you in a libation, dearest Ambrosia?" The spacey sound of Gliese came as if out of nowhere as there she stood at the ready, stationed directly in front of me with a tray full of drinks balanced on one hand.

For a moment I was taken aback, seeing her there. "Gliese…how strange of you to ask, I was actually just coming to see you."

"And so here you find me," Gliese concluded as she moved to put the tray of drinks on our table. From this large order of assorted beverages she grabbed up two of what looked like those we already had and placed them down where we were sitting. "For you, unless something else is of your fancy?"

"No, Gliese, these will be fine, I think. Wouldn't you say, Summer?"

"Thank you," Summer said.

"Yes, thank you, Gliese, you really didn't have to do that. I was getting up."

"I took the liberty of getting the next set ready when I saw you two come this way," she told me, a gentle smile pressed upon her face.

"Well that's right nice of you, Gliese." I regarded her kindly, again taking my chair. "So, didn't get a chance to see you downstairs. The demands of the crowd keep you away?"

"I go where I am needed," she said as she lifted the tray onto her shoulder.

"I'll take that as a yes."

"I'll be round again when you run out," she said. Then she was gone, the tray held above her so as not to spill anything as she weaved through the scattered faces.

"Well, that was awfully kind of her," I projected towards Summer as I grabbed my beer.

"Yes, it was."

Another dead end. At least with my getting out to the bar I could have had time to think of how to best steer the conversation. Now I was left with nothing. I surely couldn't bring up anything from earlier in the night that might make her upset a second time.

Just let her be, lean back, and take in the atmosphere. Just enjoy that which is now, and what needs be asked will find the opportune moment.

So with my cold beer in hand, I relaxed back into my chair and took in the scene. The beer, it was as crisp and clear as the mountains surrounding my one true home.

*****

The night drew on, and with it came a fairly ample supply of liquor couriered our way. Yes indeed, it seemed whenever I found the bottom of a bottle, another cold one would be waiting to top me up, all provided by Gliese, who continued to make the rounds. It was actually quite alarming, her precision of arrivals, appearing at each instance I needed refilling.

The dance floor was packed and the people on it infected with the bug. So many bodies moving to the beat. I wanted to be part of it so much that I at points found it hard to sit still. Yet I couldn't leave Summer alone there.

As for Summer, while I did eventually make attempts to engage her over top the music, it became little more than idle chit-chat that seemingly went nowhere. So when nothing took, neither straightforward banter nor any attempt at in-depth conversation concerning such topics as the arts and culture of our time, I became frustrated.

As she strived to continually shoot down every possible effort at verbal progression, I was made to feel less inclined to continue. Summer, I thought, had made her obvious feelings of rejection towards me more than adequately clear; not by acts of ill-natured callousness or any snide behaviour, mind you, but by using inaudible whispers to answer any queries made. Tired of getting the cold shoulder, in the end I just gave up asking.

So with nothing left to say I focused instead on the music. The wave of its boom roared much like a rockslide might in the awesome power of earth falling; its monolithic tour de force sent hurtling, tumbling down the mountainside, doom fast approaching like a reaper for all those unfortunate enough to be caught between its narrows. Oh, what a thrill it was.

All but for me, who couldn't help risking a return to the places I had been shunned away from. I could not help it, and so again my thoughts ran back to her if only to wonder where the girl I'd met but a few hours prior had gone. I looked towards this vision of loveliness set out before me, with an ever--somber expression on her face, still nursing a half-full glass of wine, and I wished for nothing more than to remedy this feeling of vexation. Perhaps she wanted only that I left her alone for a while…? No, she hadn't been quite right since the events of downstairs. Or perhaps it was even before that. At first, I presumed I must have done something to cause her this level of distress, a riff I'd somehow placed betwixt us, maybe to do with the way I'd acted earlier. That I had failed to include her was something I wish only that I could reverse and allow that my conscience be clear of. That was my guilt to carry, but it was not what was bothering her.

I was an expert in reading body language, or so I believed, and what she was telling me was a story of weariness. She twitched at the bolting music on each crescendo, and the vivid light parade of vibrant twirling spectrums and strobe luminescence hurt her eyes. She seemed intimidated by the crowd and the visible flesh on those the bodies of the people who passed her by, too self-conscious of the skin she was in. The dress that cleaved to her gorgeous dimensions she kept closed off, trying to hide what pulchritude showed through its revealing blazon. She was far too exposed to the room, taking her out of her comfort zone, far away from the reach of safe refuge, throwing her to the wolfs and leaving her in places she rather not be.

Had this been Mona's plan? To make her feel so awkwardly out of place? It was intolerably cruel of her if this were true. Or had the plan simply backfired? In trying to unmask the girl and allow the flower to take bloom, had she instead further buried the stem? Should Mona have gone a different route, by a careful hand laid to the unearthing of sprouting buds reaching out to touch hold the warmth of the sun? If she had only been there I might have asked her.

This wasn't Summer's place, clearly, and these weren't her people. The dress she wore wasn't reflective of the woman inside. She belonged somewhere else, a region free of noise and fools dancing (I was fast looking to become one of them, as with each drink consumed the beat drew on me deeper).

What she really needed was quiet, an area where she could collect her thoughts, shining conceptions that they were, and mould them into sheer brilliance. I mean, who knew what sensational things she might be bringing to life if not stuck where she was. A creative intellect as beautiful as Summer's needed constant peace of mind to flourish. She had been pulled out of her work by being made to go down to the club, and so the process had been interrupted. Such a thing was never acceptable.

I felt like asking her if she wanted to leave, but I didn't. She was an adult capable of making up her own mind, after all, and had she wished to do just that then I was sure she would have left ages ago. Also, my asking her to leave may have come off sounding too much like I was probing for an invite to accompany her upstairs. *What would you say if she did ask?*

So why did she stay? I searched it over in my mind, and the only thing I could come up with was that Mona had asked her there. Was that enough to keep her tied to the post? I guess it was. They seemed pretty tight, those two.

So then where was Mona? I'd not yet seen her, and I had a pretty good vantage point of the floor. Had she chosen to stay upstairs? Was she too tired? No, I couldn't see her missing out on her daughters' birthday. Perhaps she was just running behind, really behind. Yes, that sounded like the only plausible explanation.

Mona wasn't the only one missing in action. I hadn't seen hide nor hair of Star since she'd left us in a tear. Strange, considering she had come up to dance. I couldn't see her on the dance floor, although it was possible that she existed somewhere in the middle of the madness and menagerie. She also could have been somewhere else, such as at the bar.

I would have liked to know where she was. I bet she danced like a demon.

Gany was out on the main stage, grooving hard to the sounds he was spinning. Gliese I could see from across the floor with tray in hand. Oh yes, and the ever so wonderful Nashira patrolled the perimeter or stood at attention beside the door leading upstairs. Nashira, Matron of a Dark Nebula.

I must also note that on that night I saw another who, like Nashira, stood watch. He could be found somewhere close to the main entrance, unmoving for most of the evening. He appeared large and muscular, and I wondered if he was not also part of Mona's crew.

I didn't want to leave Summer, but for every drink I had—and there had been quite a few as time dragged on—the more I felt the call of the unknown, could feel the blow and clap of the electronica scratching at my back, channelling through my cavity, calling me to join in its masquerade of cadency. The music had found me, there was no denying it. Sitting there beside her I could not help asking whether she'd accompany me out onto the floor. I knew the answer ever afore she stated it, but it didn't stop me from trying. Initially, it didn't bother me when she said no. Things slowly began to change, however, as I proceeded further into the depths of the alcoholic binge. I caught myself swaying to the tune that played, bopping my head to the beat manifesto, and I didn't want to stop. I was definitely more than a little intoxicated, for a second consecutive night.

So I waited, hoping things would change. When they didn't and at last I could take it no more, I decided I would go with or without her—but hopefully with.

"Come on, Summer, bet you're a real angel on your feet," I said, my toe tapping. "And that dress, oh, but I would love to see how it moves, along with you in it."

"I said no!" She used the same raised voice she had used on her sister. It should have been enough to silence me, and yet still persisted.

"Right, right. Well, do you mind if I…"

"Go ahead," she said, resting her head in her hand. "Have fun."

"Really…!?" I was surprised and elated. "You're sure now? Because I could just as easily stay and…"

"It's what you want," she said, and then she herself was on her feet, leaving her seat for the first time in hours.

"Wait, you are coming?" I asked, excited to see her standing yet confused at the sudden change of heart.

"No," she said.

"Then where are you going?"

"Just going." She wasn't giving any ground.

"But…to where? You don't have to go, you know. Look, I'll stay here and we'll get ourselves a couple more drinks." Though I didn't really see the point, as she had hardly touched her wine.

"Ambrosia, I'm going to the bathroom, all right?!" she hollered over the noise.

"Oh." I wasn't sure how to respond to that. "Well... I'll accompany you then!" I was also feeling the pressure.

"Really, I don't need you to accompany me," she said.

I hoped she didn't feel I was smothering her. "No, actually, I have to go myself. Just didn't know until—"

"Fine."

I knew enough not to say anything more, even in my inebriated state. As we made our way through the crowd, I had to be careful not to fall into her, which almost happened more than once.

The booze, it seemed, had managed to hit me harder than I had previously determined. My steps fast turned into a stumble. Vertigo held sway over me like a fog barrelling in off a harsh bay wind. Still, I did my best to follow Summer, who wasted no time in reaching her destination.

Half-clad individuals of both sexes packed the restroom. Most were just standing around talking as though taking a break from the music, with some doing more than that, and none showed me any bother as I quickly went in and did my business.

Upon leaving the lavatory, I immediately noticed just how much closer I had come to the dance floor. The center stage was just a little across the way and the pull was almost more than I could handle. But I could handle it. I didn't go, not right away anyway. It almost killed me, but it was after all only polite to wait there for Summer and see her back to her seat.

So I waited, and I waited, and when that came to pass I waited still more, further on than ever I would have liked to. The longer I stayed there watching the bodies turn in epic rhythm to the song, the greater the urge to join the dance stirred within me. Nevertheless, I stayed where I was. What was taking her so long? I wondered. Could it be she had already gone, made her way back before I had ever emerged? No, that wasn't possible. Peering out over the crowd I didn't see her anywhere, not anyone resembling her back at the tables. The line to the women's lavatory appeared as rather lengthy too. *Should have used the men's.*

Perhaps if I just move into the crowd a tiny bit while I wait. I found myself departing my station, if only briefly, to move a step closer into the nightlife that beckoned me onward. But I didn't want to stop there, resting on the outskirts, doing what I could to avoid bumping into those around me, and it was proving difficult to both pay attention to the beat and watch for Summer too. So I made my choice and moved further into the crowd, swearing to come back and check on things during the next moment's passing.

The instant I hit the floor, I was gone—lost to the sound. What once stayed fresh in my mind was too soon led to stray, and the watching for her dwindled until it was all but forgotten. The music was too good, I was too drunk, and I couldn't care enough to give a damn about anything else, not anymore. All that mattered was the now I was in, the heartbeat of the collective; all of us offering ourselves to the night. I was fooling myself if I'd believed anything otherwise—the rhythm had me all along and just needed me to take its hand. I'd heard the call, I'd answered, and so it gave me to the greater part of many.

It was then, when captured by tourniquet of wrenching desire, that she came to me, revealing herself from within the darkness and taking the stage. Oh, heavenly body ferried earthward, would I be the one to catch you, precious Star.

"We 'ave someone special 'ere with us ce soir. It's her birthday, so might 'ou make some clamour?!" Gany's voice projected out over the masses, and so in unison we echoed back our esteemed gratification. "She az agreed to sing us a song! 'aven't you, Star?!"

"Faen yeah!" she screamed into the microphone put to her hand.

I guessed her mood had changed for the better. It was more than I could ask for, and immediately I began to make my journey forwards, wanting desperately to find myself closer to that stage. The crowd was in an uproar, yet I managed to squeeze into what limited space there was available for me. Then, as in a mad fever, I continued to push past those in my way. No one could stop me from reaching my destination, and I was prepared to go through whomever and whatever to get to the forefront of the lady's worship.

"Then shall we, mon amour?"

"Let's go!" Star bellowed.

Gany spun on his electronic din as Star took full control, chanting:

Is this the end of us?
Feels like I've somehow
lost you now, now, now, now, now, now.
Precious dreams to me
falling down around
feet dead on the ground, ground, ground, ground,
ground.

Have you had enough?
It all comes as too much
The things that you must think
in thoughts of me and his touch.

I am no innocent
I am the flirt,
I lack true discipline.
Stay with me and you
will end up getting hurt.

And now I've gone too far
clearly I've crossed a line.
The risk in dealing with this
is the high cost fit for the crime.

Mark of the broken heart
Makes hard to fight your way back in, in, in.
You think you know me so well
But know I'll do this again
And again
And again.

You lie in innocence
I am the scourge
I should be disciplined
You best steer clear the oncoming disaster.

Is the love lost therein?
Moral compass of a self-serving nature.

It's now on my conscience
Where to me there's no other
nearer or dearer

No other consequence
Seems so severe as that
which you come to fear

I'm not the only one out there
You deserve better.

This is the end
of me and you

The line has been severed
in two.

With her final words the crowd cheered, and it was the most amazing spectacle of intensity I'd ever witnessed. She possessed such passion, her words filled with rapture, flirted with disaster; it turned loose my last refrain. I yearned for her only.

Star left the stage, and in descending to the dance floor locked her gaze onto me. She shot me up with a smile and made a raise of her eyebrow as if calling me closer. I took the last few steps that would bring me right to her.

"Star, wow, that was… Listen, I just wanted to say, about before, I'm—"

"Hush," she said as pressing fingers to my lips, "let's not fret on what was."

Gama Mao, but she was beyond perfection. The droplets that perspired down her cleavage drove me to hysteria.

"Star, you were—are...incredible." I was so lost in her I'm not sure how I was able to form words.

"Mmm, I like that. But I wouldn't be," she leaned in to whisper in my ear, "without you."

A spasm engulfed every origin of my anatomy. She grabbed my hand and led me deeper into the coterie. In the center of the room, the grinding of gears turned with the pulse of the crowd, forming on collective seam.

Much like a dream, I had no idea how I had entered there, but that no longer mattered. What mattered was the now we were in. Dancing beside her, I was swept upward within a dream. My senses were on fire, emotions blazed on high so that I could feel no more the touch of ground beneath my feet.

She had me flying. Her motions riveted the flesh, an ache that fastened to the core of my burning for her. The beat came on hard, and Star with it, pushing herself in, allowing for less than a hair of space between us. She locked in against my pelvic throw.

When Gany threw down a pulse-go echo, we were the both of us grabbed within its pull. Together we heard the call of its bellow:

I'm so intent on you
to see this fantasy through
For every hour spent not by your side
makes me want to turn back the tide

Where nearby bodies jolted and leapt with the anthem's rise, we grappled onto one another—vessels in epic motion, thrusting deep as along a fluid stream.

I am filled
with the need to feel
something real
within this heart
So torn apart
I can't remain still,
It's an out of time scenario
A life calling up for the kill

Arms flailed in undulation, and hair thrashed wildly on reeled heads. A heat that rose off us was fast becoming more than I could take.

For the sake of all

that is right and true
It's always been you
the better part of me
Please do what it is
that is necessary
and save this life tonight

Suddenly a trumpeting of pulse-pounding beats took rise, and we with it.

It's unlike a design of any
Kind of beautiful
Beyond the realm of the individual entity

A seducing voice bounced in further off the air stream as the bass grew heavy with intensity. "Faen, this track takes me," she moaned in my ear, and I fell far from the point of no return.

These things are meant to be
between us only
One look from you
is enough to bring
me such sweet release

Desire and energy in the room pumped blood heat, its ascension showing no signs of stopping. Never had there been anything like this in life before, nothing that should feel this good. *Please never let the feeling end, eternal freefall.*

There's nothing more

without the two of us here
Now let me find where your heart beats

She spun around on me, and quickly I engaged her from backside. As I raised her arms up behind her, they moved to the touch of my face, tracing along to the nape of my neck. We grinded to the fever pace that bled out and got lost in the sound as she slid her body up and down. I seized hold of her thighs, squeezing tightly as I rubbed along the length of her curves. The palpitation of my heart was sent racing as we moved on in heavy oscillation, unbreakable as the drive of the sea. The need was beyond bearable.

It's unlike a design of any
Kind of beautiful
Beyond the realm of the individual entity

When the music didn't let up, neither could we. Time spun off its axis. I had been brought into Canaan and once there had found true infinity. And when turning to me she implored that I leave there with her, I told the lady I'd follow wherever forever, beyond the boundaries of other worlds.

These things are meant to be
between us only
One look from you
is enough to usher
me such sweet release

“And you’ll rescue me should I fall?” she asked me.

“In me you’ll find always someone there to hold onto.”

So she secured these words through a press of her lips to my mouth, her tongue swept up inside with a kiss to dispel any shroud of a lingering doubt. Passion coursed as I found her there and so met with the ever sweetly drawn desires. Our vessels moved in sync, bodies entwined deeply, a feed to the hunger’s craving.

Lay me down baby
in the shine of your light
Lay me down baby
As much as you like...

Taking my hand in hers and pulling me in stride, Star pushed through the crowd as we exited the dance floor, made haste for a destination of a different kind. We soon found ourselves at the gate leading to upstairs, and again we embraced, grabbing at each other by a sultry showing of doted lust. Star threw the door back to expose the red-lit stairwell that would grant us passage to a more private setting. To our surprise, however, we found the enclosure already occupied.

“Ooooooh...” Gany let out a groan of pleasure for the boy on his knees in front of him. “Bonjour, mes amis,” he said, looking up. ‘You...oh...enjoying this bon nuit...?”

“How…?” I trailed off. How had he gotten there so quickly? He was still at the turntables just a second ago. Yet to my added surprise, I looked back and found another man I did not know now at the helm. *Must have gotten a friend to cover him again while I was preoccupied.* I had, it seemed, been rather elsewhere with my mind on other things, devoted to pursuing the temptress beside me.

"Disgusting," Star said under her breath, spitting the word in Gany's direction as she pulled me upstairs. I couldn't for the life of me figure out why, though. Were they not doing just what we set out to do, to seek out the pleasure of another's embrace?

We entered the foyer, and darkness held us as she thrust me against the doorframe, my weight hitting the door still partly ajar and slamming it shut.

"Which room?" she asked in haste. As I bit her neck, I answered back, "Hmm...?"

"Which...uh...which room are you in?"

"The first…room one. And yours?"

"Seven."

Seven? So she shares a room with her sister.

Star quickly grabbed my hand again and pulled us through the black, up onto the next landing, feverishly searching for the door handle.

"You have your key, right?"

"Key...? Yes, or…" *Did I remember to grab it off the bureau?* Suddenly the most intense sickness hit me square in the stomach as my heart plummeted. I let go Star's hand and began to search my pockets, knowing in the panic that my efforts were futile.

"It's fine, the door's open," Star said. Relief passed over me with the sound of a creaking that let us into the starlit room.

Inside she closed shut the door behind her, locking us in. Without further need for hesitation she heaved herself onto me, and we clung to one another like two wild animals in heat.

Taking hold of my shirt, she tore it open and sent buttons flying to the floor. The article of clothing was cast off me as returning the favour, my fingers wove through the ties of mesh on the teddy she wore, ripping down from top to bottom.

Not stopping, looking to find access in, my index finger then forced its way between the cups made to cradle her, pulling a cut to the cloth that binds. Breasts lay out bare before me, my sex now so like a rock it pained, crying out for release.

As I was sent barrelling into the wall, she drove a hand in to meet me there and grasped tightly.

"Now grab me my long sword," she jested as a groan of satisfaction escaped me. So I parried with a quip of my own, and slipping in past her buckled thong, moved to help bring on an emergence of true wonder-filled serenity. A flush of exuberance came over her, rushing in as written upon the face, and felt down in the knees. What followed was a further plea for pulling her closer towards jubilant ecstasy; something that no prior act of outwards hostility could ever hope to conceal, not from me. I would go a thousand kisses deep if need be to expose the vulnerability within.

With her inseam already encouraging me onward, the journey inwards to her most erogenous places was all too easy and only the slight of a motion away.

Sighs of rapture spilled out with pressure instilled on the highest, most sensitive nerve centre located on all of her creature. This flooding of carnal pleasures crashing through dam walls sent Star into a mad frenzy. She grappled hold of me, scratching down the lines of my back, breaking the skin in a most delectable way.

Tongues toiled and bodies pressed still deeper in. The constriction of Star's passage on fingers sparked in me a simultaneous firing of all synaptic receptors. I was made to rocket skyward as clasping firm the buttocks, I propelled us into the nearby open closet. Crash colliding against the fabrics that hung there, I dropped to my knees and buried my face down in her. The taste, tantalizing. No sweeter a nectar could have been reared by Goddess or nature.

Provoked by this feeling, this opulent exhilaration and the need to greater satisfy, I dug deeper still within, meeting her every quarter. My hands gripped her bustier, wrenching it off. Pressed to body convulsion, I feasted on Sauvignon Blanc.

So when at last she could take it no longer, a wail of pleasure rising as the quiver ran through her, I stayed on to savour the nectar of muscle spasm, walls given to rupture.

Then rising in want, with no time to waste in the come down of splendour, I unfastened to the release of my member. With hands placed securely around her hips, I then raised a Star up on high.

Those legs, they clung to the either side of me; spiked heels dug hard into my back. Above her, she grasped the clothing rod for leverage and made ready to receive my offering whole. I launched my attack, penetrated the every layer of her being, and by the grappling of thighs a further tightening of the organ brought to surface the spearhead of an ever-greater intensity.

Heavier I sank in, rooted to the canal, the fervor filling in my loins, bringing me closer to rhapsody. With each thrust the surmounting heat burned still more out of control. *Let it take you now.*

It was a feeling so consumed that the order was to press on ever deeper therein.

I obeyed, relentless in my volley to firmly bolt myself to her moist chasm and breach the lesser-known regions of her inner sanctum with all of me. *Now run hands down the flesh of her back, kiss the line of her breast, latch hold of the nipple gently in your mouth. Hold it in your teeth til the breath catches in her.*

Star gasped.

But she was not the only one with the urge for feeding the flame, as I too dared to let the very same envelop me. Fever stricken with the heat, we two were caught under a strict cover of sensuality, and struggling for air, finding there not enough.

With the music pulsating in the downstairs beneath us and I sheathed in her, matching its every beat, we soon came to the brink of a surge that had been swelling there within us since the very beginning. In this most intimate moment, this precious pressing on of pre-eminent points poised in the axis of amour, the crescendo was near reaching its critical juncture.

Still hoisting her higher, I watched as she lurched her upper body forward and braced a hand to my chest as she climbed further towards that momentous peak, doing what was necessary to bring forth that intense feeling unlike any other this side of heaven's gate—beautiful grace, the rapture of tides.

She cried out, "Don't stop! Don't stop."

And I won't. So I rotate on the pivot to deliver her another.

Succumbing to a groan, drawn on by the passion of a pleasure principle, I watched with a prolonged shudder as her head shot back. She gripped me with all she had before finally letting go of the bar, dropping feet to the floor, essentially forcing me out...

Star then took the helm, swiftly spinning herself around like a prima ballerina. When she again asked me to take up the dance, bracing her hands against the shirts, I was reminded of our first performance as I took to the backside position.

She had tattoos that covered the length of her upper posterior: a spread of wings appearing in the moonlight coming in from window space, feathered darkly. As I looked on them, bringing myself close into her, I could feel the body tense as if for hardened collision.

I put my hands on this vision, clasping onto front hips, pulling them in as I moved my own forward, and in the seizing of she who would gladly have me, I bore myself deep into her den.

Star cried into the night, but still held on. Through the piercing push onto her tapered regions, the stress of constrictions, she endured. To her inner zones I travelled, breaching the area and meeting with sheer intoxication. I brandished her fury like an approaching tidal wave. There was no escaping the sensation, spearheading a vessel onto the break of an opposing tide's yearnings.

She bemoaned me, to the pleasure and pain both captured in the sensitivity, as a contraction of her interior walls led me to wail just the same, clutching at the threads of her hair held tightly round each my fingers.

On and on it came, we belonged to the song. Until, with bodies wound, a shock-like tremor so profound passed its way through me in the torrent and by the rage of a high-octane rhythm. The echo shot down through the underground: detonations of the full-blown, unabridged pleasure. Inside that moment she became a part of me, the other missing piece—an explanation for this one heart's beating.

So it was to be, complete; the need to feed the fires of bodily necessity had been fulfilled.

Exiting the closet and collapsing to ruin upon the bed, our breaths trembled to a slow, and the pummel of our heartbeats lessened until a final feeling of idleness crept in. We lay there in silence, saying nay a word, naked atop the sheets. Touching her head on my shoulder, she held close to my body as the darkness overtook us.

CHAPTER 9
◊
DELIRIUM TREMENS

"*Natarehsla Mihtrasem.*"

Eyes open, I lay naked upon a hard ground. Sky above me, shadowed. Rising to my feet, I feel a gentle breeze across my body. *Where am I? How did I end up here?*

Something soft extended from the earth, alive, standing tall to either side of me. Too dark to see, I feel the touch of its brush against my shoulder, the smell of incense inciting the senses.

An eerie voice sounds on the air.

"*Natarehsla Mihtrasem*"

The voice, it pulls at me, as though beckoning that I come forward. Where eyes cannot see it does not matter, for I know the way. It is a path I have often taken. And still the call of a name heralds me on.

"*Natarehsla Mihtrasem.*"

It is louder now, the need becoming more severe, controlling. In heed I push onward, travelling en route towards where the voice lay its origins down, and with each pressing advance a greater excitement gathers within me.

"*Natarehsla Mihtrasem.*"

Until when reaching my destination, the voice centers over my placement; my body ceases to go on any further, for I know she is there. Though I cannot observe her, I perceive of her coming all the same, like an extension of my core infrastructure come back in to frame. I feel the heat off her breath on my chest, as she stands there beside me and takes hold of my hands.

"Lover."

My heart beats for her as we press lips together in recognition of the esteemed miracle that's come and brought us here, at long last. It's the miracle of love as held by kindred spirits, for I've known the lady longer then I've known myself, and it wasn't until our first meeting that I was able to find the true self in me. And so it happens that here again I am born anew, a fledging bird taking first flight with her by my side to guide me along the way to wherever this life takes us.

She showed that to me, and for it, I vowed to never let her go.

"NATAREHSLA MIHTRASEM."

I leapt up with a start, sweat pouring off me. Light of a new day poured into my room. I was safe in my new home.

With a deep breath I crashed back down onto the bed that held me. My body, still naked from the night before, lay drenched in cold sweat.

It was just a dream, that and nothing more. But damn if it didn't feel real. It was just like the others, those that had been occurring since the spring, but with one notable difference. This episode was at least somewhat comprehensible. The place was familiar somehow. Someone I felt I knew was there also… Who was it? A person from my past?

Nonsense. You've only known four people in your life before now, and none of them would be cast in such a scenario. A representation for something then?

And what of the voice? Finally I could hear what the voice was saying, but what good did it do if I couldn't understand the words? Some other language, perhaps? Something from former teachings I'd all but forgotten and repressed from memory? Would it need to be deciphered before I could grasp onto any understanding of what was going on? My head hurt just thinking about it.

It doesn't mean anything anyway, just your mind running away on you. Let it go, remember not the girl whom you cannot see because she does not exist. Instead, focus on the beauty who lay there beside you.

So I turned to the space beside me that held her…only to find the lady not there.

But where did she go, and why? I put a hand on the empty space, cold. I lingered over the memory, letting it take me. She had left some time ago.

I guess she just had some place she needed to be. I pulled myself out of bed and grabbed the pants that still hung around my ankles. I would just have to catch up with her later.

As I stood up, I quickly discovered my head to be pounding, and with a flash of malt beer and pipe weed, the recollections of the previous night bowled through my skull. My second hangover is as many days.

I shuffled over to the closet, and, seeing a pile of shirts cast off their hangers and onto the floor, memories of the erotic endeavours traded the pain momentarily aside for a smile.

I grabbed one of the few still hanging shirts available to me, a long-sleeved burgundy pull-over. It had a nice look, I thought, as I inspected myself in the mirror. I couldn't say the same for the pale face looking back at me.

"Gama Mao," I spoke aloud as I tried to get the knots out of my matted hair. Fussing only seemed to make matters worse and helped increase the throbbing sensation in my head.

It was then by chance that I caught from out the corner of my peripheral something falling, or moreover floating toward the ground. It was there by the window that I'd seen it drop, spiralling down towards the floor. I walked over to where it landed and knelt down, picking up the article in my hand, a solitary crow's feather.

I immediately looked up and found above me, hanging in the window, the dreamcatcher.

Funny, I had all but forgotten it up to that point. Now thanks to recent events, I was reminded of the story that Mona had told me. *Could it be that...? Nah, ridiculous to think.*

I stood level with it and reached out a hand to inspect.

Flash of white light across the eyes, burning and blinding them. I stumbled, as through the room I wandered in this state of intense unsteadiness. Reaching out I looked for something, anything to hold onto.

At once I hit what I believed to be the table, and only because it was the closest thing to my proximity.

Grab hold of it!

Anchoring myself there, my eyes began to focus…onto the blank sheet of paper placed out before me, and on the pen—in my hand? For it seemed I'd lost all control of my body as I watched in horror as my hand began to drag itself across the page. I wrote lines of nonsense words, of what I do not know. Was it even legible? It was a language I could not place.

And like that, I was back in control. I threw the pen down and ran for the door, wanting to be anywhere but in that room. As I grabbed the knob, however, I stopped. I waited. I felt compelled to stay.

I turned back towards the table, towards the paper and its indecipherable scrawl—scrawl written by my own hand. *Madness… Now pick up the parchment, fold it up, put it into your pocket.* And I did, shaking uncontrollably.

I then exited the room with one thing on my mind: Mona. *Got to go find Mona, get some answers, make some sense of this.* It was all too crazy to think about.

In the hall I could hear the sound of voices coming from the parlour. My only hope was that one of them might be the woman I pursued. I entered, and the light that shone down before me by the canopy glass said it was now late morning. There, a familiar face sat on the V-shaped couch.

"Ah! You've come about at long last. Is good to see 'ou again, mon ami. You 'ad a bon nuit, oui?"

I took a deep breath and tried to forget my anxiety.

"Yes, Gany. It was a night like no other." *Should I tell him what just happened, not believing it myself? No, he would think me mad.*

"And 'ou are all right, mon cher?" he asked.

"Yes, Gany, I'm fine. Just didn't sleep well is all."

I steered my gaze towards the sound projecting from out the wall stationed above the fireplace mantle, and to where a picture was being cast upon the screen. It had been the sounds that I'd been hearing when standing in the hall. Still weird to see it there, without signal scramble. The television screen showed an older gentleman sitting at a desk. I was pretty sure it was the news, as what else could it be? He reported on a landslide in Peru burying a suspected three thousand people. *Monstrous.*

"Not sleep well? I see, and 'ou are sure that is all? You look a slight out of sorts."

I might say the same about him, dressed in the same attire from the night past. Had the man slept at all?

"I'm sure, Gany. Just a slight more to drink than I should have, I guess." I tried hard to dismiss my obvious shakiness and take my hand away from my pocket. "Gany, what is it you're watching?"

"Why, is the tele-vision, Ambrosia. Is, how you say, a transmitter of signals that—"

"No, Gany, I know what it is." Just because I could never before be in the room without the picture scrambling didn't mean I did not know what it was. "What I meant was, what's on?"

"Oh, is the news, of course. Reports of current events, ah, 'ou know, happenings around the globe and such."

"Of course." I turned my attention back to the man onscreen, glad to have this break in conversation.

The man's report had changed to that of another natural disaster, this time a flash flood running through the west coast of South America.

"Hmmm, seems sad."

"Ah, oui, monsieur. Sad indeed."

I steered my eyes away from the brutal images playing out before me. "Gany, you haven't seen Mona or Star this morning, have you?"

"Ah, non. Non…I 'ave not yet seen the lady Star come in, and—"

Hold up a minute. "Wait, what do you mean come in?"

"Oui, she az not returned since she left sometime in the middle of the last night's passing...but 'ou do not know she left?" he asked, finally clueing in on my lack of following. "Je m'excuse mon ami. I was unaware."

"That's fine, Gany." It wasn't, and I was a little more than blown away by the news. "Just when was this? Do you know where she went?" Or why?"

"She a left shortly following closing. Do I know where she is gone, you ask? Pardonnez moi, but Star never tells where she is going."

"Oh." I was a little crushed knowing she must have left no sooner than my having passed into sleep's realm. I told myself there must be a reason.

"As for Mona, mon frère, alas but I am afraid you 'ave gone and missed her too."

"What? Really?" Couldn't catch a break.

"I am afraid so."

"Well, where'd she go?" I demanded.

"To the safe house, but of course."

"I'm sorry, safe house?" The man was just full of information that I knew nothing of.

"Ah, 'ou will see, 'ou will see. All in good time," he said quickly, as though tired of all the questions. "Now if you please, I must hear this."

I watched as Gany then pointed the remote control towards the television, causing an increase in volume. I at once was steered back towards the news anchorman in his reporting:

"Now in local news, we turn you over to on-scene correspondent, Cyntia Medea."

The screen then left the newsroom behind, switching to a shot of a city street and a woman with long blonde hair posed in front of buildings in a red skirt suit. Behind her a sign read Alcazar Cabaret.

> "Thank you, Tom. It was here, at the Alcazar Cabaret, an all-night dance club located on Lesser Water Street, that this sad tragedy occurred. This morning, at approximately 3:33 AM, twenty-one

year old Allen Rodrowski, son to wealthy industrialist Greg Rodrowski, was sent to Hartland General Hospital after collapsing. On arrival there, he was said to be in critical condition, and was later pronounced dead. Today, family and friends seek to understand the reasons behind Allen's death. No family member was available for comment, but a source close to the family was quoted as saying they are devastated. Much at this time still remains unknown about what caused this young person's demise. At this point, officials aren't saying whether foul play is suspected. Police are looking for anyone with information pertaining to these events to contact them at 555-0956. Greg Rodrowski's only child, Allen, was heir to the Rodrowski fortune. We will stay with this story as further developments arise.
Cyntia Medea,
Channel Eight News."

The woman finished her report with a small wink of her eye as the screen returned to the anchor.

Gany again pointed the controller to the screen. It went black.

"Grizzly," I said. It was the only word I could come up with to describe the events. I felt horrible for the poor individual, and my stomach felt like it was tied up in knots. Worse though, was that someone felt the need to report on such a tragedy. I was sure the family would have preferred not to have had their personal matters of grave misfortune disclosed to the public so soon after the fact. And so coldly, like it was nothing to say. I was beginning to see why my Mothers had always said I was better off not seeing such things.

"Is a tragedy, no doubt," Gany said, saddened by the news.

"And this happened here, in the city? Is this a usual occurrence?"

"Ah…" Gany removed his hat and rubbed the hair beneath before readjusting it firmly back into position. "The city nightlife, it can be dangerous at times. Is not something I enjoy seeing either, Ambrosia. Alcazar Cabaret is place not unlike that of the Nebula. We are a close-knit fabric, and when thread gets pulled, we are all quick to unravel. The children of the evening tide need not wash across shore by morning's rise." Gany met my gaze with sorrow in his eyes.

"And so you believe foul play is suspect?" After everything I had read about the horrors of modern civilization, still it was a bolt from the blue when first exposed to such cold reality.

"No idea," he said. "Listen, Ambrosia, I 'ave got some things to do, but why don't 'ou go get something to eat. Summer, she made breakfast before setting out."

Summer gone, too? Had I managed to miss everyone? Dear Summer—I had not thought of her since our departure the night before. I only hoped she had made out all right after we had parted ways. Not like she wanted to be there anyway, not like Star. *Oh, Star, where have you gone!*

"Then, once you've 'ad the chance to clean up a little, I will take 'ou out, show 'ou around some while on way to the safe house."

And so inevitably to Mona.

"But now I must be off. See 'ou in little less than an hour." He got up off the couch and, giving a touch to the brim of his cap, exited the room.

Alone again and with my mind swimming, I made my way towards the kitchen as my thoughts turned to the girl and her sister with whom I had laid in the dark hours before dawn.

I, however, never made it to the kitchen, as on first entering the dining area and the glow off its canopy light, I found there on tabletop a place already set out for me. A folded sign atop the plate had on it my name, and with a few water spots appearing next to. Beside the plate a vase stood with a solitary lotus flower inside, its sweet fragrance filling me with the divine notion of another place, one I'd left behind to pursue the chance at a better life…

A series of concave bowls of various sizes were stationed in front of the plate and silverware, each with a cover placed upon it. I took my seat before the meal that presented itself, and removing the lid off the first bowl was met with the sights of a delectable-looking omelette. I took in a whiff and immediately my glands began to salivate. So suddenly I was transported back to my home and memories of mornings, of fetching fresh eggs from our chickens. Putting the omelette on my plate, I began to peruse the other bowls. There was fresh fruit, steamed vegetables, and hash browns coated with shredded fermented cabbage.

Feverish with hunger, I started in and immediately noticed something going on with the eggs, they were not like what I was used to. Not bad per say...just different. The fruit was fresh, a feast of melons and berries. The hash browns too had a nice spice to them. Yes, a lot of heart went into this meal. Summer outdid herself, and for that deserved my thanks a thousand fold.

I'd do just that, just as soon as I saw her. Until then the best I could do was clean up after myself. But first nature called, and perhaps a wash, too. There was no denying it; a questionable tang had risen from me.

I headed back down the hall, past the living room en route to the lavatory. On the way, I saw a face I knew but had not yet had the chance to engage. She met me halfway down the hall, dressed in a green pantsuit and a white T-shirt with polished shoes. She seemed ever as stylish as during the evening past, her dark hair streaming past her shoulders, and with a complexion as innocent as first light cast down about the unmarked clearing. Simply sensational was she to take in.

"You're the girl from the bar last night, right?" I asked.

"Oh, yes, I am. Hello." She seemed a bit shy, but her smile told me to continue.

"And you live here?"

"Yes, I do."

"Well, it's nice to meet you. I'm Ambrosia, and I guess I live here now too. So, good."

"Yes, it is," she answered, obviously nervous. Her dark brown eyes fluttered like a butterfly's wings.

"It is…and you are?" She wasn't giving me much.

"Oh, sorry, I'm Heze," she said.

"Well, Heze, happy to make your acquaintance."

This was followed by a short, awkward embrace as we each nervously stepped first to the same side and then to the other before finally coming together with kisses on cheeks before stepping back.

So it was time for someone to talk again.

"So yeah…Heze, it's good to finally have the chance to greet you." Had I already said that? I was finding it hard to come up with things to say.

"Yes, I've been wanting to meet you also. You are liking your stay so far then?"

So she knew of me, and still she spoke shyly. I suppose it didn't help that I was acting awkwardly also.

"Yes, I am. Enjoying myself, that is." Aside from the bad dreams. "Thanks."

I watched the extent of her features to spot small gestures that may give away something about the creature before me. Heze had large, soulful brown eyes and a warm, innocent smile. It was an expression that went perfectly with the rest of her rather plentiful attributes, registering one with the feeling of pure virtue as fresh and untried as the fall of a virgin snow laid bare over a pristine pasture. That, with her highlights hinting a shine off her straight, dark, shoulder-length hair was enough to curve the straightest arrow; yet all I wanted to do was shelter in the bud to see it flower.

"Oh, and you? Are you, doing well?" I at last came back, really not knowing where else to go.

"I am, doing well…thank you." She spoke with such a sensitive tone it made me smile.

A brief passing of silence then followed. I, who might have liked to converse longer, was reminded of my reason for being there—relieving the surmounting pressure placed upon my kidneys.

Having to move this train along I broke back in, trying desperately to get things back on track. "So, yeah, it's been great running into you."

"Yes, it has."

"And I hope we get another chance to talk really soon."

"I hope so, too. That is, if you want to, if you have time..."

"To get better acquainted? I'd like that. Soon then." I really needed to go.

"Yes, soon."

With that I made my move to slide past her on a mad dash for the throne. With teeth swimming I made hard for the bathroom, tugging at the zipper that still managed to perplex me. Getting my pants undone, into the room I ventured forth and let loose…all the while unknowing that the area was already preoccupied.

"Hello, Ambrosia. How are you this fine morning?" A voice grabbed me, so much so that I was caused to jolt.

I gave a quick semi-turn to face the sound, and there she was, her legs crossed as seated upon the bathroom counter. A soft yellow Lycra dress flowed from her left shoulder down to the knee. "My, but I hope you were done."

"Uh, yeah, thanks," I said, zipping up.

"Amply so."

"Uh…Gliese, what are you doing in here?"

"Me? Well…" She got off the counter, carrying in her hand a green cloth. "I do so often frequent this room. I enjoy it. The atmosphere is welcoming." Her expression and the look of her wide eyes were enough to hypnotize a person.

She then proceeded to sit on the floor, there in the middle of the room. She laid the cloth of sea green out in front her, a series of stone runes in its blanket.

"And last night, you had an enjoyable experience?" she asked whilst arranging the stones in a line.

I decided to humour her. "I did. It was…beyond enjoyable."

"Yes, everything went according to plan. I only wish Mona could have been there to see it."

"I'm sorry, what?"

"Trials of a bedtime mosaic." She stopped there, as though there were no need for further explanation. She continued to look down at the runes.

"Uh, could you maybe explain that further, please?"

"That's what she called it. I speak of course of those events of the last evening past. They were the result of Mona's desire for a diverse decor of ardent concupiscence. As you are very well aware of, she is linked to the Goddess, and it is believed that by holding a celebration of sex and the fortification of souls, you would be made to feel more welcome into this new extension of home. And so came the trials of a bedtime mosaic." She rattled off the words as if by an eloquent dream.

"She planned it that way…?" So it had been all for me? Such an extravagant endeavour for undertaking, I was overwhelmed by the notion.

"So you're telling me everything that went on last night, the get-ups and the people, the silken lingerie, all of it was done for my benefit?"

"The exposition of the skin, yes, it is something of a differing turn of events from the usual sort of club behaviour. Not that we wouldn't like to, but societal norms being what they are." She paused to look over the runes. "We do, however, like to bend the rules on occasion," she said, a slight smile on her face.

"Humph." So Mona knew all along what I was being led into, yet she said nay a word. I suppose it was to be a surprise. Yet after our discourse concerning my need to renounce the faith long instilled in me, I couldn't help wondering why she had not mentioned her plans for the night. I also couldn't help wondering why she had made such a fuss about Summer wearing that dress. Although, I suppose, the night was as much for her as it was for me, for her and Star's birthday.

"Like your runes to be read to you, would you then?" Gliese's dreamscape voice pushed its way through the menagerie of contemplations swimming through my head, thus bringing me out of my cranial drift.

"Uh, sorry?"

"It's just, you're still here. Thought you might be intrigued about the runes, what it is they hold in store for you, for your future."

Well of course I'm still here, we were talking. Barking mad, this one.

"Um, that's all right. You know what, yeah, I'm good." I really did not want to get into the politics of make-believe with her. I had already had my fair share of nonsense rune readings in my time. Dear Mother Linnea, sacred caster of stones, she used to have me ask her all sort of nonsense questions. The arrangement of certain patterns that specific rocks fell into supposedly were meant to show me insight into my own life. Trouble was, I never had anything worth asking. It didn't stop her from making me participate, no less handing me some abstruse, incomprehensible statement to do with providence and the like. I was sure this would be no different.

"Come, sit down." She wasn't about to let me go so readily.

I gazed up to the ray from the stained glass atop me. The sun was long in the east.

No use arguing the matter, lest I come across as being disrespectful. Sauntering over to the yellow dress and green cloth laid out on the linoleum, I sat down, maybe a bit too fast for my liking. Hard rush of blood to the head. *Okay, overshadowing hangover still in full effect; err on the side of caution with all sudden downward movements.* I took to rubbing my temples.

"If you wanted something to speed up the process of solving present vexations, may I then be of some assistance?" Gliese said, watching me, reaching into her cleavage (really, where else was she going to hold it to her body?) and handing me a small vial filled with a kind of dark potion.

"What is this?" I asked as I uncapped the lid, taking a whiff of the contents within. An aroma of citrus and spearmint, among others.

"Completely natural herbal remedy," she said.

I looked at the vial in my hand. "And you happened to be carrying it on you why?"

"An after evening pill, I thought maybe you could use it, following last night's festivities."

"You'd be right." I guess she knew better than any on just how much alcohol I'd consumed. Again I studied the vial held in my grasp and thought what could it hurt? I downed it all. The taste was much like that of its aroma and made a tingle on the center of my tongue, almost numbing.

"So, a reading then?" Gliese wasted no time in reengaging me.

What could I say? "Knock yourself out."

"Wonderful." She gathered up the runes, shaking them between her hands. "Now Ambrosia, what is it you desire to know most?"

I knew before the words left my mouth. "I desire to know…"

"There is no need for troubling me with such details, Ambrosia. Just focus on the thought, let it breathe out from within you…"

Strange, I had not ever done it like that before. I rather liked it.

"You have it?"

"Yes, I do."

"All right then."

She let go of the stones, so falling they hit along the cloth, cast about in all direction. When examining the pattern that did emerge, the way the runes fell they took on a kind of zigzag design, though loosely based. They almost seemed to resemble the makings of a W, with the central peak taking on a triangular, arrowhead appearance.

"Oh, there is much to see here, much to see indeed," Gliese said as she searched over the stones. But if what she saw there excited her in any minute way, I wasn't able to tell.

She spent the next few moments examining the stones while I waited for her to continue. Until at last I could wait no longer. "Well, out with it then."

Gliese looked up straight into my eyes, those oddly drawn hazel bulbs she wore, transfixing as ever. "The road you travel on is a dark and misbegotten path."

She pointed to the arrowhead. "Here at the center, sign of the Sun represents you."

She then pointed to the right outer line in the pattern. "Symbol of need, you journey upon its wiles, unbeknownst of the tragedy that awaits you if you do not stray from its keep."

She then moved a finger to the other branching line. "Here we find another path, one you've touched but not pursued. This road is similar to its other, in that it's conflicted, difficult to travel, and can only lead to nowhere. Each these paths you are linked by, and each onto its other, yet by taking either one you will be driven farther from its adjoining path." Gliese pointed again to the centre arrow.

I was impressed by the complexity of the riddle she spat out at me, not to mention a little confused. "So…I cannot risk either one path?"

Gliese nodded as she looked down on the runes.

"Only by a balance of both sides may you bridge a connection to the whole and bring about a lost harmony." She then returned eye contact. "Does this help answer your question?"

"Oh yes, helps a lot." Even more unintelligible than what I was used to, more broken and so unsettling.

I wasn't sure why it piqued me so. I had only asked about Star's true feelings towards me. Had I any faith in the runes themselves I probably would have asked about the sudden seizure episode I'd just experienced following the dream…that I had somehow managed to put aside until just that point in time of remembering? True, it had left my mind for the most part since the moment I'd left Gany to take a seat at the breakfast table. *Guess a good meal will do that.* Nice to escape, too, if only for a short while.

"Understand that much of what the runes tell us often come as shrouded in mystery, only to be deciphered in time," Gliese told me, as though sensing my quick dismissal of her comments. She then gathered up the stones, bundled them in the cloth, and stood.

"So, how's the head?"

"It's...good?" I hadn't even noticed, but I no more had the sting driving its way through my temples as I rose up from my seated position.

"We are happy then?"

"Uh…sure." Though I was anything from content, now returned to the catacombs of my own personal vexations.

"Well, think I will be taking my leave then."

"Really…?" I said, somewhat surprised of her decision to go and offer me some much needed privacy, if only to clear a restless mind. Good thing too. I had there, for a moment, actually contemplated revealing the things going on in my own head, and had she not been about to leave I very well might have. But again I couldn't do that, not to someone I'd barely just met. Yes, better to not have anyone else think me crazy just yet. "Things to do? I understand."

"No, but I imagine you do."

I was alarmed at her words, as to what she could possibly mean by them, when she then moved in close to me and whispered, "A shower would be to your best benefit, to cleanse body and mind."

"Oh."

Following these words, Gliese made for the south exit, saying, "I bid to you fine fondness of day, Ambrosia."

Gone, finally. I was alone at last with just my thoughts, thoughts that indeed needed to be cleansed. Not wanting to be disturbed I closed both bathroom doors, and decided to take the lady's advice.

I stripped off all my clothes and jumped in between the glass panels of the shower stall. Hot water found me and, standing there, letting it wash over my body, feeling the heat upon my head that spread out along my shoulders, I couldn't help but think again of Star. Maybe it was due to the sensation of scratch marks running down my back. It was a gentle reminder of the perfect night, and of the perfect woman for whom I shared it with.

These thoughts then led to other events that transpired following our passion-filled rendezvous. I became stuck on the images that came to me during a state of steady unconsciousness, playing them out over and over again in my mind: a dark place, familiar somehow; another felt there beside me, a connection; a voice on the air, calling; someone, or something, beckoning me that I come forward. What was it being said?

"Natarehsla Mihtrasem."

I almost fell out of the stall. The words, they were right at my ear, like someone had been right there beside me. I shut the water off and opened the glass panel door. Looking around, I took a pass over the entire area, but nothing, no one was there.

"Hello?" I called out just to make sure but got nothing in response. My thoughts swimming, I was left to wonder, could it be just all in my mind? I had been trying to remember my dream, so it wasn't unlikely that the experience be recreated, a piece of my unconscious sneaking up to the surface. *But it felt so real...*

I decided not to go back in, but instead towelled off and clothed myself quickly, doing what I could to put what had just happened, and the dream itself, into the farthest recesses of my cerebral cortex. Allowing no time for anything else, I hastened to leave the lavatory behind me, but not before taking one last glance back on the room as I left it. Nothing, of course, as I knew there would be, just the awareness of a cold chill running up the root of my spine.

Trying hard not to think, I decided to wait out whatever time I had left back in my room. I was turning the handle of my door when suddenly and from out of nowhere Gany appeared, startling me.

"Pardon moi, mon ami, it was never my intent to scare." He wore a blue blazer, blue-grey pants, and charcoal fedora—very sharp.

"It's fine, Gany. Really."

"Ah, bien. So, Ambrosia, ready for the big city?"

I let go of the knob. "Sure." Anything to get me out of the house, put my mind on other things. Like finding Mona…and who knew, maybe by chance I'd even run into Star somewhere along the way.

Grabbing a coat on Gany's advice, we then travelled downstairs to make our way for the outside. This, of course, meant first crossing down through club space.

It was surreal to see it there in the daylight, even with the semi-darkness of blinds half pulled down over the bay windows. To think that only hours ago the room was filled with bodies, unfixed on the dance floor, clinging together as they rallied to the music. You could almost feel the aftershock of feet reverberating off those floor panels.

Looking to the corner at the south side of the house was a darkness residing there still, as it had been when last we journeyed through its shadow. So I hadn't imagined it. Honestly, it was hard to tell what was real anymore, though of the events passing through the last hours, the journey into the underground foundations by a blackened gate seemed to be the most concrete.

Yet did my eyes deceive me, or had I not seen, on closer approach, what seemed to resemble more that of a permanent corner listed behind the penumbra? I ventured still closer to further inspect.

As I approached my fears only became further realized, for it was unmistakably apparent to me that I had indeed not been seeing things. So it was that I could not stop myself from reaching out for reassurance, allowing for a hand to hit up against the wall.

I knew then that it was true, and so I subsequently turned towards Gany with panic.

"What is this!?" *Does nothing make sense anymore?*

"What is what, monsieur?" he coolly answered back.

"Don't give me that, you know what!" When I received no response, I continued. "This wall! What is it doing here?"

"Wall…? I am not sure that I follow," he responded, a look of general confusion on the face.

Does he really not know?

"Last night, here in this dark corner, there revealed a hidden passage…and the passage, it led out to a stairway going down below house foundations." Even I thought it sounded crazy when hearing it come out of my own mouth.

Gany gave a surprised snort as he walked closer towards me. "A hidden passage…? This wall?" he said, putting a hand on it. "I see…"

"Don't talk to me like I'm crazy. I know what I saw." I was starting to get more than a little upset.

"And are you sure 'ou saw what you think 'ou saw?"

"It was you who took me there, you who insisted I go!" I yelled back.

"And I suppose it was I who walked through walls also?"

"Yes! In a manner of speaking."

"Did I now?" he joked, laughing at my pain.

"I know what I saw! What I experienced." But I didn't know, not anymore, what was real and what was merely offset by delirium. I felt I was walking a very fine tightrope, the ground having already given way beneath me, my fragile world fallen into shadow, shattered by a crumbled sense of false reality. This final instance proved it—I didn't know what was sane anymore. It all happened so fast…

"Ambrosia, 'ou didn't by chance share in anything with mademoiselle Mona leading up to our experience of night's past?" Gany calmly questioned at the sight of my little breakdown.

"Why, yes, I did. However did you know that?" I asked, putting my focus squarely on him.

"It wasn't a clouded liqueur she served up in a wine glass?"

"Yes, yes it was!" Now I was really paying attention.

"Ah, 'ou see then."

"See what?" I was more lost than ever.

"Why, the things you're describing, mon ami. They sound as though they might have had some help coming about is all."

I pieced my thoughts together. "You mean to say the things I saw were naught but hallucinations of the mind brought on by some mystery beverage I had taken? That my perception of reality was not more than a twisted sensory derailment of chemically altered proportions?"

Gany only answered by a shrug of his shoulders, leaning up against the wall with his arms crossed.

I was taken aback. "Gany, if this is true then I was drugged unknowingly…and it was Mona herself who allowed for it to happen!"

"But you did take it willingly?" Gany asked.

"Well, yes…"

"After not knowing what it was?"

"She never told me it had hallucinatory effects!"

"Did 'ou ask?" he parried by a composed measure.

"Well, not specifically, no, but…"

"Then there is nothing left to argue," he said, cutting me off.

I gave an exasperated sigh but decided to let it go. I already had enough anxiety without adding this to the mix. "So does Mona offer this kind of thing to all new house guests?"

He leaned in closer to me. "Only the ones she really likes." Then, returning to his position, "Ah, mademoiselle Mona, she likes to entertain."

"So it was all in my head, everything…" I was half-glad I hadn't gone into explaining the underground coliseum to any great detail.

"You tell me, cher. We were here last night," Gany said, gesturing to the tables before us. "But did we move beyond this corner?"

"No," I answered for him—still, it was hard to believe. It all seemed so real…but in a way it was a relief to know I wasn't going crazy.

"Just still can't believe she would do that…"

"She is just trying to open your eyes, mon ami."

"Yes, and broaden my mind. I understand. She definitely put a bend to my reality, that's for sure."

"At least she did not break it," he joked. "And 'ou enjoyed the experience, no?"

"Well, I guess," I said when suddenly I started to wonder what other things may have been hallucinated. Had Star really been there at all?

"Gany, last night, what do you remember of the stairwell?"

He blushed a little. "Oh, yes, well… I hope we did no startle 'ou two."

"But it did happen, and Star was there?"

" Of course, monsieur." He looked at me as though I had two heads, like it was such an outrageous thing to ponder.

"All right, good." That was all I needed to hear.

"Not everything is a dream, cher…come, we 'ave been here I think for long enough, and we should probably be off," he said as we both turned to go.

As we made our way through, I continued to wonder if the elixir hadn't perhaps left any minor residual effects, ones that may have transferred through to morning. So it was that I could not stop from asking as we approached the main doors.

"Gany, these hallucinatory states, how long do they usually last? I mean, have you ever heard of someone still being affected for hours after the fact even into the next day by something they've taken?"

He paused for a second to look at me, his hand on the door handle. "Garcon, are you no feeling okay?

"Me? Why yes, of course," I said back, maybe a tad too quickly. "I was just wondering is all."

"Well, is hard thing to say, Ambrosia. I am not sure I can give 'ou a proper answer."

"Oh, I see."

Gany then pulled back the door to expose the outside. What I'm saying is: how long these lingering effects of delirium last may all depend on the person affected."

"So it is possible?"

"Anything is possible, mon ami, 'ou only need believe." He smiled and gestured me ahead. "After you."

Exiting, I was surprised to find that the sky above our heads was starting to cast over. "That was fast."

"Hmmm...?"

"Oh, just the sky, not too long ago it appeared spotless when looking out my room window, and now…" A chill overtook me as I remembered that morning, and I tried to let go my demons.

"A change to the weather—happens on a whim around these parts." Gany snapped his fingers. "Just like dat."

We made our way to the garage, and when getting to the car Gany stopped and turned to me. "I think...why do you not drive?" he said, tossing me the keys.

"Me…? But I can't, I mean, I don't know how is all," I proclaimed as I caught them, standing in awe of his proposal.

"No better time to learn, mon frère."

"Seriously?" I asked, looking on the Porsche with hungry eyes.

"Is calling your name, I see the fever growing there in your eyes. You love it. Who am I to take such things away, eh?" Gany smiled, and with a slight nod of encouragement gave me the go ahead.

Wasting no time, I at once made for the driver's side door. I got in and put the key to the ignition as I saw Mona had, excitement all the while rushing through my veins like burning gasoline. Turning her over, Lenore then lit up. Feeling her start to run, it had an almost dreamlike effect on me. It was more than I could have imagined, being there in the driver's seat.

Gany, who had gotten in on the passenger side, looked at me with his hand on the shifter. "Think you can handle a stick?"

"I think so." Or so I hoped, having invested much of my free time (and there was a lot of it) imagining just such a scenario, preparing for the chance should it ever find me. I had studied the mechanics and had read enough about how these things worked to feel more than able behind the wheel. Also, having watched Mona helped, and what she was doing really didn't look all that complicated.

"Then mon ami, when 'ou are ready, put it in the reverse."

Before I knew what was happening I found myself going through the motions. Looking behind me, I pulled out of the garage and onto the street, all without a hitch. It was the most amazing feeling, those wheels turning round, treading on the concrete beneath us. To know I made that happen…

"So where are we off to then?" I asked, looking to the man beside me.

"I will guide 'ou. To the end of street. When you get there take us left."

"All right." I put the car in gear, hit the gas, and…stalled it.

"Well, can't get it right every time," I said, a little embarrassed, and glad there was no one else on the road to see my mistake.

"Try again. This time ease off the clutch." He seemed understanding.

"Right."

Again I started her up, and this time took things slower. Before I knew it, we were off and headed for the end of the street. From there I proceeded to turn left.

"Look out!" I heard his voice yell beside me, warning me of a car fast approaching from the alternate direction. As I realized we had entered into the wrong lane, I tried to swerve, to stomp down on the pedal and propel us in an alternative direction, but it was already too late. As everything became a blur, I prepared for the worst. We somehow, someway averted tragedy. It was however, due to the other vehicle swinging around us and across the center line. No time for loosening up, by a screech of brakes a second car aimed to stop from coming at me. Panicking, I swerved and sent us barrelling towards a line of pedestrians who scattered along the sidewalk. I again gripped the wheel, and steered hard away, sending us back into heavy traffic. Horns blew from all direction as I tried desperately to gain control, and my feet pushed on whatever pedal they could find as I wrestled the wheel in a vague attempt to put us straight again. It was to no avail, for Lenore was made to fish tail as everyone in her path did what they could to get out of the line of fire.

It was then that it happened, when a truck twice our size, unable to steer clear of the hazard, put itself on a collision course with our front end. I tried to move, to get out from under the impending millstone, but it was just too late. Realizing there was nothing left to be done, I braced for the inevitable assault with eyes closed.

A violent jolt propelled out over the car, and I felt the steering wheel jerk to the right as we were sent flying. Then nothing. Everything came to a standstill. Yet there was no crash, no sound of twisting metal or sudden jarring.

Opening my eyes, I saw that we were no longer on the road. Instead we had landed somewhere back on the sidewalk, as watchful onlookers stood on either side of us. Further down the street the truck remained, stopped and unscathed.

"I don't understand. What happened? We didn't crash. Why didn't we crash!?"

Gany let out a heavy sigh, putting the car in park. "It is enough that we did not. You can take your foot off the brake now, mon ami."

I did my best to ease up.

"I should mention that when turning, do gear down, come to a full and complete stop if 'ou would, and do look both ways for oncoming traffic before proceeding. Oh, and please do try to keep on the right 'and side of the road, s'il vous plaît."

I couldn't help but continue to look at the road behind us. "Gany, I don't understand. If we didn't hit, how did we get over here?"

"I took the liberty, and the wheel. You did not see?"

"No, no I didn't. Guess I freaked and just, you know, seized up." I said, prying my hands from off the wheel, feeling embarrassed and a little ashamed in knowing I really could have hurt someone.

"Eyes always on the road, mon frère."

"Yeah…"

"Now, I believe it may be in best interest to be leaving here. Shall we try again, no?"

"Wait, you want me to try this again?" I looked him square in the eye with awe.

"Of course, best to get back on the horse, no? Now, let's be off." He pointed at the road ahead.

A bit shaken still, but ever eager to prove myself and get back in the saddle, I returned my hands to the wheel. As luck would have it, no vehicles seemed to be coming in our direction just then. I wish I could have said the same for the people amassed on the sidewalk. The audience only added to my sense of nervousness.

"Just put them out of your mind."

I took in a deep breath, put the car in gear, and came out onto the road.

"Gany, this little ordeal isn't going to cause any trouble for us, is it?" I asked as carefully pulling away from the scene.

"I do not think so." He sounded confident.

"Really?"

"The car, she is recognizable, but no crime was committed; no 'arm came to anyone. If it is the police 'ou are concerned about, trust me when I say they 'ave more important things to worry about than giving pursuit to the near accident of a negligent driver. Is much crime out there that would better deserve their time."

"All right then," I said back, wanting to believe him but still feeling a bit jittery all the same.

"Now if 'ou would take the next left. And this time…"

"Do gear down, come to a complete stop, and check both ways before proceeding. Yeah, got it."

"Oui. And do use turning signal also. Is located to the left, above wheel."

"Sure thing," I said, going through the motions and making a clean go of it as I successfully pulled out onto another crowded street and only after the road was clear.

"Bien. Now at lights ahead, stop on red, and green means go. Another left to the main road. Heavy traffic, take care to keep space between vehicles."

"You mean this isn't heavy traffic?" I asked him as I looked around at the placement of vehicles and people in the general area.

"Oh, garçon, this is minor," he said, and I thought I heard him give a slight scoff. "Now, allow me to show 'ou a few sights before coming to our destination.

"Agreed, as long as it's along our route and doesn't take too long." Not that I didn't want to see the city, but we had people we needed to find. I also felt the need to keep my first driving lesson a short one.

"Relax mon ami, is on way."

"Good, just point me in the right direction then," I said, stopping on the red.

"Of course, monsieur. On green then, take us right."

Together we travelled the city, and I managed to impress myself by making only a few more minor errors of miscalculation along the rest of the journey. Insignificant things like the failing to use my signal light, not coming to a full and complete stop, running a red light or two…nothing too major, at least not like before.

Gany was true to his word, showing me some of the metropolis' major sights as we travelled along its roads. I saw the clock tower that survived the Hartland Devastation of 1913. Gany explained that on one grave December morn, two ships, one an Italian vessel carrying munitions supplies, the other a relief supply ship hailing from Spain, collided within the harbour waters. On impact, the Italian vessel at once caught fire, and the explosion that soon followed registered a blow that on impact destroyed more than two square miles of the region. The blast killed more than two thousand people and sacked the city area's infrastructure. The ship's anchor itself was found no less than two and a half miles away from where the explosion took place. Yet the clock tower, made of brick and styled after Georgian architecture, characteristic of its well-balanced and proportioned design, was made to sustain through the force of destruction.

All, that is, but the mechanism itself, for intact though it was, the clock stopped the minute the blast went off. Never since that time did its arms turn again, left as a mark of remembrance for those who perished in the tragedy, and of a city that in a time of turmoil prevailed against odds most overwhelming. Gany called it a minute paralyzed in the standstill of the mind.

Stationed behind the clock tower and at the height of the metropolis stood Bastion Hill, a vast dominion complete with fortified walls covering its peak. This fortress, or citadel, finished around the mid-nineteenth century and beginning some thirty years prior, held to the shape of a star and supported an ample courtyard within, and a commanding view of the harbour below. Bastion Hill, the prime reason for British interest in the land in 1749 (aside from the behemoth harbour itself, one of the largest natural anchorages in the world), was chosen for its height and reach over the mouth of the harbour. It made for quite an attractive sight, from a defensive standpoint. While in times past the fortress was once used for military purposes, housing an immense supply of artillery within its walls and hidden mostly beneath ground, at present day it held the need for no such purpose and functioned as more of a main historic site to the metropolis. Though it should be mentioned that on the high noon of each day, a tremendous clamour arose from atop the hill, the tremulous boom of cannon fire denoting the role played by the citadel in shaping the city—"Through issue of its ceremonial thundering bellow, we are made to remember."

Further on to the city's south end was a beautiful landscape. Gany called it "Point Park Place". An amply forested area, and in centuries previous, a peninsula that held British armoury outposts. Originally it was intended to provide fortification (not unlike Bastion Hill) against any oncoming threat of enemy ship appearing in the waters. Its present use, however, was as a recreational land site for public use, including a host of walking trails, points for ocean viewing, and Shakespearian theatre performances throughout the day along the various areas of the forest grounds.

Among other historically relevant facts Gany sought fit to point out—and one that really stuck out in my mind—was a stone effect on the beachfront that led into forest dwelling. It was at one time a place for the execution of criminals, left to hang on a gibbet. Deeper within the forest was Corsica Tower, a nineteenth-century structure built by (yet again) the British Empire[v] during the Napoleonic Wars[vi], being completed thereafter. The tower stood about forty feet high, with thick walls carved from out solid rock, held to a rounded design. With its height and concrete defensive posturing it made the perfect spot for the mounting of heavy artillery, weapons of measure placed atop the roof platform, able to access a 360-degree arc, and provide the region's people with a fitting line of protection across the bordered harbour.

Yes, it seemed the city had a vast and rich heritage to it. It was quite fascinating to discover. It was especially interesting by a military aspect, something that always fascinated me. It seemed the city had to it a keenness for the art and the language of war, like a well-played game of chess—position is everything.

Aside from those historical points of reference, there were of course other parts to the region that Gany decided to show to me. Many of them things I'd already identified on my journey into the city a day earlier, but they nevertheless managed to mesmerize and hold me still in an arresting state of awe.

I stood amazed at the buildings of glass with their imperial proportions, imposing cathedrals crowned in pointed steeples, the monumental feats of architecture cast around every street corner. It was in the roads too, grids the city was built upon, a series of ascending and descending avenues and boulevards, channels and thoroughfares, parkways and, well, you get the picture.

In addition to the traffic, a fair magnitude of persons littered the streets, going this way and that, crossing in front us, and held up amongst the many intersections we passed. Such a vast variety of groupings there were, so many shapes, sizes, colours, and garb. Such an assortment of ages and cultures all collected here in this thriving metropolis. They painted the streets, filled the parks and cafés, indiscriminately scattered over the places we passed through. Yes, the city was alive with the light and sound of life experience. I absolutely loved it.

"So, mon ami, what do you think of our little slice of outside haven, hmm?"

"It's amazing, Gany. It really, really is," I replied, my thoughts engaged on the pretty thing crossing the street to the left of me. Blonde bombshell dressed to the nines, exposing the finer things around the line of her short miniskirt. I would have liked to help her with a slip into something warmer.

"You would do better to watch the road and less the girl 'ou so readily address, or undress as the case may be." He gave another scoff. "Please, for both our sakes."

"Oh...uh, yeah," I said, coming back to earth and disengaging the attractor beam she had on me. Lucky thing too, as I looked ahead again just in time to miss an oncoming car I'd been haphazardly steering us toward. Seems I'd gone and drifted a bit into the opposing lane again. Oops. "Sorry, Gany. She just grabbed my attention is all..."

"Is all right, mon ami, trial and error."

"Guess it is..."

When at last our trip came to an end and we arrived at the safe house, Gany allowed me to back into the parking space and readjust for correctness.

The three-storey building that stood somewhere near the harbour seemed somewhat dilapidated along its outer ridges; the lengths of its walls that stretched long were graffitied with words and images along them.

So this is it, I thought. Wow, not at all what I expected.

I followed Gany through a set of metal doors and down a series of long, bland and battered hallways. Many doors were opened slightly, with the voices of individuals coming through them.

Soon we let out into a lobby area. Here I saw many youths younger than myself, and appearing in some cases greasy and rather unkempt. There were, I noticed too, some clean-cut faces, but they were outnumbered by the rest.

Then there were a few faces that seemed reminiscent of the night past—leather jackets, coloured hair, piercing rings, tattoos…and again my thoughts ran back to Star.

It was then that I noticed that where Gany was once standing there beside me, now only emptiness remained. *I wonder where he went off to?*

I did a quick inspection of the area but could not find hide nor hair of him. That's when I saw a door stationed off to the side that remained ajar, with the words "Main Office" stapled across the top of its frame.

I made my way over and was about to take a peek inside when I heard a familiar voice coming from within.

"What do you mean it's not there?" The voice was then immediately followed by a hacking cough.

"Mona," I whispered to myself.

I then heard Gany talking back to her. "I mean is not there, just gone."

"Already...what's their angle?" She sounded perplexed and more than a little stressed.

"I surely do not know."

"Know what…?" I said as I poked my head in to see a small room littered with papers tacked up over the walls. Gany stood in front of a small desk where Mona was seated, hands folded and placed on the desk. With a pair of chained glasses and her hair tied back in a knot, she looked evermore the serious one, dressed in an earth-toned blouse. She moved her gaze almost immediately towards me as I made my way into the room, closing the door behind me.

"Ah, lad! Good to see you! Come in, come in," Mona said as her hand drifted over to an ashtray smouldering with a lit cigarette. "It's nothing, really, just a little thing happening at home, nothing to get too concerned over. Worry yourself not, my young friend." She then took up the cigarette and pressed it between her lips for the long haul.

"Of course, didn't mean to pry."

"And you didn't, my boy. So, Gany here tells me you had a chance to see the town."

"Yes, there's a lot of culture here I didn't know about. It all paints an interesting picture." I looked at her and thought she seemed as though a slight paler than yesterday.

"I'm glad you think so. And how about last night, hmm? Tell me, did it meet with your expectations?"

"Uh, yeah, was an…experience. You, weren't there?"

"So sorry, my boy. I guess I was a little worse for wear following the long trip home last night. Jet lag will do that."

"Jet lag?" I had never heard the expression.

"Never mind. So what do you think? Of the place I mean."

"She is meaning the safe house, mon ami," Gany said.

"Oh…of course. It's all very…" I really wasn't sure what to say about it. "I'm sorry, but what is this place?"

"Why it's a house of refuge, son," Mona said, extinguishing her smoking gun, and placing her hands on the desk again as intertwining her fingers. "Station for the wayward soldier, sanctuary of the unsown thread, solitude's point off the road wrought with calamity's misfortune; may all your worn and weary travellers seek shelter here. Let it be that you no more tread along this barren road only."

"I see." I again turned to Gany for answers.

"Is, eh, a place where the city's less fortunate may come, those who seek shelter, a hot meal, warm clothing, the use of sanitary facilities."

"Less fortunate, you're referring to the homeless?"

"No, Ambrosia, it's for anyone down on hard times; tabernacle of the disheartened human being, vagrant voyager, or even the troubled teen as the case may be." She seemed as though to turn a gaze to Gany a moment then, and rising from the seat that held her, walked over towards me. "Does the explanation suffice, or would you prefer I take you on a more intimate interaction of these facilities?"

"Tour the grounds? Sure, Mona. I'd love nothing more." And perhaps I'd get the chance to speak with her about what happened since we last saw each other.

"Ah, good. This way then, my boy." Mona then went to the door, opening it.

"You coming?" I asked the Frenchman to my left. I was, however, secretly hoping he had other things to do.

"Gany has some things in need of attending, child. Worry not, we won't be away long. Come!" And as quickly as Mona said it, she was gone.

"You 'ad better follow too, if 'ou want not to lose 'er, monsieur." Gany said, urging me on.

"Right, well…until later then," I said, slipping out the doorway.

"Au revoir, mon ami."

I ran to catch up with Mona, who was out the lobby and halfway down the hall by then. As I went, I passed a young man who had with him a large breed of dog. The animal automatically started barking as I passed by and tried to go after me. It would have had me too, if not for the rope bound around its neck running to the man's hand. I was thankful for it.

"I think you riled up our friend there," Mona noted as I came up beside her.

"Friend? Friend is not the word I would have chosen."

"Oh? And what word would you choose to use?"

"Beast." I called it as I saw it.

"Hmm." She just smiled and looked ahead, walking. "No greater a beast than you or I, I suppose."

"Yeah…wait, what?" I couldn't fathom a relation between myself and that allegedly domesticated animal. *Seems no less wild than the sort I'm used to.*

"Friend doth not judge thee, stray from thee, and by thy side comforts be. But a beast, a beast yields to passion's keep, savage in instinct—hostility's strain is the enemy. The animal was only taking guard over his companion. Would you not do the same?"

"Instinct, eh?" I was finding it hard to follow. Was she for or against the animal, this man's best friend?

"And where did instinct lead you last night?" she asked as we began up a set of stairs to the second floor.

So that's what she was getting at. But what did she know? Just who had she been talking to?

"Last night? Last night I…"

She turned to me as we reached the summit.

"You had the dream again, didn't you?"

"Yes! But how did you know?" I was more than a little thrown by her question.

"Something unresolved usually doesn't just go away, my boy. And I could see something was vexing you. What else if not that?"

Plenty, but my Star could wait. I decided then would be the best time to show Mona the words I'd somehow written down, and so took the page from my pocket. "I…have something to show you." I handed the folded note to her, my nerves so shot I was shaking. "What do you make of it?"

She unfolded it and looked over the words.

"Ambrosia, where did this come from?"

"I wrote it, following the dream." I couldn't believe the words I was saying.

"You did...?" She gave me a raise of her eyebrow in intrigue. "And the dream, was it the same? Was there anything different about it?"

I hesitated, unsure what I should tell her. I wanted to share something, but not everything. And definitely not what happened there afterwards, the losing control. It honestly still scared the Sheol out of me.

"Yes…it was, but it wasn't. Not exactly..."

"How was it different?" she pressed.

"Only that it was more specific, I think…"

"I see…and what do you remember?"

"Not a lot. There was someone there, a girl. But…I couldn't see the face…and there was a voice, words on a dead air, but I couldn't comprehend them." I was getting frustrated just talking about it. "That's it, I guess."

"Well, that's clearer than before. The words you heard, could they be what's written here on the page? Or is this a description of the things you do remember?"

"Wouldn't know. It's in a language I don't understand."

"But…am I not to believe you wrote this on waking? If you do not understand it, mind telling me how it is that you were made to come upon the words at all?"

"I…don't know that either. They just sort of, you know, came to me." I felt sick to my stomach. Should I not tell her everything? My mind kept screaming *no.*

"And you are sure of this? This couldn't have been something your Mothers taught you, something you might have learned and forgotten from when you were younger, perhaps?"

"Not that I remember." Though possible it was, I thought it an unlikely possibility. "I mean, maybe, but I really don't think so. I hate to admit it, but I was never very good at languages, and the ones I did learn I don't have a very large grasp of."

"So you really don't recognize any of the writings then?"

"No, that's why I was hoping that you would. I mean, do you have any understanding…?"

"Of the language?" She took another look over the note. "Sorry son, but it's all Greek to me."

"It's not Greek." I knew that much, my Mother Isaura hailing from Greece.

"Just another turn of phrase, my boy," Mona said with a small sigh. "No, I'm sorry I can't help you."

"Oh, well thanks for trying anyway." I couldn't hide my disappointment.

"Although…" Mona said as though in contemplation, and at once the wave began to lift.

Although…

"I may know someone who can. Very good with things of this nature."

"Really?" I was to the moon.

"Absolutely, and I'm sure she would be happy to help. Here, let me write down her information."

Mona took a pen from her blouse pocket. She then had me turn around, putting the paper to my back where she wrote a series of digits down before returning to me the folded page in hand.. It was then that she took from out the same pocket the phone she had travelled with.

"This is the cell phone I showed you the night we met, Ambrosia. And now, it's yours. I'm sorry, I meant to give it to you before, but things seem to slip your mind when you're older. To call, just slide to unlock, press the digits, and put it up to your ear like so."

"Yes, I am also familiar." Her having already described it to me the night we met.

"Good." She handed the phone to me. "When you have time I want you to call that number I gave you and ask for Regina. She may be able to give you some answers."

I looked at the little instrument in my hand, so small. "Thanks, Mona."

Together we rounded the corner to make our start on the second landing when something hit me in the ribcage, knocking the wind out of me. I looked up to find the source of my vexation, a metallic cart on wheels. "Ugh!" I winced at the stabbing sensation that shot through my diaphragm, as both phone and paper fell out my hands to the floor.

"Oh, ah! AH! Sorry! Sorry! Sorry!" Came the fanatical ravings of a soiled and sullied nomad found at the other end of the cart. A tower of portly ruin, he had long, strangely greased down hair and a scruffy beard. His face, what I could see of it anyway, was grimy, with shaggy eyebrows and eyes like grey storm clouds—dead inside. He wore a large rumpled trench coat stained with bird droppings and a shabby hat to match. Never a more tattered and bedraggled creature could I fathom by any measure of design.

Catching my breath again, I cried out, "Gama Mao! Watch it, you silly oaf!" Grabbing the cart full of bottle-filled bags, I swung it hard away from me.

"Ambrosia!" Mona shouted.

My actions appeared to startle the gargantuan, who threw his arms up in the air and began to dance around clumsily in bulky rubber boots.

"What's zat!? What's zat!! Who dat did it, by?!"

His smell was so putrid it nearly knocked me off my feet.

"Easy, Kelbin. Calm down. It's all right," Mona urged the giant to relax with a calm hand held upward.

"Miss Mona? MISS MONA?! Yue zurp erda meade beshiz ries zen! Fei ding awfth ebah lud, thym azkum!" Nonsense words spewed from out his mouth.

"I know. I know. But it's okay now. No harm done." She placed her hand upon his chest. "Calm now, calm."

To my surprise she seemed to quiet the mastodon with her touch. "There now, see. Everything is all right."

"It's a far cry from all right!" I barked back. "See how hard he hit me? I mean, I could have internal bleeding!"

"Ambrosia, enough!" Mona would have none of it. Her stare, like two ice daggers, shot shivers straight to the heart of me.

The colossal thing bowed his malformed head.

"Is good, Miss Mona. Is good." His voice, it was like sandpaper against rock.

He stood there a moment in standstill, but then something must have caught his eye, or so I thought, for he bent his colossal body over and began thumbing around his boot. When he rose again, I saw he had picked up the parchment with the words written on it that I had been made to drop.

But I wasn't about to let this go.

"Hey now, that's mine! I demand you give it back!" I shouted, but the time for words was over.

"*An lámh dhearg abú!*" came the thundering battle cry, and like a great Nordic avalanche he was at once down upon me, pushing Mona over in the process. In his rage he meant to crush me, yet quickly I countered, arms raised high to disarm much of the onslaught. His hand came down hard, hitting me like a hammer and drilling me down onto one knee. Ignoring the pain, I managed to throwback his appendage, only to find the full weight of his storm soon falling down upon me. I dodged to the right just in time, giving a solid kick to his side. It was like hitting a brick wall, and just as effective.

I could hear a violent cough coming from Mona, like the winds sweeping in off a foul tide's gale. The goliath boomeranged, catapulting his upper limbs, his fists held together in upwards volley, nearly clipping my neck in the process. I could feel the breeze pass as I leapt back. It brushed by me, mere centimeters from clear-cutting my head clean off my torso.

A sheer instant remained for a counter attack, so I made haste to offset the situation. Landing multiple blows, I hit on all the fundamentals in trying to bring the giant down; a beat to the clavicles, a strike to the sternum, and a kick to the knees—all in fluid motion.

Where the final axe sunk in and this tree trunk of a man turned to timber, was when his bottom left leg detached itself from his body and spun across the hallway. A mighty wallop resounded as he met the floor with a bang.

I couldn't believe what I had just seen—I was fighting an amputee. As Mona's hackings continued, I gazed at the leg in horror, only to be caught off guard by the man coming toward me, crawling on his hands and knees and grabbing at me. I went down hard.

Unable to recover, he was on me in an instant, with his entire body weight pressing the life out of my being. There was nothing I could do; I was paralyzed. I thought I heard Mona scream out. But then everything was getting dark, suffocating. As I came to the realization that this could very well be it, I thought of the guiding light that I had only now just found—my Star was fading—fading fast.

But she did not go out.

The veil was at once lifted, and as the blur that was my eye line cleared, I could see the massive figure being hauled off me, restrained by a chokehold and a grappling around the arm. Holding him were both a man and a woman. The woman I knew to be Nashira, and the dark-skinned man gripping the neck I recognized only as the person I'd seen but not talked to the night earlier, who stood watch over the Nebula's entry.

They managed to keep him held there on the ground, the two of them, though he struggled to free himself. So soon there came another who stood between us, facing the restrained. It was Heze.

I could only look on as she knelt down before the brute, held an open hand before his face, and gently blew onto her palm. The contents of a dust then carried off the hand and fell over the giant's head.

"Sleep. Sleep," was all she said.

And like that, his struggle came to a slowing, then to a stall, and finally to a dead stop. The two holding the man let go and laid the giant down to slumber, out cold upon the floor.

Heze immediately went to help a wheezy Mona to her feet. "Are you okay, Mother?"

"Yes, child…thank you. I'm fine now," Mona said between breaths.

I slowly got to my feet. The pain elicited through my cavity like a knife stabbing from within and I groped at my chest, in some ill attempt to remedy my condition. I could now see that a large group had amassed in the hallway, watching us. Strange that none had come to offer any help.

"What…was…that?" I managed to force out, my sting only dwarfed by my sheer amazement of the situation at hand.

Nashira turned and looked at me with an icy stare, but said nothing. She resembled the same person I engaged the night prior—perfect posture, controlled state, hair supported well behind her, shirt pressed and dress pants dark—but seemed even less impressed with me now.

"Nothing more than a simple herbal concoction, one brought to engage the individual—" Mona stopped to take a moment, obliviously due to the strain. "—under the tranquilizing effect of slumber."

"What herbs could be used to do that?" I was beside myself with the thought.

"Valerian root, hops, lotus blossom, passion flower. All highly sedative, given the right circumstances," Heze, still holding Mona, interjected.

"Circumstances, kind of like the sleeper hold I had him in, yeah." This came from the rather stocky looking man to my right in the denim jeans and grey shirt. Very wide he was through the chest, with other broad attributes, and defined characteristics. From eyes set somewhat apart and an overhanging brow, to the mouth stretched mandible of his pronounced jaw. Large enough, still he seemed miniature in stature when compared to the brute he just helped to take down.

I walked over to the dozing giant. Even in sleep he looked a menace, as though captured by a great internal nightmarish struggle. He issued out a low growl-like whimper.

I looked back at his detached limb, still unable to believe it.

"Mona, I…I'm sorry. You have to know, I had no idea."

"Hmph," Nashira scoffed.

"I was only defending myself!" I cried. "You don't understand, you weren't there. He came…no, he came at me for no reason! He's crazy!"

Mona, helped by Heze, limped over my way and put a hand on my shoulder.

"Really, it's all right, how could you have known…? Oh, my dear boy, but I'm sorry this had to happen. I'm sorry it had to happen to you. You have to understand, Kelb here is a little…unbalanced. He is generally quite gentle, but then, you just never know."

"I guess." Still, something set him off. At once my thoughts turned more to the wounded woman by my side as I heard her exert a troubled sigh. "Mona…are you okay, Mona?"

"Just a little winded, thank you. Think though, I might have to go back downstairs now. Sorry to have cut short our little tour, my boy."

"No need to apologize, Mona. There will be other times, I'm sure. Do you need any help?"

"I might." She turned her gaze towards the other two. "Praesepe, Nashira, if you will please take Kelbin away from this crowd and into the closest room available. Do re-attach the leg, and watch over him until he wakes. Shouldn't be long, I would think."

"Sure thing, Mona," Praesepe replied.

"You're Praesepe?" I blurted out.

"Yes, I am, Ambrosia. Not quite what you were expecting?" said the robust man as he looked me over calmly.

"No, it's just…" He really wasn't what I had pictured. Though I had little basis to go on.

"You can call me Tegmine," was all he said back to me, and then went to preparing the brute that laid out before him on the floor. I accepted it as a nickname.

I returned to helping Mona. "But what if he attacks again?" I asked as I braced her arm around my shoulders.

"Well, that depends, are you going to be there when he wakes?" Nashira said. "I'm sure we can handle what you could not."

"He won't be any trouble, I can assure you," Mona said. "When all this is over, our friend shall awake in a much relaxed and meditative state. Poor, poor soul. Such a tragic tale of woe."

"Tragic tale…?"

"Yes…but now is not the time to speak of such things. Now let us go…and please Ambrosia, don't forget your cell phone."

"Oh, of course," I said, and ever so gently let go of Mona a moment only to retrieve the lost property. The crowd I could see was dispersing as I went to locate the fallen phone. Thankfully, it wasn't far from where it had flown from my clutches when the transgression first began. Still feeling the remnants of the massive weight thrust upon me, I carefully knelt down, grabbed up the phone, and that's when I saw it: the note I'd written discarded once again on the floor. Suddenly I remembered how the juggernaut had first inspected it before going on the attack. *Why?* I wondered. *What could have been the cause of his alarm? Had he somehow understood it?*

"Ambrosia," Mona called out, rushing my thoughts back to the present.

"Oh, yeah coming."

I seized the page, stuffing it along with the phone in my pants' pocket. Running up to Mona I wrapped her right arm once more around my shoulder, and Heze was there to provide stabilization on her other side.

"Is there any other way downstairs?" I asked as we began to take our first steps together.

"Fraid not, lad. Just take us slow, you'll do just fine."

Reluctantly so, we slowly made our way towards the stairs. As we did, Mona said something in passing.

"The beast walks on two feet."

A strange thing to say, I could only really think to relate it to the ordeal we had just gone through. Of that I wondered, of which one of us was she referring to? Him, or me? Perhaps both.

Back in Mona's office, Gany was busy at the desk and typing on an opened laptop computer. He immediately got up and ran to our aid on noticing us. When we got her close enough, Mona then broke from our carry and took her chair, immediately going for a cigarette.

"You all right, chérie?" Gany inquired, sounding worried.

"Yes, Gany, I am fine, thank you. Just had me a minor mishap is all," Mona assured him, though I was sure that wouldn't be enough to reassure Gany.

"A mishap?"

"Yeah, one going by the name of Kelb," I said, filling in the missing blanks.

"I see. So what is the bother with Kelbin?"

"You mean other than that he mowed Mona down while in his attempt to throttle me?"

"Ambrosia, stop, please," Mona was quick to ask of me before pausing to exhale. "Really, it was nothing."

"I don't know if I would call what just happened up there nothing," I interjected even though the better part of me said not to.

"Anyway, now is not the time," Mona sharply cut me off.

I did not fully comprehend but decided to concede to her request.

"Right, now that that's taken care of, there are other things that need attending," Mona firmly stated as she blew a line of smoke. She turned her attention on Gany. "I trust you have made the proper arrangements, that things have been set into motion."

A machine next to her computer began to elicit electronic noises. It was the same kind we had back home, where my Mothers would receive pages upon pages of literature with which to feed a thirsty mind. This was, however, the first time I had gotten to see one working up close. The sound I knew.

"Ah yes, of course, chérie. Your ticket, it is being printed as we speak."

I wondered what they were going on about when my answer came in a slip of paper that shot out the machine ensemble. Mona grabbed the sheet of paper from out the printer tray.

"Mona, what is that?" I questioned her, but I already knew.

"Why, it's my itinerary, my boy."

"Okay…for what, exactly?"

"It's her flight ticket," Heze answered my question for me, standing there looking down at the page in Mona's hand and sounding more than a little distressed.

"Flight ticket…?" Oh. "But wait, what do you need that for?" Didn't Star say she never stayed for very long?

"Well, to travel, of course. And I best not doddle about, either. According to this ticket I'm set to leave within the next few hours."

I was more than dismayed to hear the news.

"But I don't understand…? I mean, didn't we just get here? Why leave now?"

"Correction, Ambrosia, you have just made it here. I've always been 'here'. However I am afraid that my specific brand of services are again needed elsewhere, for the time being, so I will extend those roots."

"You really have to go do this?"

"It is the duty I am fortunate enough to be bestowed with, son. I must answer the call. You understand?" She smiled at me as though looking for validation, and still she sounded somewhat winded.

But I didn't understand, not at all. All I could think was: *Why would she just pick up and leave me like this, at a time when I need her most?*

"And what are these services you speak of? What is so pressing that you have to leave us now?" I demanded of her.

"Why, to help those in need, of course. You've seen the news, the chaos happening across the globe.

I cannot just sit by and idly watch," Mona said as though there was no other option to be had.

"And must you go? Shouldn't you maybe rest awhile, Mother?" Heze jumped in, feeling obviously much the same as I.

Mona slowly got up from her chair and moved to face Heze while putting a reassuring hand on the girl's shoulder. "You know I must, and I cannot risk any more time to fall through the hourglass, child."

Mona then nodded a gesture of goodbye. "Gany, my cane, if you would please?"

From behind a small filing cabinet I watched Gany pull out a thin wooden staff, its head curve sculpted to resemble a serpentine creature, exquisitely contrived. And to his shoulder held the bag Mona had travelled with less than a day ago. He ushered towards us, placing the cane in Mona's hand.

"Ah, thank you," she said, and then turned towards me. "Fret not, my son, for I will return soon."

"Yeah?" I wasn't sure.

"Count on it," she said with conviction in her voice.

Mona then turned from me and alongside Gany moved herself towards the room's exit, cane in tow, letting it fall ahead of her as with each passing step there came a clack to the floor. Though it seemed she used the cane for precautionary sake rather than for absolute necessity, the question remained why she had the cane at all.

Then exiting, just like that, they were gone. I wasn't at all partial to this disappearing act she was pulling, couldn't help but feel somewhat abandoned in my time of need. So again I was left not knowing where to go next.

Until, that is, the lady reappeared in the doorway. "Almost forgot," Mona said as she dug into her blouse pocket, holding something there in her hand. "Well, come hither, son. It's for you, after all." She directed herself towards me.

She handed me two items. I looked at the contents I was holding, a bit bewildered. "What are these?"

"These are your tools for getting round. One is your passport with picture ID. It identifies who you are, something you might need for getting into certain places."

I perused through the thin black book's pages and was more than a little shocked to find that indeed there was a picture of me inside. Or what looked like me, but with shorter hair. Beside it was a series of information that included both my name and birth date, at least the day we chose to celebrate: April 16, 1991. I couldn't help wondering how Mona had managed to secure the documents in question.

She went on, "The other is your own personal charge card, and you can use it in order to pay for the things you need, should you ever need them," Mona said as pointing out the card she had handed to me. "Spare no expense."

"Uh..." I really wasn't sure what to say. Still I had to ask, "Mona, about this picture..."

"I assure you it will work well enough to do the trick. As you know, it's worked once already."

"No, you're right, it looks just like me." And that's exactly what I was getting at.

"Well, it should," she was quick to tell me, the need for departure apparent in the sound.

I ignored the indication. "But how, I mean, when did you have the time to put this together, let alone get a picture of me?"

"My dear boy, I really don't have time for this now. Do you not remember I took the picture of you on my phone the night prior to our leaving? Actually, on the phone I gave you."

I had remembered the photo not taking. "Still, doesn't explain how it got on here, or why my appearance is altered."

"Well, modifications were made on my part, and suppose I forged the documents the morning we left with painstaking effort? I'm very meticulous that way. Now if there isn't anything else…"

There was everything else. "No, that's alright, I'm good, I guess."

"Good. And oh, I do apologize, son, but we will be taking Lenore for a spell. Heze, if you would be so kind as to show Ambrosia here the way home."

"If it would please you," she said.

"It would."

"Can you at least tell us where it is you're going?" I jumped in, looking to stall her. There were still so many questions that needed asking.

"To Peru, South America."

The places on the news devastated by natural disaster.

"And how will you help?"

"In whatever way I can."

She then went to go when I grabbed her arm.

"Mona, wait!"

"What is it, son?"

"Well…it's just…"

"No point in arguing the subject anymore. I have to do this," she said firmly.

"I know." Although, I wasn't sure in what way. "There's something I need to ask you first, before you go." I lowered my voice. "It's about Kelb."

"And what is it that you would like to know?"

It had been on my mind since the moment the words had been returned to me. "What he said, right before he attacked. Do you know what it was?"

"I'm sorry, but well…gibberish is gobbledy-gook."

"What's that?" I wasn't understanding her.

"What I mean is, try not to read too much into it, Ambrosia."

"Yes…" But how could I? There were too many questions left up in the air, too many things I didn't yet know. "But the words on the page, what if he understood them? Don't you think that maybe he might know what they mean? Is it not worth looking into?" I was at the point of exasperation.

"Some would say no." She was curt in her retort. It was not what I wanted to hear.

"Well, why not then? Why couldn't he…?"

"Because, son, he's blind."

To be continued in
The Psyche of Ambrosia - Part II:
A SWAIN'S AFFRAY

References

[i]Dreamcatcher – Wikipedia, the free encyclopedia, Mar 26th/2012

In some Native American cultures, a dreamcatcher (or dream catcher; Lakota: iháŋblagmunka, Ojibwe: *asabikeshiinh*, the inanimate form of the word for "spider" or Ojibwe: *bawaajige nagwaagan* meaning "dream snare") is a handmade object based on a willowhoop, on which is woven a loose net or web. The dreamcatcher is then decorated with sacred items such as feathers and beads.
https://en.wikipedia.org/wiki/Dreamcatcher

[ii]Ojibwe – Wikipedia, the free encyclopedia, Mar 26th/2012

The Ojibwe (also Ojibwa), or Chippewa are a large group of Native Americans and First Nations in North America. There are Ojibwe communities in both Canada and the United States. In Canada, they are the second-largest population among First Nations, surpassed only by the Cree. In the United States, they have the fourth-largest population among Native American tribes, surpassed only by the Navajo, Cherokee, and Lakota.
https://en.wikipedia.org/wiki/Ojibwe

[iii]The Darkside of the Moon – Wikipedia, the free encyclopedia, Mar 26th/2012

The Dark Side of the Moon is the eighth studio album by the English progressive rock band Pink Floyd, released on 1 March 1973. It built on ideas explored in the band's earlier recordings and live shows, but lacks the extended instrumental excursions that characterised their work following the departure in 1968 of founder member, principal composer, and lyricist, Syd Barrett. The themes on *The Dark Side of the Moon* include conflict, greed, the passage of time, and mental illness, the latter partly inspired by Barrett's deteriorating mental state.
https://en.wikipedia.org/wiki/The_Dark_Side_of_the_Moon

[iv]Lord Byron – Wikipedia, the free encyclopedia, Mar 26th/2012 George Gordon Byron (later Noel), 6th Baron Byron, (22 January 1788 – 19 April 1824), commonly known simply as Lord Byron, was an English poet and a leading figure in the Romantic movement. Among Byron's best-known works are the lengthy narrative poems *Don Juan* and *Childe Harold's Pilgrimage*, and the short lyric *She Walks in Beauty*.
https://en.wikipedia.org/wiki/Lord_Byron

[v]British Empire – Wikipedia, the free encyclopedia, Mar 26th/2012
The British Empire comprised the dominions, colonies, protectorates, mandates and other territories ruled or administered by the United Kingdom. It originated with the overseas possessions and trading posts established by England between the late 16th and early 18th centuries. At its height, it was the largest empire in history and, for over a century, was the foremost global power. By 1922 the British Empire held sway over about 458 million people, one-fifth of the world's population at the time. The empire covered more than 33,700,000 km^2 (13,012,000 sq mi), almost a quarter of the Earth's total land area. As a result, its political, legal, linguistic and cultural legacy is widespread. At the peak of its power, the phrase "the empire on which the sun never sets" was often used to describe the British Empire, because its expanse around the globe meant that the sun was always shining on at least one of its territories.
https://en.wikipedia.org/wiki/British_Empire

[vi]Napoleonic Wars – Wikipedia, the free encyclopedia, Mar 26th/2012
The Napoleonic Wars (1803–1815) were a series of major conflicts pitting the French Empire, led by Emperor Napoleon I, against an array of European powers formed into various coalitions. They revolutionized European armies and played out on an unprecedented scale, mainly owing to the application of modern mass conscription. The wars are traditionally seen as a

continuation of the Revolutionary Wars, which broke out in 1792 during the French Revolution. Initially, French power rose quickly as the armies of Napoleon conquered much of Europe. In his military career, Napoleon fought about 60 battles and lost seven, mostly at the end of his reign. The great French dominion collapsed rapidly after the disastrous Invasion of Russia in 1812. Napoleon was defeated in 1814, and then once more in 1815 at Waterloo after a brief return to power. The Allies then reversed all French gains since the Revolutionary Wars at the Congress of Vienna.
https://en.wikipedia.org/wiki/Napoleonic_Wars

About the Author

Byron Fortin is a dedicated writer with a background in classical literature, theatre, and romantic poetry. He also holds degrees in both healthcare and electronic engineering, with a great interest in the future of alternative energies and a passion for the natural sciences. In 2012 he won the Diamond Century of Service Challenge Award for volunteer services. When he is not writing Byron prefers to try his hand at painting, and also enjoys the art of spontaneous adventuring as a way of sourcing inspiration. Having spent his early years in the Annapolis Valley, Byron now lives in beautiful Peggy's Cove area of Nova Scotia, off route 333.

Currently available from Byron Fortin in the

WORLDS BEYOND SCRIPTURE

Series:

Book

1: Through the Psyche of Ambrosia
Part I: A Nexus of Numen

Book

2: Through the Psyche of Ambrosia
Part II: A Swain's Affray

And Coming Soon in 2016...

Book 3: Two if by Dark Reverie - Part I
A Call to Away Kin

Book 4: Two if By Dark Reverie - Part II
A Rose with the Echo

63010369R00180

Made in the USA
Charleston, SC
26 October 2016